Alice-Miranda
in Scotland

Books by Jacqueline Harvey

Kensy and Max: Breaking News

Alice-Miranda at School
Alice-Miranda on Holiday
Alice-Miranda Takes the Lead
Alice-Miranda at Sea
Alice-Miranda in New York
Alice-Miranda Shows the Way
Alice-Miranda in Paris
Alice-Miranda Shines Bright
Alice-Miranda in Japan
Alice-Miranda at Camp
Alice-Miranda at the Palace
Alice-Miranda in the Alps
Alice-Miranda to the Rescue
Alice-Miranda in China
Alice-Miranda Holds the Key
Alice-Miranda in Hollywood
Alice-Miranda in Scotland

Clementine Rose and the Surprise Visitor
Clementine Rose and the Pet Day Disaster
Clementine Rose and the Perfect Present
Clementine Rose and the Farm Fiasco
Clementine Rose and the Seaside Escape
Clementine Rose and the Treasure Box
Clementine Rose and the Famous Friend
Clementine Rose and the Ballet Break-In
Clementine Rose and the Movie Magic
Clementine Rose and the Birthday Emergency
Clementine Rose and the Special Promise
Clementine Rose and the Paris Puzzle
Clementine Rose and the Wedding Wobbles

Alice-Miranda in Scotland

Jacqueline Harvey

RANDOM HOUSE AUSTRALIA

A Random House book
Published by Penguin Random House Australia Pty Ltd
Level 3, 100 Pacific Highway, North Sydney NSW 2060
penguin.com.au

Penguin
Random House
Australia

First published by Random House Australia in 2018

Addresses for the Penguin Random House group of companies can be found at
global.penguinrandomhouse.com/offices.

A catalogue record for this
book is available from the
National Library of Australia

ISBN: 978 0 14378 601 6

Cover and internal illustrations by J.Yi
Cover design by Mathematics www.xy-1.com
Typeset in 13/18 pt Adobe Garamond by Midland Typesetters, Australia
Printed in Australia by Griffin Press, an accredited ISO AS/NZS 14001:2004
Environmental Management System printer

Penguin Random House Australia uses papers that are natural, renewable
and recyclable products and made from wood grown in sustainable forests.
The logging and manufacturing processes are expected to conform to the
environmental regulations of the country of origin.

For Ian, who introduced me to the delights of Scotland, and for Sandy as always

Chapter 1

Alice-Miranda leaned forward and rested her head on Bony's neck. 'Well done, boy,' she cooed. 'That was a good effort.'

The pony's nostrils flared and his sides heaved. Next to him, Chops looked as if he'd just been for a walk in the park instead of a race across Gertrude's Grove.

'Someone's a bit out of condition,' Millie remarked. 'Although ten points to Bony for trying super hard to beat us.'

Alice-Miranda sat back upright in the saddle. 'Yes, but he shouldn't be puffing quite this much. It's my fault – I haven't been riding him enough lately, and I suspect his breaking into the vegetable patch last week didn't help. Thank goodness Mr Charles found the little monster before he devoured more than a few brussels sprouts.'

'You shouldn't be so tough on yourself,' Millie said, giving Chops a congratulatory rub between his ears. 'We have had quite a lot of homework. It's tricky to stay on top of everything these days.'

The afternoon was sparkling and unusually warm for the time of year. Bonaparte whinnied as the stables came into view.

'Look, there's Miss Grimm and Mr Grump and Aggie!' Alice-Miranda exclaimed. She waved to the headmistress and her husband, who were pushing a pram along the path towards them.

Both girls slipped down to the ground and pulled the reins over the ponies' heads.

'Hello!' they chorused.

Mr Grump greeted them with a broad smile. 'Well, hello to you too.'

'How was your ride, girls?' Miss Grimm asked.

'Fast and furious,' Millie replied. 'We couldn't resist a race.'

'And Millie and Chops beat us, as always,' Alice-Miranda added with a grin.

Bonaparte bared his teeth at the same time as lifting his tail and expelling an eye-watering gust of wind.

Alice-Miranda glared at the beast, who looked for all the world as if he were smiling. 'Where are your manners, Bony?'

'Oh, not to worry. Our little one does the same,' Mr Grump said, gazing adoringly at the occupant of the pram.

Miss Grimm pulled back the hood, and the girls and ponies peered in at the tiny baby.

'We call her the smiling assassin,' Mr Grump said with a cheerful chortle. 'Steer clear if there's any hint of a smile on that angelic face.'

The infant lay on her back, kicking her legs and stretching her arms above her head. Her hazel eyes sparkled as the sunlight glistened off her crown of wispy blonde curls.

'She can't possibly be as bad as Bony – and, I have to say, Fudge has been pretty stinky too lately,' Alice-Miranda said, referring to the school's pet cavoodle, who these days divided his time between the junior and senior boarding houses.

'I can't believe how fast Aggie is growing,' Millie remarked. 'She'll be at school before you know it.'

Mr Grump lifted the baby out of the pram and cradled her in his arms. 'Oh, I don't even want to think about that.'

'Are you enjoying parenthood?' Alice-Miranda asked.

The headmistress glanced across at her husband, a blissful look passing between them. 'It's wonderful,' Miss Grimm gushed. 'Some days I think my heart might burst – it's so full of love for that little stinker.'

Aldous Grump placed a hand on his wife's shoulder. 'I never imagined I'd be a father again. After what happened, we dared not hope for our own little miracle – but here she is.'

The man's first wife had tragically died early on in their marriage, leaving behind a young daughter, Amelia. With a large business to run, Aldous had decided it best to send the child to boarding school. It was there that he met and fell in love with Ophelia. They were set to be married until a second tragedy befell the man. An illness claimed his daughter's life and, consumed with grief, Aldous called off their engagement. He spent ten years roaming the globe in search of solace while Ophelia locked herself away from everyone, angry at the cruel hand fate had dealt her. It was Alice-Miranda who reunited the pair, when she stumbled upon Mr Grump while on a camping challenge in her first year at the school. Realising they were still very much in love, the headmistress and Mr Grump married almost immediately, but the pregnancy was a surprise. Agnes Grump had just passed the six-month mark, and to say that she was adored by everyone at the school and in the village would have been an understatement. Miss Grimm couldn't go anywhere without being stopped a dozen times by people wanting to see the baby.

Bonaparte stretched his neck in an attempt to nibble Aggie's curls. Fortunately, Alice-Miranda had cottoned on to what he was up to and pulled sharply on the reins.

'Bony, Agnes is not a cabbage!' the girl chided.

'Mmm, I don't know – she looks a bit like one of those Cabbage Patch dolls to me,' Aldous said, making everyone laugh.

Alice-Miranda suddenly remembered there was something she'd been wanting to ask the headmistress all week. 'Miss Grimm, has there been any news about the Queen's Colours leadership program? It seems ages since we sent off the applications and I'm ever so excited, although I try to remind myself there will be lots of competition for the places.' Alice-Miranda tugged on Bony's reins. The naughty pony had turned his attention from the baby to nibble her pram instead.

Ophelia Grimm frowned. 'That's a very good question. I'll check with Mrs Derby and I'd best decide which of the teachers is going to accompany the group as I'm sure there will be at least a few students accepted. Miss Reedy has her hands full doing most of my work while I'm looking after Aggie and I can't imagine Mr Plumpton will be keen to go without her.'

'What about Miss Wall?' Alice-Miranda said. 'She'd be excellent at the Highland games.'

'That's an interesting idea,' the woman said, nodding. 'I am keen to give Benitha more leadership opportunities.'

Millie sighed wistfully. 'I hope we get into the program. After all, I've got Scotland in my veins.'

'Really?' Mr Grump said, sneaking a sly wink at the others. 'I would never have guessed.'

Millie's mouth gaped open at the slight. 'Seriously? With my surname?'

The man grinned. 'I suppose there wouldn't be too many who can lay claim to the McLoughlin, McTavish, McNoughton *and* McGill clans in one name.'

'And I've been preparing for a ceilidh, just in case,' Millie said. She put up one hand, bent her opposite leg at the knee and performed a vigorous Scottish jig.

Try as she might, Alice-Miranda couldn't help but giggle along with the others. Chops joined in too with a loud whinny while Bony looked on in mild distaste.

'I'm so glad we ran into you girls,' Ophelia said, catching her breath. 'The campus here isn't the same now that you're over at Caledonia Manor. I know it isn't far, but it's different to seeing you around the school every day.'

Alice-Miranda nodded. 'It's different for us too, but I'm so grateful you let me go with Millie and Sloane.'

'I second that,' Millie said. 'It's not as if Alice-Miranda couldn't handle the work. She already beats us in most of our tests.'

7

'It wasn't a difficult decision at all in terms of whether you'd cope with the work, Alice-Miranda,' Ophelia said. 'Mind you, there will be things you'll find tricky as you get older, and I don't know if you'll be quite ready for university when the other girls go, but I'm sure you'd be an excellent gap student here with us for a year or two, if you wouldn't mind staying on.'

Alice-Miranda's eyes widened. 'What a wonderful idea. I could help Mrs Howard with the younger students, and do some tutoring and look after the ponies. I suppose it's still ages away, but it's something to think about.'

For the last few months of the previous school year, Alice-Miranda and Millie had been doing a very good job of not talking about the inevitable – that Millie and Sloane and lots of the other students were going to transfer over to the boarding house at Caledonia Manor, where the secondary campus of Winchesterfield-Downsfordvale was located. Being almost three years younger, Alice-Miranda knew that she'd just have to cope without her best friend – as they'd all done when Jacinta had gone the year before. However, unbeknown to the students, Miss Grimm had met with Alice-Miranda and her parents over the holiday break to discuss accelerating the girl's education. Given her obvious talents and maturity, there was little doubt she could handle the transition and it just didn't seem fair to keep her behind.

When Alice-Miranda had shared the news with Millie, her flame-haired friend had hugged her so tightly she'd knocked the breath out of both of them.

The hardest thing of all had been saying goodbye to her beloved Mrs Howard. There had been tears all around, but Alice-Miranda had promised to visit Grimthorpe House as often as possible and so far she'd kept her word, dropping in at least once a week.

'How's Petunia managing everyone?' Aldous Grump asked.

'Mrs Clarkson is firm but fair,' Alice-Miranda said. 'I think she's worked out most of the girls already and she doesn't tolerate an ounce of nonsense. Mrs Howard must have clued her in over the holidays.'

'What about the food?' Ophelia asked with a pre-emptive grimace.

Millie wrinkled her nose. 'I'd say Mrs Jennings

is Mrs Smith's standard *before* she had cooking lessons with Mrs Oliver.'

'Millie!' Alice-Miranda admonished.

'Did you taste that cauliflower cheese last week?' Millie shivered. 'We could have used it for wallpaper paste.'

Alice-Miranda bit her lip, recalling her own recent experience. 'Actually, Millie's right. It's just that Mrs Jennings is so lovely. I would hate to hurt her feelings. It's lucky we have a good supply of bread in the common-room kitchenette as most of the girls make cheese toasties before bed. Would you like me to ask Mummy and Daddy if they can spare Mrs Oliver for a few weeks? I'm sure she'd be happy to help out again.'

'Oh, that sounds dire,' Ophelia sighed. She tapped her chin thoughtfully. 'Don't you worry about it, Alice-Miranda. I have an idea. Anyway, say hello to everyone for us, and if you see Hephzibah and Henrietta, tell them I'll bring Aggie over for a visit on the weekend.'

The girls nodded. 'They've been busy sewing,' Alice-Miranda said. 'I think they have a special surprise for you.'

The woman shook her head. 'We get a special

surprise every time we visit. Aggie will be so spoilt I'll have to send her to some horrible boarding school to make sure she knows a bit about tough love.'

'Well, you won't be able to send her here then,' Millie said with a grin. 'Although a couple of years ago I mightn't have said the same.'

Ophelia Grimm raised an eyebrow. 'Sadly, you're right about that, Millie. I do hope I've changed and you girls are no longer terrified of me – or rather the legend of me, given how long I locked myself away. What a misery guts I was.'

Alice-Miranda stepped forward and enveloped the woman around the waist. 'But not any more. Everyone loves you and Mr Grump and Aggie. Winchesterfield-Downsfordvale wouldn't be the same without you.'

'Thank you, darling girl.' Ophelia brushed a tear from her eye. 'Sorry. Ever since the baby I've just been so emotional.'

Alice-Miranda and Millie looked at Mr Grump, who seemed to be battling tears too. He fished a handkerchief from his pocket. 'Men must get pregnancy hormones as well,' he said, and blew his nose loudly. 'At least, that's my excuse.'

Millie glanced at her watch. 'We'd better get

going. I promised Chops a good rub-down after our ride and a treat for winning the race.'

'And Bony needs some attention otherwise I'm sure he'll be up to no good again,' Alice-Miranda said. She leaned in and kissed Aggie's soft cheek.

'Right, I'll see if there's any news regarding the leadership program this afternoon,' Ophelia said.

The girls called their thanks, then swung up into the saddles and waved goodbye.

Chapter 2

Davina yanked on the wad of white pages and cursed the machine for the third time since she'd started. The motor whirred but the paper was stuck fast.

'Everythin' all right in there?' a cheery voice called from the office next door.

Davina's heart sank. 'Yes, fine and dandy. Just a wee jam is all,' she called back, hoping her boss would leave it at that. The door to his office squeaked open and she could hear his footsteps in the hallway. Davina wrenched open the door of the shredder and upended the full bin onto the floor. Then she replaced the container, slammed the door shut and flicked the switch, watching the last of the paper disappear through the metal teeth at the same moment Mr Ferguson's head appeared around the door.

The man caught sight of the mess and paused. 'Ah . . . Miss Stuart, did ye manage to get all of those letters in the mail?'

'Yes, of course, Mr Ferguson. They were sent on Monday, actually – ahead of time,' Davina replied.

'Ah, I see,' he began.

She prayed the man wasn't about to go galloping into another one of his meandering anecdotes. It was hard enough with Morag, who had a knack for popping up out of nowhere and asking a hundred and one questions. But for that Davina could only blame herself.

A few months ago, Davina had come to Morag's aid when the woman had her handbag stolen in the street. The poor soul was so shaken that Davina offered to take her for a coffee to calm her nerves. It was there she learned that Morag Cranna, a teacher, was looking for a new role. The timing couldn't have been better. With twenty years' experience, Morag was more than qualified for the job of school liaison officer. She and Mr Ferguson hit it off immediately, most likely due to their penchant for longwinded stories and Morag's capacity to hang off the man's every word. Within a week, the woman had become part of the team. It helped that she seemed to quite genuinely think Barclay Ferguson was the most inspiring person she'd ever met and that she frequently told him so.

Barclay Ferguson strode into the room and over towards Davina's desk. Her breath caught in her throat as she watched him pick up an envelope that was poking out from under a sheet of paper Davina had been scribbling on earlier. He held it aloft, his brows knitting together.

Darn, she'd missed one. She swallowed hard, realising what he had in his hand.

'Not quite all of them, by the looks of this,' he said, waving the envelope that bore the royal crest. 'But it's not too late. We'll get this last one off this afternoon and then we'll have all our ducks in a row.'

'My apologies, sir,' Davina squeaked, feeling the colour rising in her cheeks. 'The rest have all gone.

I'm certain of it.' As for the ducks – good grief, the man could win a medal for the worst use of business jargon she'd ever heard. Apart from being incredibly annoying, most of the time it made no sense at all.

Barclay looked at the name on the front. 'Ah, Neville Nordstrom. The lad is a rock star in the makin'. I'm sure his parents will be very happy for him to be involved in the program. I'm so glad I came up with the idea to have children nominate candidates from other schools around the world. I must say that the calibre of the essays was quite outstandin'. Hard to believe the age of the writers. I can tell ye the world is in very good hands with this lot.'

'Yes, sir, I'm sure it is,' Davina said, nodding fervently. She wondered whether Neville was actually a rising rock star or if that was just another of Barclay's dreadful sayings. 'They look to be a canny group of wee lads and lassies.'

'Ye know, Miss Stuart, when I had the idea to start up an adventure travel business, everyone said I was daft. Scots don't like to leave home, I was told! The world is a dangerous place, they said! No one wants to go further than Aberdeen for their holidays! But did I listen? No, I had a helicopter view and that's why it worked!' the man exclaimed, causing Davina's nerves to jangle. 'My primary school headmaster – he was the one who planted those seeds – said I could do anythin' if I turned my attention to it properly, and he was right. But it took me a lot longer than it will for these youngsters to do somethin' amazin' – because they are lucky enough to be involved in the Queen's Colours, one of the very best programs for nurturin' our next generation of leaders. This event is the icin' on the cake, the cherry on top and the cat's pyjamas too!'

Davina muffled a yawn.

'And to think that we have now rolled out the Queen's Colours in more than ten countries,' the man continued. World domination was one of Barclay's secret goals, although he wasn't about to reveal that to anyone until it was achieved. Perhaps then Her Majesty would bestow him with a knighthood. He thought 'Sir Barclay' had quite a nice ring to it. 'Many of them are republics with nothing to do with Her Majesty other than a deep admiration for her leadership. That's quite an achievement, don't you think, Miss Stuart?'

Davina nodded again, plastering a smile across her face. Her boss was an inspiring man, there was no doubt about that, but he did have a tendency to go on. 'Sir, if you'd excuse me, I must hurry to the post office,' she said without a hint of impatience.

'Oh.' Mr Ferguson looked at the envelope in his hand, as if he'd forgotten it was there. 'Not to worry. I'll drop it off meself.'

'But the mail's my job,' Davina said gently. 'I can't have the CEO running about doing menial tasks.' She reached out to take the envelope, but Barclay danced away playfully.

'Miss Stuart, I have to walk past the place – and that way I'll know for sure it's been actioned,' he said, arching a bushy grey eyebrow.

Davina smiled through gritted teeth.

'Rightio, see ye in a bit. I'll bring us some treats for afternoon tea and ye can put on the kettle. Be back in a jiffy.'

Davina sighed and surveyed the mess in front of her. She had far more important concerns than making pots of tea. There were things that needed sorting – preferably before the boss returned.

Chapter 3

Alice-Miranda tapped her pen on the page as the bell echoed through the boarding house. She'd almost worked out the last Maths problem and was determined to finish it before dinner. She still had Science homework to do later. Millie wasn't back from tennis training yet, although she couldn't be far away. The overgrown tennis court in the garden at Caledonia Manor had recently been refurbished and another added so that the senior girls no longer had to trek over to the junior school for their lessons and matches. The builders had constructed a beautiful summer pavilion too, with change rooms and a kitchenette.

Alice-Miranda and Millie now resided in the converted stable block at Caledonia Manor, where the school's secondary facilities were located. It wasn't too far through the woods from the junior campus, especially as a more direct road and path had been paved during the holidays. Their new residence, however, was quite different to Grimthorpe House. The pair had been thrilled to find they were sharing one of the double rooms. Several of the girls had rooms to themselves while others were in larger bunk rooms for four, which Millie had been praying they wouldn't get as she was certain they'd be unlucky enough to end up with Caprice Radford as a room mate. Fortunately, Caprice was sharing with Sloane again. Despite the odd war every now and again, the pair were surprisingly good together as long as Sloane kept her side tidy.

While Grimthorpe House was all high ceilings and elaborate cornicing with double-hung windows and the odd chandelier, the decor at The Stables was much less grandiose. The stable boxes had mostly been retained and converted into bedrooms, with dark timber linings. They even had some of the original features such as the metal feed bins, which the girls used for storage. Alice-Miranda had made a bed for Brummel Bear in hers.

The girls' room had matching oak bedheads and bedside tables, and there were built-in desks on either side of the room as well as two wardrobes. It was functional and simple and adorned with family photographs and posters that they were encouraged to put up to make their rooms feel like home. It was all so lovely and new, it was hard to imagine the broken-down building that Alice-Miranda had stumbled upon the first time she had gone out riding with Millie and some of the other girls.

For decades, Caledonia Manor had provided many a midnight tale for the boarders, who claimed that a witch lived in the woods in an overgrown mansion bursting with cats. Of course, that wasn't true – well, not the part about the witch. The house had certainly been a wreck and its hermit-like inhabitant, Miss Hephzibah Fayle, did own an awful lot of cats. The poor woman had been horribly scarred in a fire when she was young and, although she had once lived in the house with her sister, Henrietta had long since married and moved out.

The sisters had lost touch many years ago. Under the vines and creepers, Caledonia Manor was a carbon copy of the main building at Fayle School for Boys, which was known as McGlintock Manor. Both had been owned by the same family and in its early days Caledonia Manor had been the location of the boys' school before it was moved.

When Alice-Miranda uncovered a plot to bring down the Fayle School, she also reunited the two sisters and secured their future. The child's father had insisted on bringing in the builders right away to restore the mansion to its former glory and give the elderly ladies a home they could properly enjoy. Both the stables and manor house underwent a stunning transformation, with the intention of using the facilities as a teachers' training college, until the council red tape proved insurmountable and a new plan was hatched. When Miss Grimm decided to expand the school through to leaving age, Caledonia Manor proved the perfect solution, providing all the classrooms and accommodation they would need for the secondary students. The school expansion also gave Miss Hephzibah and Miss Henrietta new leases on life. They loved being part of such a vibrant community.

Alice-Miranda had just written the last numeral in her Maths solution when there was a sharp knock on the door. 'Come in,' she called.

Jacinta poked her head around the door. 'Have you heard from Lucas lately?' she asked without so much as a hello.

Alice-Miranda spun around in her swivel chair. 'No, but that's not entirely unusual – they seem to be very busy over at Fayle this term. I gather you haven't heard from him either?'

Jacinta shook her head, her face crumpling. 'Not for a week,' she moaned, walking over to sit on the edge of Alice-Miranda's bed, 'and when I've called over there the past couple of times, the housemaster said that he was out and that he'd pass on the message that I'd phoned. Do you think Lucas is having second thoughts?'

Millie barged in through the door, red-faced and puffing. 'Miss Wall wouldn't let us go – we told her we'd be late for dinner,' she huffed, before spotting Jacinta and her glum face. Millie threw her tennis kit in the corner. 'What's the matter? Has Lucas done a runner?'

Tears welled in Jacinta's eyes. Her brows knitted

together and she looked as if she were about to say something she might regret.

Alice-Miranda rushed towards the girl and put an arm around her shoulders. 'You know Millie didn't mean anything by that.'

'Sorry,' Millie said, realising she may have hit a little too close to home. 'Alice-Miranda's right. I really didn't mean anything. I was only teasing. Has something happened?' She quickly pulled a tissue from the box on Alice-Miranda's bedside table and passed it to Jacinta.

The girl sniffed and wiped away her tears. 'Yes. No. I don't know.'

The door flew open and Caprice marched inside.

'You could knock,' Millie snapped. 'It's called manners.'

'I heard blubbering and I was worried there was something wrong. Is there?' Caprice appraised the three girls with an icy stare and noticed Jacinta's red eyes. 'Your boyfriend's dumped you, hasn't he?'

Alice-Miranda sighed. 'Caprice, could you please try to be a little more sensitive?'

'I saw Lucas this afternoon in the village shop,' Caprice added, a smile playing at the corners of her mouth.

Jacinta immediately sat up straight as a post. 'Did you speak to him?' she demanded. 'What was he doing? How did he seem?'

The tall, willowy girl flicked her copper tresses and shrugged. 'He didn't mention you at all. I think he was buying a card. It had a love heart on it, so I presumed it was for his girlfriend, but maybe not, or maybe that's not you any more,' Caprice said, and flounced out the door.

'Seriously, did you really have to say that?' Millie called after the girl. 'And if you hadn't got everyone's phones confiscated, we wouldn't even have this problem.'

'I wasn't the only one who ate those pizzas!' Caprice yelled back.

A door slammed, reverberating through the walls.

The girls' headmistress, Petunia Clarkson, had been surprised to see a pizza delivery driver speeding away from the premises after dinner one night. The strong smell of pepperoni wafting from Caprice's room also didn't escape the woman's detection. When questioned, the girl confessed to organising a late-night feast, citing that everyone was starving and Mrs Jennings's corned beef had all the taste and texture of shoe leather. While Petunia couldn't exactly argue, having just prepared herself some beans on toast in her flat, she decided ordering in was not something she could condone and the only course of action was to lock up the phones for the rest of the term.

Jacinta's tears began to flow. 'What if Caprice is right? What if he doesn't like me any more and he's just too scared to tell me?'

Alice-Miranda turned to face the girl. 'Jacinta, haven't we been through this before? You need to talk to Lucas before your imagination gets the better of you. I'll try to call him after dinner, if you like.'

There was a knock on the door.

'Go away!' Millie roared.

But this time it wasn't Caprice. The door opened to reveal their housemistress, who looked unimpressed to say the least.

'Millie,' Mrs Clarkson reprimanded. 'I think you need to remember your manners.'

Millie blushed from head to toe. 'Sorry, Mrs Clarkson. I thought you were someone else.'

'Clearly.' The housemistress gave a small nod and clasped her hands in front of her. 'Girls, you'd better hurry to dinner. I hate that bell as much as you do, but I really didn't think I'd still have to patrol the corridors like a commandant. You're older now and you need to take more responsibility for yourselves.'

'Our apologies,' Alice-Miranda said, rising to her feet. She grabbed a cardigan from the end of her bed and shrugged it over her shoulders, then headed for the door with Millie and Jacinta following behind her.

'Jacinta, could I have a word?' Mrs Clarkson asked. 'I need to speak with you in private.'

The girl bit her lip and nodded.

Alice-Miranda and Millie both cast worried glances back towards Jacinta, hoping she wasn't in trouble, then hurried out the door to the dining room.

Chapter 4

The dining room, located in a wing that ran perpendicular to the original stable block, was thrumming with the usual evening chatter, but there was also a hint of excitement in the air. After a few moments, the girls realised the smell of charred meat they had become accustomed to was missing. Alice-Miranda and Millie headed for the servery and were surprised when Mrs Smith walked out through the kitchen doors. The woman waved hello with a slotted spoon.

'What are you doing here, Mrs Smith?' Alice-Miranda asked.

'Well, Miss Grimm has finally put on a young lass – Ginny – to help me over at the main school and it turns out she's a whiz. Her father is a chef and she wants to take over his restaurant once she has more experience under her belt. Anyway,' Mrs Smith said, lowering her voice, 'I heard a whisper that Mrs Jennings was feeling the pinch – apparently, there had been some complaints – so I offered to swap for the week. I think Ginny will teach her a few things and I get to spend time with the girls I love best – not a word of that to the others, mind you, or I'll be in trouble.'

Alice-Miranda was positively beaming. 'It's lovely you're here, but I hope Mrs Jennings isn't too upset.'

'Oh, on the contrary. I think poor Rachel's relieved,' Mrs Smith said, wiping her forehead with the back of her hand. 'She was telling me that she's been feeling out of her depth and hasn't been able to get the knack of cooking for so many at once. There's nothing worse than knowing your food isn't up to scratch – believe me, mine was ghastly for a long time until darling Dolly intervened.

We all need help from time to time and, while it's a difficult pill to swallow, there's no shame in putting your hand up. I'm glad I finally did – or you girls would be as thin as rakes.'

'That's true. Your food was terrible,' Millie said, flashing a mischievous grin. 'Sorry, Mrs Smith. That sounded like something Sloane would say.'

'What would I say?' Sloane asked, sidling up to them.

'It doesn't matter,' Millie said, and Mrs Smith winked.

The girls filled their plates with spaghetti bolognaise and garlic bread and wandered off in search of their friends. Jacinta was sitting with Chessie in the far corner. Millie glanced around and was relieved to see that Caprice had taken up residence with Sofia Ridout and some of the older girls. She wove her way through the maze of tables and sat down next to Jacinta and Chessie, who had chosen a spot tucked into the far corner of the dining room.

'So, what was that about with Mrs Clarkson?' Millie asked, sliding along the bench seat. She couldn't help noticing the girl looked much perkier than twenty minutes ago.

A brilliant smile swept across Jacinta's face.

'Lucas. He called twice this week while I was out. Mrs Clarkson had mislaid the paper she'd written the messages on. She said that I could phone him straight after dinner and, look, he sent me this.'

The girl held aloft a card with a love heart on it and passed it around.

'That's sweet,' Alice-Miranda said.

Sloane looked up to see Miss Reedy walking in with Miss Wall beside her. 'There must be something going on – those two hardly ever come over for dinner. I hope they don't take up too much time with whatever it is. Mrs Clinch has gone way overboard on the trigonometry homework. I don't know why we even have to learn it in the first place. It seems utterly useless to me.'

Alice-Miranda's stomach fluttered. 'Maybe they're here to announce who's been accepted into the Queen's Colours leadership program.'

Over the chinking of forks on plates and the occasional slurp, the girls participated in loudly whispered speculation.

'Well, I won't be in the program,' Chessie said. 'I haven't even started the Queen's Colours yet.'

Having previously been a student at Bodlington School for Girls, Francesca Compton-Halls was a relatively new arrival at Winchesterfield-Downsfordvale Academy for Proper Young Ladies.

Alice-Miranda smiled at the girl. Although they weren't allowed to say so, students who had already completed several levels of the Queen's Colours had been invited to nominate a peer for the program and Chessie had been top of her list. Alice-Miranda thought it would be a lovely surprise if the girl got in.

'I wonder if any of our friends from other schools will be going,' Millie said. She munched on a slice of garlic bread, wishing she'd picked up another piece. It was deliciously crunchy on the edges, with the softest warm dough inside. 'Wouldn't that be fun?'

Miss Reedy and Miss Wall filled their plates and sat down with Mrs Clarkson and several of the teachers from the secondary school. The academic staff didn't always eat with the Caledonia Manor girls the way the staff in the junior school did, but tonight Mrs Reeves, Mrs Clinch and Mr Pratt were in attendance.

Philomena Reeves was a stocky, well-covered woman with dimply arms and a round tummy. She taught secondary English but with none of the warmth and fun of Miss Reedy. She couldn't have been much more than forty-five. However, her choice of floral dresses and short hair set into a permanent wave made her appear a lot older.

Mrs Clinch taught Mathematics and had a peculiar penchant for spelling her name at the start of every lesson. Her coal-coloured eyes gazed out from under a dark fringe that skimmed the bridge of her nose. Millie had remarked that it was sort of like having her own private curtains to peer through and it was quite unnerving given you never really knew who or what the woman was looking at.

The third teacher present was Percy Pratt, who taught Science and was an utter genius. He looked a bit like Einstein, with untamed silver hair and a huge caterpillar moustache. He also wore his lab coat around the clock and even on weekends. The man had one of those minds that never forgot a thing, which was good and bad, as he could always recall a misdemeanour or two of any of the girls. Professor Pratt could actually remember his entire life, which Alice-Miranda thought must be quite exhausting.

As the girls enjoyed their dessert of home-made apple pie and vanilla ice-cream, Miss Reedy and Miss Wall took to the podium at the end of the room.

'Good evening, everyone,' Miss Reedy began. 'It's a pleasure to see you all. I know that many of you have been anxiously awaiting news about the Future Leaders Opportunity Program, which, as you know, is an extension of the Queen's Colours for students who have shown great leadership potential. Those chosen will spend eight days in Scotland – six days in the program plus two travel days. The students will participate in activities designed to test their strengths, identify their weaknesses and allow them to build their leadership skills. There is an incredible line-up of guest speakers too. It sounds like the most wonderful event and I'm very pleased to say that we have seven girls who will be representing Winchesterfield-Downsfordvale. Your essays and applications were judged by a panel of experts, and I stress that Her Majesty had absolutely nothing to do with the final decision.' Livinia Reedy glanced at Caprice as she said this, wanting the girl to know for certain that there was no favouritism on Queen Georgiana's behalf. 'Could the following girls please come up to collect their letters of offer?'

There were audible gasps and congratulatory shouts as the names were read out. Sofia, Millie, Jacinta, Sloane, Caprice and Susannah Dare hurried to the podium in quick succession.

Millie sat back down and grinned across the table at Alice-Miranda. 'You must be lucky last.'

But the name everyone was expecting wasn't the one that was called.

'Francesca, it seems you have received one of the special offers. A classmate who recognises your potential has applied on your behalf,' the teacher said.

Chessie's eyes widened. 'Miss Reedy, there must be a mistake. What about Alice-Miranda?'

The girl with the chocolate curls shook her head. 'I wrote the letter endorsing you. How exciting that you were accepted! Congratulations!'

Chessie felt an awful jab in her stomach, as if by doing nothing herself she'd just done something terrible. 'But you should be going, not me.'

'Obviously, I'm disappointed,' Alice-Miranda said. 'I would be lying if I said I wasn't, but you know, life isn't always about getting things your own way. As Miss Grimm says, we all have to develop our disappointment muscles.'

'There must be a mistake,' Millie whispered. 'How did Caprice get in and you didn't? She's not a leader – she's a monster.'

Caprice sucked in a sharp breath. 'Miss Reedy,'

she called out, her lip quivering while fat tears threatened to spill onto her porcelain cheeks. 'Millie's being horrible to me *again*.'

Jacinta glared at the girl. 'Oh, give it a rest, Caprice. Everyone knows what a brilliant actress you are.'

'Girls, stop that at once. Alice-Miranda is absolutely right. We don't always get what we want and her attitude should be a shining example to you all.' Livinia smiled at Alice-Miranda, still coming to terms with the result herself. She made a mental note to speak to Ophelia and see if there was anything they could do about it – although having just made her big speech about Queen Georgiana having had no say in the final decision, it probably wouldn't look good if Alice-Miranda was suddenly invited to go along. 'Miss Wall will be accompanying you on the trip and I know she's looking forward to it immensely,' Livinia added.

Millie squeezed Alice-Miranda's arm. 'It's not fair. I won't go.'

'Nonsense, of course you will,' Alice-Miranda said, mustering a brave smile. 'And you'll all have a wonderful time.'

'I wouldn't be taking the news as well as you,'

Sloane said. 'I'd be crying in the corner by now, thinking how unjust life is.'

That was putting it lightly. Sloane had been a terrible brat in the not-too-distant past, but she'd come a long way since her early days at the school, when her behaviour would have given Caprice a run for her money.

'Miss Wall would like to speak to the girls who will be attending the program in the sitting room. The rest of you, please finish your dessert,' Livinia instructed.

Everyone at Alice-Miranda's table stood up bar her. The girls gave stiff waves as they walked out to speak with Miss Wall. Except Caprice, who slinked away like the cat with the cream.

Livina Reedy walked over and sat down opposite the child. 'I'm sorry, Alice-Miranda,' the woman said. 'I can't imagine what's happened.'

'It's okay. Really, it is,' Alice-Miranda assured her. 'I'm sad not to be going, as I put a lot of time and thought into composing my essay and completing my application, but writing is a fickle business. The other girls must have made more compelling arguments, that's all.'

'Just by the way you've taken the news, I think

they should let you go,' Livinia said. She couldn't have been prouder of the child if she were her own daughter. 'Well, how about we take a trip to the theatre in Downsfordvale while the girls are away? I hear a fantastic production of *A Tale of Two Cities* is about to start soon.'

'That's very kind, Miss Reedy, but wouldn't Mr Plumpton want to accompany you?' Alice-Miranda asked.

Livinia grimaced. 'I'm afraid he's not a huge fan of Mr Dickens, but he *is* quite keen to do an evening at the observatory, so perhaps he could go there while we go to the theatre. Although the stars are lovely to look at, you could spare me hours of hearing about planets and the universe.'

'That sounds perfect then,' Alice-Miranda agreed.

Livinia looked at the clock on the wall and realised that she had to get back to do some marking before it got too late. She promised to be in touch soon about their outing.

'Thank you, Miss Reedy. I miss our lessons,' Alice-Miranda said. 'Mrs Reeves is very good, but it's not the same.'

'Maybe I can suggest we swap classes next term,' Livinia said with a twinkle in her eye. 'After all,

I am acting headmistress. What's the point of having all that power if I can't use it to my advantage just once?'

Alice-Miranda giggled and, after Miss Reedy bade her farewell, the girl found herself sitting on her own in the large dining room. Before long, she was overcome with a strange feeling. But this wasn't anything like one of her usual strange feelings. It was completely different. It made her tummy twist and her heart sink all at the same time and, no matter how many happy thoughts the girl tried to invoke, tears welled in her eyes. So, this was what proper disappointment felt like, Alice-Miranda thought to herself.

Chapter 5

Alice-Miranda lay on her bed trying to read. Trouble was, as much as she was enjoying revisiting *A Tale of Two Cities* before her planned excursion with Miss Reedy next weekend, she just couldn't concentrate. She rolled onto her side and looked at Millie's neatly made bed. It had been bittersweet saying goodbye to her best friend and the other girls this morning.

Alice-Miranda slotted her bookmark between the pages and sat up. It was just after ten o'clock on Sunday morning and she wondered if Miss Hephzibah and Miss Henrietta might like a visit. Perhaps she could bake a batch of scones to take up to them. Mrs Smith had still been in the kitchen at The Stables that morning – apparently, she was staying on for another week as Ginny and Mrs Jennings were getting on famously, and Mrs Jennings wanted to get the hang of a few more dishes.

Alice-Miranda wandered out into the hallway. The house was so quiet you could have heard a pin drop. She walked into the empty sitting room and was surprised that there wasn't anyone about at all. She then remembered Mrs Clinch had taken a bus load of students to Downsfordvale for a Mind Benders tournament. According to the rules, Alice-Miranda was still too young to take part and, while she could have gone as a spectator, she'd completely forgotten to put her name on the list in time.

The girl continued into the dining room, where she could hear Mrs Smith's voice drifting from the kitchen. Alice-Miranda was just about to knock on the swinging doors when she heard Mrs Smith say something that made her wince.

'I can't believe it, Dolly. Fancy that dreadful

Caprice going ahead of our girl. It just doesn't bear thinking about,' Mrs Smith tutted.

Alice-Miranda shook her head. She wished everyone wasn't so upset on her behalf. It only made things worse in a way. She knocked loudly then poked her head around the doorway.

'Oh, speak of the devil. Here she is now,' Doreen Smith said into the phone. She smiled at Alice-Miranda and held out the receiver. 'It's Dolly, dear. She'd love to say hello.'

Alice-Miranda nodded and took up the handset. Mrs Smith busied herself about the kitchen while the girl had a quick conversation about what was happening at home. Alice-Miranda's parents were both away at the moment, with her mother in New York and her father doing the rounds of the organic farms Kennington's owned. Dolly and Mrs Shillingsworth were home alone and causing chaos as they'd decided to give the side sitting room a bit of a makeover. Alice-Miranda asked after Millie's grandfather and was pleased to hear that he and Mrs Oliver had been out several times in the past few weeks and he was coming over to the house for dinner that evening. Alice-Miranda had been secretly hoping that Ambrose might ask

Dolly to marry him. Dolly finally took a breath and, realising that she had something about to bubble over on the stove, told Alice-Miranda she'd call Doreen later.

'Well, this is a lovely surprise, but what are you doing here?' Mrs Smith asked after Alice-Miranda had hung up the phone. 'I thought everyone had gone out today. Mrs Clarkson said I was off the hook for lunch.'

'You are. I forgot to put my name on the list in time,' Alice-Miranda said.

Doreen Smith's brow furrowed. 'You? Forgot something?'

Alice-Miranda nodded.

'That's most unlike the girl I know and love,' the woman said. 'It doesn't have anything to do with your friends heading off to Edinburgh without you, does it?'

Alice-Miranda shrugged. She was mortified when a fat tear wobbled in the corner of her left eye. She brushed at it quickly, but not before Mrs Smith spotted it.

'Oh, darling girl, come here.' The woman enveloped the child in her bony arms.

Without a moment's hesitation, Alice-Miranda

hugged the woman right back and for a minute or so she sobbed her little heart out.

'You know, I feel so much better having had a good cry,' Alice-Miranda said, gently kneading the dough.

'There's nothing like it,' Mrs Smith agreed with a hearty nod. 'We all get overwhelmed from time to time and I find that tears are a great release valve. Some people swear by exercise, but a good old bawling seems to do the trick for me.'

Alice-Miranda grinned. 'I've always been quite good at keeping my emotions in check and I really don't know why I'm so upset about this. I suppose I have been telling myself that disappointment is all part of life and I've experienced it before, but mostly it's been on behalf of others – for my friends and people I meet, not me personally. Those tears have been bottling up since Miss Reedy's announcement.'

Doreen Smith sprinkled a handful of flour over a section of the stainless-steel benchtop. Alice-Miranda tipped the scone mixture onto it and picked up the rolling pin, which was also dusted in flour.

'Well, how about I join you on your walk to see Hephzibah and Henrietta?' Mrs Smith said.

Alice-Miranda nodded. 'That would be lovely. Miss Grimm is going to bring Aggie to see them this morning. That baby would cheer anyone up.'

Alice-Miranda finished rolling the dough and picked up the scone cutter. She pressed it down onto the mixture and then placed each of the perfect circles in neat rows of six on the metal tray.

'I can only agree with you there. She has the sweetest disposition. Reminds me a bit of someone else I know,' Doreen said, giving the child a nudge.

Alice-Miranda grinned and did the same. 'I really am the luckiest girl in the world,' she said without a hint of irony, because she truly did mean it.

Chapter 6

Millie looked around the conference room with its tartan carpet and thistle wallpaper. The decorators had certainly gone all out on the Scottish motifs. During the bus trip from the airport, Millie had been glued to the window, taking in the sandstone buildings and gasping when she caught a glimpse of Edinburgh Castle high on the rocky outcrop above the city, but she couldn't shake the niggling feeling that had started when they'd left Caledonia Manor.

Chessie deposited her daypack with the other bags at the back of the room and hurried over. 'Isn't this exciting?'

'Absolutely,' Millie said without her usual dose of enthusiasm. 'It's just . . .'

'Not the same without Alice-Miranda?' Chessie felt the familiar twinge of guilt in her stomach. 'She should be here instead of me.'

Millie shook her head. 'Don't be silly. Alice-Miranda would be so cross if she knew we were moping about. She'd want us to enjoy every minute of the program, so that's exactly what we'll do.'

Caprice, who happened to be loitering behind the pair, rolled her eyes. 'Are you two still upset about Little Miss Perfect missing out? Until I saw your droopy faces I'd completely forgotten she wasn't here.'

'I wish I could forget you were here,' Millie rebuked.

Caprice narrowed her eyes. 'It's not my fault Alice-Miranda's essay wasn't up to scratch. To be honest, I don't even care about the program. I just want to meet Clotilde Heminger. I overheard Miss Reedy telling Miss Wall that she's one of the surprise guest speakers. She's my favourite actress and we have *so* much in common. I hope I get some time alone with her. I want to ask her about her agent. I'll definitely need one as soon as the film comes out because the offers will be flooding in. Maybe she'll give me an introduction,' Caprice mused.

It was Millie's turn to roll her eyes. 'Or maybe not,' she muttered to Chessie, who giggled into her hands.

Sloane nudged Jacinta. 'Do you think that lady likes cats?' She motioned towards a woman who was standing at the front of the room. Her skirt was patterned with various cats wearing a selection of navy and pink waistcoats and tam-o'-shanters. Her own waistcoat matched theirs and a pair of ginger pusses dangled from her earlobes.

Jacinta grimaced. 'Just a bit.'

A slim man entered the room, grinning from ear to ear. He had a full head of grey hair, a matching beard and wore a natty tartan suit in navy and red. Apart from the fact that he was tall, he might have passed for a Scottish garden gnome. He cleared his throat and waited for everyone to find their seats.

'Good evenin', everyone!' he began. 'My name is

Barclay Ferguson and I am the CEO of the Queen's Colours program, which sits under the auspices of the Queen's Trust for Children. Along with my colleagues, Miss Cranna and Miss Stuart –' he gestured to two women standing off to the side – 'I'd like to welcome ye all to the inaugural Future Leaders Opportunity Program or, as it's affectionately known to us in the office, FLOP. But there will be no floppin' about this week, I can assure ye! We have the most extraordinary program in place and I canna wait to share it with ye all. My background is in the travel industry – ye might have heard of Fergusons; we invented adventure tourism. It all started with a single idea! Then there was lots of brainstormin' and runnin' it up the flagpole before the business took off. It soared to great heights beyond expectation!' he shouted, raising his left arm in the air to emphasise the point. 'I have stepped down from the day-to-day affairs, I am very proud to employ over ten thousand people around the world. But now I work for Her Majesty and, together, we are goin' to leave no stone unturned searchin' the globe to find the leaders of the future.'

'What's he talking about flagpoles for?' Sloane whispered to her brother.

Sep shrugged. 'Must be some sort of business jargon.'

'I hope he doesn't speak in riddles the whole time. It's hard enough to catch the words with that accent of his,' Sloane grumbled.

Barclay Ferguson's Edinburgh accent seemed to become increasingly Glaswegian. He'd actually grown up in a tiny village on the outskirts of Glasgow and had only moved to Edinburgh when he was at university, where he did his best to cultivate a posher dialect. The man frequently reverted to type, though, especially the more animated he became. Presently, Barclay Ferguson's grey hair seemed to stand higher on his head the longer he spoke and his face was as red as a beetroot.

'He isn't short on excitement, I'll give him that,' Lucas noted.

'I am lookin' forward to gettin' to know all of ye over the comin' days and learnin' what drives ye to be a leader. And we have some amazin' surprises in store for ye all. I'm goin' to find it hard not to tell, but one thing I've learned as a leader meself is that confidentiality is key. Now, please welcome our school liaison officer, Miss Morag Cranna.' The man tittered before adding, 'The woman likes cats, if ye hadn't already worked that out.'

The children applauded the man and he took a rather fancy bow before retreating to a chair in the front row.

Morag Cranna stepped forward. She held a clipboard in one hand and had a pen poised and ready for action in the other. 'Good afternoon, everyone. If you could please quiet down while I take the roll, that would be very helpful,' she called in a singsong voice.

With thirty students in her care, Morag was determined not to lose anyone. Mr Ferguson had expressed his disappointment that quite a number of the children had for one reason or another declined the invitation to attend. Morag, on the other hand, was quite relieved that there weren't as many as he'd originally planned. Working with young people was like herding cats at the best of times and she knew a lot about that, having five of the creatures herself. With the influx of this lot, though, the churning feeling in her stomach that she'd managed to avoid for some time now had returned with a vengeance. She needed to keep on thinking positive thoughts. FLOP was her redemption – she could feel it.

Just as Morag was about to begin reading the list of names, she felt her phone buzz in her skirt pocket. It was the fifth time in as many minutes. She sighed and took it out, her eyebrows knotting in consternation as she stared at the screen.

Davina Stuart hopped up from her seat. 'Is everything all right?' she whispered to the woman. 'Would you like me to call the roll while you answer the phone?'

Morag shook her head. 'It's fine, thank you.'

'Are you sure?' Davina asked. 'Sounds like someone is desperate to get hold of you. Could I help at all?'

'Um, it's my contact at the castle,' Morag said hastily. 'She never stops pestering me. I don't know what she could possibly want this time. Everything's been arranged for weeks.'

Davina gave a sympathetic smile. 'You probably should give her a wee bell. We'd hate for anything to go wrong at our first activity tomorrow.'

Morag bit down on the end of the pen, which was already looking worse for wear. 'I suppose you're right,' she said, handing Davina the clipboard. 'I promise I won't be long.'

Davina turned to address the audience. She pushed up her spectacles and took a deep breath. 'I'd like to offer my welcome too. My name is Davina Stuart and I'm Mr Ferguson's assistant. I do hope you'll all have the most wonderful time. I can't tell you the amount of planning that has gone into this – years and years.'

Barclay frowned at the woman. 'I think ye mean months and months, Miss Stuart,' he whispered.

'Oh, of course. Perhaps it just seemed like years – in a good way.' Davina blushed. 'First things first. We need to make sure that everyone is here.'

The woman proceeded to read out the name of a school first followed by the students from each one. Barcelona International College was first up with only one candidate, Neville Nordstrom. Millie had got the shock of her life when she'd charged through the entrance of the Royal Hotel to find the boy standing on his own in the front foyer. She hadn't seen him since Charlotte Highton-Smith and Lawrence Ridley's wedding, when the lad had accidentally boarded the wrong ship and thought he was steaming towards America, only to discover he was actually on the Royal Yacht *Octavia* sailing from Barcelona to Venice. Poor Neville had been scared to death, but with Alice-Miranda's help, his mistake was sorted and he even met the man who could save the rare species of butterfly that was at the heart of his ill-fated mission. Millie had rushed over to say hello, the pair embracing a little awkwardly while Neville's face turned the same colour as Millie's hair. Sloane and Sep Sykes were thrilled to see the boy too as they often spent time together during their trips home to Spain in the holidays. Neville's parents were firm friends of Smedley and September Sykes these days. It transpired that it was Sep who had nominated Neville for the program.

Chessie gasped when the name of her old boarding school was announced. She hadn't noticed anyone from Bodlington School for Girls among the crowd and glanced around, grabbing Millie's arm when she caught sight of her archenemy, Madagascar Slewt. How on earth that bully had garnered an invitation was anyone's guess. Although, when your father was the Chairman of the School Council, it probably wasn't that difficult to convince the headmistress.

'Not her!' Chessie gulped, and put her hand over her mouth.

Millie turned to see who she was looking at. 'Oh my goodness, it's Maddie!' She jumped up and waved her arms in the air.

Madagascar Slewt peered out from under her mouse-brown fringe and pulled a face that made it clear she had absolutely no idea who the idiot with the red hair and freckles was. Then it dawned on her. She gasped and waved back, grinning from ear to ear.

Chessie shrank down in her seat. 'Do you know her?'

Millie nodded. 'She's my cousin – the one at Bodlington. Well, she's really my first cousin once removed because her father and my mother are cousins. We used to play together sometimes when we were very little,' the girl explained in one breath. 'I haven't seen her in yonks.'

When Millie had previously mentioned a cousin Maddie at Bodlington, Chessie hadn't for a second entertained the notion that it could be Madagascar Slewt. No one at school was allowed to call the tyrant by anything other than her full name. Plus, Millie was far too lovely to be related to anyone so vile and ruthless. Chessie felt as if she might be sick. The week she had been looking forward to disintegrated before her very eyes. She would somehow have to become invisible and stay well out of Madagascar's way if she were to survive to the program's conclusion.

Fourth on the list was Fayle School for Boys, represented by Sep Sykes and Lucas Nixon. Jacinta flushed with pride when Lucas's name was announced, clapping long and loud. They'd spent the whole journey to Edinburgh talking and plotting how they might be able to spend some time together in the next school holidays.

The other fantastic surprise had been seeing Lucinda Finkelstein, Ava Lee and Quincy Armstrong from Mrs Kimmel's School for Girls in New York. Millie had almost fainted when she realised that Alethea Goldsworthy, who was now known as Alethea Mackenzie, and her best buddy, Gretchen, were also along for the event. That didn't seem possible given Alethea's track record, having once been the biggest bully at Winchesterfield-Downsfordvale, but apparently everyone could change. Alice-Miranda was always saying that. Millie had embraced Lucinda, Ava and Quincy like long-lost friends, although they were sad to hear that Alice-Miranda wasn't attending.

There were several other schools before Winchesterfield-Downsfordvale Academy for Proper Young Ladies was called. Davina Stuart rattled off each of the girls' names, but there was one in particular that stood out.

Millie's ears pricked up and she turned to Chessie with wide eyes. 'Did she just say what I thought she said?'

Chessie bit her lip and nodded.

The Winchesterfield-Downsfordvale girls looked at one another along the line then at Miss Wall, who was sitting at the end of their row. Benitha shrugged and held her palms in the air, as confused as the rest of them.

Davina glanced around the room. 'Alice-Miranda Highton-Smith-Kennington-Jones, where are you?'

Millie jumped up out of her seat. 'She's not here. She wasn't invited.'

Davina's eyes widened and she swallowed hard. 'Of course she was,' she said uncertainly. 'She *has* to be here. I mean, her essay was clearly the best of them all.'

Millie nodded proudly. 'You won't get any argument from us about that,' she said, earning a scoff from Caprice.

Jacinta turned and glared at the girl, who ignored her and inspected her fingernails instead.

Meanwhile, Barclay Ferguson had been thinking about a hundred and one other things, as he was prone to do. Registering a change in the air, he abandoned his runaway train of thought and returned his attention to what was happening in the conference room. 'Is there a problem, Miss Stuart?' he asked, just as Morag Cranna scuttled back into the room.

Davina seemed reluctant to say. She was racking her brain, thinking where she could have misplaced the invitation. 'We're missing one of the students,' she whispered.

Morag's heart jumped. 'Don't tell me we've lost someone before we've even started.'

'Apparently, the lass never received her invitation,' Davina mumbled. She glanced at Mr Ferguson. He would be furious with her, given that managing the invitations was her job.

The man stood up from his seat and hurriedly walked over to join the two women. 'What are ye two bletherin' about?'

'One of the children hasn't come because *Davina* mislaid the invitation,' Morag said. 'It had nothing to do with me.'

'I do apologise, sir,' Davina said softly.

'Oh dear, we'll have to send the child and their school an apology. Ye do realise, ladies, that this is not a great start to a leadership program – now we look like we canna lead a horse to water ourselves.' The man shook his head. 'Who was it?'

Davina gulped. 'Alice-Mira–'

'Not Alice-Miranda Highton-Smith-Kennington-Jones!' Barclay's face was white as a sheet. 'Ye've gone and left out the Queen's goddaughter's daughter – her favourite child in the entire world!'

By now the huddle of three at the front of the ballroom was creating a great deal more interest than they likely wanted to. The children could hear their hisses and whispers.

'Someone looks like they're in big trouble,' Millie said, craning her neck to see. She wished she could get closer to hear what they were discussing so heatedly. 'But I have an idea.'

Chessie, Sloane and Jacinta watched on as the girl trotted over to Miss Wall. It appeared she was borrowing the teacher's phone. She dashed off to the foyer and returned less than two minutes later.

'Excuse me, Mr Ferguson,' Millie said, tugging on the sleeve of the man's tartan suit. 'It's all fixed. I've arranged everything.'

The man frowned. 'What are ye talkin' about, lass?'

'Alice-Miranda. She'll be here tomorrow morning ready to start first thing.' Millie grinned. 'I just spoke to her father and, fortunately, Cyril is available and he's going to pick her up from school in Birdy and then they're going to fly here tonight in the jet,' the girl said, as if it were the most sensible thing in the world.

'Who are Birdy and Cyril?' Davina asked.

'What does it matter?' Barclay said, a smile lighting up his already glowing face. 'The child's a genius! Now, *that's* what I call initiative and leadership.' He bent down so he was eye level with Millie. 'And ye are?'

'My name is Millicent Jane McLoughlin-McTavish-McNoughton-McGill, sir,' the girl answered. 'But everyone calls me Millie.'

Barclay Ferguson clapped his hands. 'Well, Millie,' he said with a theatrical flourish, 'whichever group ye find yerself in can have ten points to start off, and I've promoted you to the position of team captain.'

'But, Mr Ferguson, I have everything worked out already and she *isn't* a captain,' Morag whispered.

'Well, she is now.' He grinned with all his teeth. 'And if we don't up our game, I suspect by the end of this week Millie and her cohort will be runnin' the entire organisation, and the three of us will be out of a job.'

The student body burst into a spontaneous round of applause and Millie was stunned to hear Sep leading the group in three cheers – all for her.

The girl's smile was incandescent. Her team was already in the lead, she was the captain and her best friend in the world would be joining them in the morning. Millie didn't think the week could actually get any better.

Chapter 7

Alice-Miranda pressed her face against the taxi window, mesmerised by the waking city. A street sweeper inched along the road in front of them, bathed in lamplight, its giant brooms whirring while early morning joggers ran past, rugged up against the cold, their breaths creating clouds in the frigid air. She was grateful that Shilly had packed her favourite navy overcoat, which Cyril had brought with him from home along with a suitcase of warm casual clothes including the most divine green-and-pink tartan skirt, matching tam-o'-shanter and a bright pink scarf.

It was a crisp winter's morning. The temperature had only just risen above freezing and a thick layer of frost covered the ground. The last stars were fading in the clearing sky, and the first rays of sunlight framed the rows of sandstone townhouses that lined the main road.

'I just love this time of day.' Alice-Miranda turned to the woman beside her. 'The way the lights are coming on and the blinds are going up, especially in the upstairs windows – they look like eyes blinking in the first sunbeams of the morning.'

'Mmm,' was all Caroline Clinch could muster in reply. She stared out of her side of the taxi, her mind so busy that she hadn't really registered anything she'd seen so far. This was the last thing she'd anticipated having to do this week. She'd argued with Livinia Reedy that she couldn't possibly leave her classes to attend such a frivolous indulgence – she'd used more temperate words, of course – but the woman didn't give her any choice in the matter. Clearly, the power of being acting headmistress had gone to Livinia's head.

'I adore Scotland.' Alice-Miranda sighed happily, oblivious to her companion's pinched expression. 'Have you been before, Mrs Clinch?'

'No,' the woman replied curtly.

'I've only visited Edinburgh once with Mummy and Daddy for a couple of days before heading south to stay with one of Granny Valentina's cousins. He and his wife live in the most gorgeous manor house. Uncle Morogh has wild red hair, although it's quite thin. Mummy thinks he dyes it because the bald bits are the same colour. He wears a kilt all the time, not just for special occasions, and drinks a thimble of whisky before breakfast, which he says is the best thing to start the day. Mummy and Daddy were both doubtful about that, but it hasn't seemed to do Uncle Morogh any harm.

'He's married to Aunt Audrina and she's bags of fun and a champion golfer. Together, they write kilt romance novels under the pen-name Audrina Morogh. Everyone thinks that's just one person, but of course it's two. I'd never even heard of the kilt romance genre until we went to stay with them. They were working on a story called *Kill or Kilt*, which Aunt Audrina said was to be a mix of romance, history and crime. I was keen to learn more about Scottish history, but Mummy said that I probably shouldn't read their books until I'm a little older. Apparently, the stories are a bit racy.'

Caroline wished the child would stop prattling on. She'd much rather be at home in front of the fire, reading or baking or even marking papers. On the rare occasions she had taken a trip away, the weather had been frightful, the airline delays disastrous and generally the whole thing had been a huge disappointment. So, Caroline Clinch had long ago concluded that it was better to stay put.

'Look, isn't that the prettiest school you've ever seen?' Alice-Miranda remarked as the taxi pulled up at the traffic lights outside Stewart's Melville College on Queensferry Road. The impressive sandstone building with its towers and turrets was truly gorgeous.

Even Caroline couldn't help but gasp. 'My goodness. I thought *we* lived in the lap of luxury,' the woman murmured.

'Oh yes, I can only agree,' Alice-Miranda said. 'We're the luckiest girls in the world to go to school where we do and to have such lovely teachers.'

In all her years working in schools, Caroline

had never encountered a child like this one. Alice-Miranda was as smart as a whip and always eager to learn. She'd never heard her say a bad word about anyone either. Surely she was too good to be true. That last comment proved beyond doubt that the child wasn't trustworthy – everyone knew there were a couple of old cranks at school you wouldn't have given tuppence for.

Alice-Miranda ran her finger down the itinerary which Miss Reedy had printed for her. 'It looks like we're staying in Edinburgh for a few days then going to Loch Ness and, after that, to St Andrew's and then New Lanark, which sounds quite familiar. I can't wait to find out exactly what we'll be doing in all those places.'

Five minutes later, the taxi pulled up outside the Royal Hotel. The door was opened by a man wearing a thick black woollen coat with gold braiding. A second fellow, identically dressed, walked around to the other side of the vehicle to retrieve the luggage. Caroline Clinch would have liked to stay in the vehicle and head straight back to the airport, although the thought of riding in a helicopter again turned her stomach.

'Good mornin', ladies.' The doorman tipped his

top hat and gave them a winning smile. 'Welcome to the Royal Hotel. I hope ye enjoy yer stay.'

Alice-Miranda's eyes sparkled as she offered the man her hand. 'Hello, my name is Alice-Miranda Highton-Smith-Kennington-Jones and I'm very pleased to meet you, Mr . . . ?'

'Campbell. Frazer Campbell.' He shook the child's hand gently.

'It's lovely to meet you, Mr Campbell, and thank you for your warm welcome. I'm so excited to be here. I'm part of the Future Leaders Opportunity Program, but my invitation got lost and that's why I'm late. I was truly disappointed when I wasn't accepted, but I realised that you don't always get to do the things you'd like to and so I was quite fine with it all in the end. Miss Reedy and I were going to the theatre to watch a production of *A Tale of Two Cities*, but then Mrs Clarkson came rushing into my room and said I was to pack my toiletries bag immediately. Ten minutes later, Cyril arrived in Birdy and away we flew – with Mrs Clinch as well. She's one of our Mathematics teachers.' The child motioned to the woman, who was shivering beside her and not one bit happy about it.

Mr Campbell blinked several times in quick

succession then smiled broadly. 'Well, that's a fine story, young lady. I look forward to hearing about yer adventures here in Scotland.'

'I can't wait to see everyone,' Alice-Miranda said.

Mrs Clinch rolled her eyes and bustled forward. 'Well, perhaps we could stop chatting and go inside then? It's a little chilly out here and I'd rather like a cup of tea.'

'Oops,' Alice-Miranda said. 'Mummy says I could talk underwater with a mouthful of marbles and I think she's probably right.'

The man winked at her and opened the hotel door, at which point Alice-Miranda and Mrs Clinch were greeted by a blast of warm air and a squeal of delight. Millie flew across the foyer and caught Alice-Miranda in a fierce hug.

'You're here!' she exclaimed.

'I can't believe it either. Thank you for organising everything,' Alice-Miranda said. 'I thought I must have been dreaming when Mrs Clarkson said there had been a mistake and my invitation had been lost.'

Caroline Clinch carried on to the reception desk to check them both in.

Millie was practically floating on air. 'You're never going to guess how many friends are here.

I'm not telling, though, because I want it to be a surprise,' she said, jigging on the spot. 'And you're rooming with me, but we're not in the same team – Miss Cranna wouldn't be swayed no matter how hard I tried. She's one of the ladies who works for the Queen's Colours and she's *mad* about cats. There's Mr Ferguson, who's in charge. If you thought Mr Lipp wore crazy suits, wait until you see him. Miss Stuart is his assistant and she's really sweet and says "wee" all the time. As in "little", not the other kind.'

Alice-Miranda giggled. She was surprised to hear there were teams, but excited by the prospect of working in a group and having goals to achieve. 'Is it a competition?' she asked.

'Sort of. There are lots of challenges and we earn points, but there's been no mention of a prize. There are five teams of six, and you're a captain and so am I. Everyone's at breakfast, but I snuck out because Miss Wall mentioned she'd received word from Mrs Clinch that you were almost here.'

'It sounds like there's been a lot happening already,' Alice-Miranda commented.

'We're off to our first activity at ten o'clock, so let's get something to eat,' Millie said. 'I've only had some cereal and I plan to graze my way through the entire buffet, although I'm drawing the line at black pudding.'

Alice-Miranda grinned. She couldn't wait to find out who else was at the forum. She told Mrs Clinch where they were going, and the pair disappeared through a set of glass doors to meet their friends.

The woman pressed her foot hard on the accelerator, urging the car to go faster. If only she hadn't stayed so long – but planning was the most crucial part of the process. If the plans were right then everything else would follow. This was far too important to mess up. There was too much at stake. She'd never forgive herself if . . . Well, it didn't bear thinking about. The stage was set. Everything was falling into place nicely and as long as she could get back in time, there was absolutely nothing to worry about at all.

Chapter 8

After greeting the girls from her own school and the boys from Fayle, Alice-Miranda was stunned to see Lucinda Finkelstein, Ava Lee and Quincy Armstrong hovering behind them grinning from ear to ear. Lucinda explained that Mrs Kimmel's School for Girls in Manhattan had been involved in the Queen's Colours for the past year, ever since their headmistress had learned of the program from Alice-Miranda's mother, who also happened to be one of her old friends.

Alice-Miranda hugged each of the girls and managed to ask how their families were before their teachers broke up the happy party and sent them all back to their tables to finish breakfast. She promised they would catch up properly during the day.

Alice-Miranda loved that lots of the children were wearing tam-o'-shanters, and Millie explained that everyone had received one upon arrival and a beautiful silver thistle pin too. No doubt Alice-Miranda would get hers soon.

'I told you you'd be amazed,' Millie said as they moved along the buffet. 'But that's not the only surprise.'

Alice-Miranda looked around the room, her eyes widening as she spied two girls she definitely hadn't expected to see. 'Oh heavens, that *is* a surprise.'

Millie rolled her eyes. 'Maybe not such a good one.'

Alice-Miranda set down her plate and made her way across the room to the girls' table. 'Hello,' she said, smiling broadly. 'How are you both?'

The smaller of the two girls stood up and for a second appeared sheepish before she hugged Alice-Miranda tightly.

The other girl shrugged. 'Okay, I guess.'

But Alice-Miranda was having none of it. 'You're here at the Future Leaders Opportunity Program, in Scotland. Surely life is better than okay? You must be doing really well at school – Miss Hobbs wouldn't have let you apply otherwise. She's not silly.'

'Come on, Alethea. You know Alice-Miranda is right,' Gretchen said, and turned to face the tiny child with the chocolate curls. 'Ever since you came to Mrs Kimmel's and accidentally told everyone who Alethea really was and we found out about her past, she's been a different person. It was as if you lifted the weight of the world from her shoulders.'

'Shut up, Gretchen. That's not what happened at all,' Alethea spat.

Gretchen glared at the girl. 'Who are you and what have you done with my friend Alethea Mackenzie? The one who totally turned a corner and became a really good human being?'

Alice-Miranda bit her lip. She hoped she hadn't started something between the two friends. 'Well, it's lovely to see you both. I'm sure we'll catch up properly later.'

Alice-Miranda was turning to go when Alethea grabbed her arm.

'Sorry.' The word came out at a whisper and Alethea released her grip. 'I'm really great and thank you for asking. I just didn't expect that you'd want to speak to me. I haven't always been especially nice to you. Actually, I pretty much blamed you for everything that ever went wrong in my life and that probably wasn't fair.'

Alice-Miranda stared at the girl, a sheen in her brown eyes. Then she reached out and hugged Alethea, who hugged her right back.

On the other side of the room, Sloane almost choked when she caught sight of the pair. 'What's going on over there?'

Jacinta turned to see what Sloane was on about and gaped like a floundering codfish. 'Wow. It seems Alethea really has changed. I always imagined she'd rather hug an anaconda than Alice-Miranda.'

Caprice snorted. 'Everyone can change, you know.'

'Yes, it's just a pity that some people choose not to,' Millie quipped as she slid onto the banquette. Her plate was piled high with scrambled eggs, hash browns, sausages and crispy bacon.

Alice-Miranda and Alethea each took a step backwards.

'How's your mother?' Alice-Miranda asked.

'She's very well. She and Daddy got divorced because he's a lying scoundrel. But Mummy is marrying again and to the loveliest man. And I'm getting a sister,' Alethea said, glancing at Gretchen.

Alice-Miranda laughed with delight. 'You don't mean . . .?'

'Yes, siree.' Gretchen nodded. 'Alethea's mum is marrying my dad and it's awesome. We're both going to be flower girls.'

Alice-Miranda wondered what had happened to Gretchen's mum, but now didn't seem like the right time to ask. She was just glad the girls were happy and there didn't seem to be any hard feelings.

'You and I are in the same team,' Alethea said to Alice-Miranda. 'You're in charge, so don't mess up. You know I don't like to come second.' Alethea raised her eyebrows then smiled.

Alice-Miranda smiled too. 'I'll definitely keep that in mind. Enjoy your breakfast. I'd better get mine or I'll be in trouble before the program officially begins.'

She gave the girls a wave and hurried back to the buffet, where she picked up her plate and rejoined the queue. The boy with sandy blond hair in front of her looked vaguely familiar, although she could only see his back.

After a few moments, she tapped the lad on the shoulder. 'Neville, is that you?'

The boy spun around. 'Hi!' he said, frowning. 'Oh, it's you, Alice-Miranda. You look older, in a good way.'

Alice-Miranda couldn't help noticing the changes in Neville too. His straight back and broad smile were so very different to the timid lad she'd met a few years ago on board the *Octavia*. It seemed Neville had acquired a healthy air of confidence about him. 'It's wonderful to see you. What have you been up to?'

'Still chasing butterflies,' Neville replied with a grin. 'I'm the Junior President of the International Lepidopterist Society these days.'

'I couldn't think of anyone who would deserve that position more. Gosh, especially considering the lengths you went to to meet President Grayson and save that species.' Neville had been on a mission to save the Euchloe Bazae, a rare butterfly whose habitat was under threat, when he set off on his ill-fated sea voyage to the United States. 'Are the two of you still in touch?' Alice-Miranda asked.

Neville nodded. 'He came to Barcelona a few months ago. My mother nearly had a stroke when the friend I'd invited over for dinner turned out to be the President of the United States. Mum was in full-on embarrassing parent mode and invited him to stay in our spare room for the night. Can you imagine President Grayson sleeping on the pull-out couch between Mum's sewing table and the elliptical machine? Thankfully, the President was a good sport about the whole thing and invited us to his place instead. So, we're going to the White House in the summer holidays and then to his beach house too.' Neville's ears had turned a slight shade of pink, reminding Alice-Miranda of when she'd first met him.

'That's fantastic. I'm sure you'll have an incredible time.' She beamed. 'We've got a lot of catching up to do.'

Neville smiled and Alice-Miranda felt a shiver run down her spine. Her skin tingled and her stomach did a little flip.

'Are you all right?' the boy asked.

Alice-Miranda nodded. 'Yes, I think so. It just felt like some of your butterflies started having a party in my tummy – or a boxing match.'

'I like that idea – can you imagine how pretty a butterfly party would be?' Neville grinned. 'Like you.' The boy's face turned the colour of beetroot. 'Did I just say that out loud? I better, um . . . eat, uh, breakfast.' He struggled to find the right words and in a split second he was gone.

A smile tickled Alice-Miranda's lips. It was wonderful to see Neville again. He really was the loveliest boy.

Chapter 9

After breakfast, Alice-Miranda made her way through the throng of students in the conference room, introducing herself in the usual way and trying to remember all of their names. So far she had met two boys from Paris as well as lads from Switzerland, Ireland and Scotland, three children from South Africa, two each from Singapore and New Zealand in addition to the girls from New York and Neville from Spain. Alice-Miranda continued on to a girl with cascading blonde curls who was wearing white tights adorned with bright pink flamingos.

'Hello, I'm Alice-Miranda Highton-Smith-Kennington-Jones,' she said with a smile. 'It's lovely to make your acquaintance.'

The girl's blue eyes sparkled. 'I'm Britt Fox and it's such a pleasure to meet you,' she said, diving straight in for a hug. 'I knew from the moment I saw you this morning that you and I would become firm friends. I get these feelings from time to time and I've never been proven wrong.'

Alice-Miranda gasped. 'That happens to me too.'

'See? I told you we would be friends,' Britt said with a wink.

Alice-Miranda took stock of the petite girl with radiant skin and shell pink nails. Her clothes were fabulous, but Alice-Miranda wondered if she'd be warm enough in just a T-shirt and denim shorts over her tights. Britt also had on a pair of cute red Mary Janes and a backpack covered entirely with silver sequins. 'Aren't you cold?'

Britt shook her head. 'Norway is much chillier than Scotland,' she replied. 'And don't worry, I have a coat for later. Your coat is so chic and I do adore that skirt.'

'Thank you. Mummy chose it. I've always wanted to visit Norway and now I'll have a friend for when I do. I love your tights, by the way,' Alice-Miranda said. 'They're fun.'

'They were mail order from Finkelstein's in New York,' Britt replied with a grin. 'It's my dream to open my own department store that only sells ethically sourced fashion. I'm hoping the program has some mentors we can link with so I can learn everything there is to know about pursuing such a venture.'

Alice-Miranda's eyes lit up. 'Have you met Lucinda? Her parents own Finkelstein's. It's the most glorious shop. I'd love to introduce you.'

The girl guided her new friend over to the American contingent and introduced her to Lucinda so they could talk all things retail.

Millie had been chatting to Chessie nearby and overheard what Alice-Miranda had said. 'Did you forget to mention that your family has an even lovelier department store on Fifth Avenue?' she chided.

Alice-Miranda raised her eyebrows. 'It would sound like showing off if I did. Besides, I'm sure Lucinda will probably tell her.'

'You never show off,' Millie said. 'Unlike

someone else.' She glanced over at Caprice, who was flicking her copper tresses and batting her eyelids at the French boys, Vincent and Philippe. 'I bet they know all about her star status.'

A bell tinkled and Davina Stuart stood at the front of the room waiting for the children to stop speaking. Alice-Miranda thought the woman looked to be in her mid-thirties, although it was always hard to tell with adults. She was dressed in jeans and an Aran jumper with taupe ballet flats. Her face was free of make-up and she wore dark-rimmed glasses with her hair pulled back in an Alice band.

'Good morning, everyone. How wonderful to see so many of you in your wee tams. I trust that you all slept well. I'm afraid Miss Cranna seems to have been delayed and Mr Ferguson is on his way, so let's get you into your groups and we can discuss this morning's challenge,' she said cheerily.

At that moment Morag Cranna burst through the doors, cradling a huge pile of folders to her chest. She looked as if she'd just leapt out of bed and got dressed in the dark. Her collar was askew inside a bold red jumper with a white Persian cat knitted on the front. She had a black cat dangling from one ear and a butterfly from the other, and her dark curls had all the styling of a bird's nest.

'Are you all right, sweetheart?' Davina asked.

Morag sighed loudly. 'No, I need to get organised.' She bustled forward and tripped over a stray daypack, sending her pile of folders scattering across the floor. The woman dropped to her knees.

Alice-Miranda raced over to help. 'Hello,' she said, 'you must be Miss Cranna. My name is Alice-Miranda –' Before the child could introduce herself properly, the woman glanced up and cut her off.

'Oh, thank heavens you've arrived. You're in charge of Team Five. You need to tell me what you're going to call yourselves.' Morag stared at the girl.

'Other than Alethea, I don't even know who's in my group.' Alice-Miranda passed the folders she was holding to Miss Cranna. 'I'll go and see if I can find them,' she said and charged off.

'Well, please hurry. We haven't got all day,' the woman said as she stood up and dumped the pile onto a table at the front of the room, then straightened her skirt and brushed the dust from her elbow. She plucked her collar from the inside of her jumper and ran her fingers through her tousled curls.

Alice-Miranda spotted Alethea at the back of the room and called to her. 'Alethea, would you be able to tell me who else is in our team? Apparently, we have to choose a name. Did you come up with something last night?'

Alethea shook her head. 'No, but we're all here.'

Lucinda Finkelstein, Sep and Sloane Sykes, Alethea Goldsworthy and a girl Alice-Miranda still hadn't met were standing together.

'Oh, fantastic! What a great group,' Alice-Miranda said with a smile. She turned to the girl with the mouse-brown hair and offered her hand. 'Hello, my name is Alice-Miranda Highton-Smith-Kennington-Jones. What's your name?'

The girl looked at her blankly, then extended a limp paw. 'Madagascar Slewt. I go to Bodlington.'

'Oh, wow, our friend Chessie used to go there. She's standing over there with Millie,' Alice-Miranda said, pointing in their direction.

'Millie's my cousin,' Madagascar said plainly.

Alice-Miranda blinked. She remembered Millie telling her and Chessie once that she had a cousin who went to Bodlington, but she'd never said any more about her. This was a lovely surprise.

'Well, it's great to meet you. Any cousin of

Millie's is definitely going to be a friend of ours. Have you met everyone else?' Alice-Miranda asked.

Madagascar nodded. Last night when Miss Cranna had announced the teams, she was seething that she wasn't going to be the captain. On top of that, her cousin was in the same team as that pathetic Francesca Compton-Halls. Madagascar had been sorely disappointed when Chessie left Bodlington. She still hadn't managed to find anyone who was half as much fun to tease.

'Miss Cranna enquired after our team name. Does anyone have an idea?' Alice-Miranda asked.

'It should have a Scottish theme,' Sep piped up.

'Quick, what are some Scottish words?' Sloane said. 'Highlands, kilts, tartan, terriers, haggis . . .' The girl frowned.

'What about Nessie's Monsters?' Alice-Miranda suggested.

There were nods all around except for Madagascar, whose lips turned south and looked as if she might cry.

'Don't you like it?' Sloane asked the girl. 'I think it's clever.'

'I just don't like being called a monster,' Madagascar replied sadly. 'We have this really mean housemistress and she calls me a monster all the time and I have no idea why. She's always trying to get me into trouble.'

'We're not really saying that we're monsters,' Alethea said. 'It's a play on words – you know, as in the Loch Ness Monster?'

Alice-Miranda reached out and touched Madagascar gently on the arm. 'We can pick another name if you'd like.'

'I think it's a great name,' Sloane said, noticing that Miss Cranna was tapping a ruler against a glass and asking everyone to be quiet.

'It's okay,' Madagascar relented. 'So long as no one ever calls *me* a monster.'

'Great, that's settled then,' Alethea said. 'I bet ours is the best name.'

'I'm sure that naming our groups is not a competition,' Sep said.

Alethea flicked her hand. 'Whatever.'

Alice-Miranda hurried over to inform Miss Cranna of their decision. She had a feeling that her fabulous group might be a little feisty too.

Chapter 10

Gordy Onslow sat on the edge of his squeaky bed and pulled on his socks. His twisted toes were crippled with arthritis, but it was his hands that worried him the most. They were white from the centre joint to the tips – and some days purple too. They ached constantly. His back ached as well, although that was more likely from the lumpy mattress, but at least it was thicker than the one he'd had previously.

The furnace had been on the blink again last

night, but it must have fired up just now – he could feel a faint breath of warm air and the icicles inside the window were beginning to melt, dripping onto the bare boards. Gordy stood up and peered through the grimy window pane into the street below. He liked being up high. You could see things. He'd seen a lot of things in his life – some he wouldn't wish on anyone. He watched a couple, wrapped in their woollen coats, arm in arm, tripping along the cobblestones, a lightness in their steps that was reserved for the young. They had the world at their feet, gazing into a future of endless possibilities. Until life gets in their way. Until there are jobs to be done and bills to be paid and people who won't leave you alone. Until the pressure builds like a cooker and there's no release – or is there? And the path you've chosen destroys every good thing you have ever known.

Gordy's breath caught in his throat. A tear trickled down his lined cheek and he wept for the things he'd lost. For his girl. For the shame. For the lost opportunities and wasted years. He retrieved a handkerchief from his pocket and wiped his face, then grabbed his beanie and gloves and the overcoat that hung on the hook on the back of the door. He picked up the huge bag of plastic bottles that was sitting in the corner of the tiny room beside the washbasin. He'd take the bus to the recycling centre first thing and then get out collecting again. Winter was always harder than summer. The tourists weren't nearly as thirsty but at thirty pence per return he could still make a few quid each day. Not that he needed much money. His pension paid for the bedsit and there was nothing else to spend it on.

Gordy opened the door and turned to look back at the room. Who would have thought he'd have ended up here? He brushed aside the thought and stepped into the cold. There was nothing to be gained from living in the past.

Chapter 11

Morag Cranna had stacked her folders on the table, straightened herself up and finished the cup of tea that Miss Wall had kindly made for her. She took a deep breath as her internal voice implored her to remain calm. She'd come so far; she wasn't about to let a few bumps get in her way. The woman cleared her throat and was about to ask Miss Stuart to write up the team names on the leaderboard when Barclay Ferguson burst into the room. One day the silly old coot would injure himself good and proper. She should have known that he couldn't resist a grand appearance and, given he'd recently been walking around the office on them, it was no real surprise that he'd brought out the stilts.

'Good mornin', all,' he called. 'What a day! What a wonderful day. I've just been gettin' some exercise.'

The children giggled. Mr Ferguson was fun, although Millie was a bit disappointed he'd toned down his suit today to pinstripes and a bright yellow tie. She'd loved yesterday's tartan.

He jumped to the ground and leaned the stilts in a corner. 'Today, yer goin' off on yer first challenge, which is designed to test whether ye can work together as a team and find the solutions to some brain-bendin' cryptic clues. I hope you'll enjoy them. I wrote them meself,' he said, clasping his hands together and doing his best impersonation of a giggly teenager. He looked at the whiteboard and, realising there were no teams written up yet, he turned to Morag. 'Where are the names?'

'I was just about to ask for them before you . . . arrived,' the woman replied.

'Well, let's action it then!' he cried. 'I'll explain once we have them.'

Morag quickly cast about the room, asking the leaders what they'd decided on.

Millie's group had named themselves Clan Mac, which was a play on her surnames and 'clan' being a word used in Scotland to describe extended family groups from the twelfth century onwards. Millie added that 'clan' was derived from the Gaelic word *clann*, which literally meant children.

'What a wonderfully appropriate name, Millie. That's terribly impressive,' Mr Ferguson said. 'It's no wonder yer the captain of yer team or, should I say, yer clan?' He grinned at Morag, who smiled on cue. She was still annoyed that he'd interfered the previous evening, particularly as she'd had to spend half the night redoing the team lists in the children's folders so Lucas Nixon would be none the wiser about losing his position as leader of that team.

The second group called themselves The Tartan Warriors. In charge was a red-haired lad named Declan. Susannah and Sofia were part of his team along with Britt Fox and the two French boys, Vincent and Philippe. Ava Lee announced her group, which included Quincy and Gretchen, and three students from South Africa, Junior, Brendan and Isabeau. They called themselves The Highland

Flingers and all of them stood up to perform a jig, which had the rest of the teams roaring with laughter. The fourth group were The Pipers, led by Aidan Blair, who whipped out a set of bagpipes from under his chair, promptly tucking the hide bag under his arm, raising the mouthpiece to his lips and belting out the first few bars of 'Mull of Kintyre'.

The door to the conference room flew open and a stream of pensioners shuffled into the room. They'd been in the hall on the way to their tour bus and were all set to see a pipes and drums concert later that day, but the noise had created some confusion.

'Och aye, is this where we're goin' to see the show?' said a lady with a walking stick. 'I thought we had to get on the bus first.'

Davina Stuart hurriedly ushered them out. Unfortunately, she missed one fellow who managed to sneak into the back row. It was another several minutes before he was discovered, after demanding that the volume be turned up. The children giggled as Sep and Lucas went to the man's aid, guiding him back to his companions.

Having had quite enough, Mr Ferguson waved his arms in the air and shouted over the skirly racket.

'Thank ye, thank ye, Aidan! Absolutely brilliant, but perhaps ye can save it for later and somewhere more appropriate.' The man dropped his voice to a whisper and added, 'Like outside in a field far, far away.'

Alice-Miranda was last to announce her team name, Nessie's Monsters.

'Although I would like to point out that there aren't any real monsters in our group,' she said with a grin and gave Madagascar a wink.

Chessie gulped. 'Don't be so sure of that,' she muttered, hoping that by some miracle Madagascar had been struck by lightning or some such thing and the event had completely transformed her personality. To be fair, so far she seemed to be getting on well with everyone and Chessie had managed to avoid any personal interactions. Still, her stomach lurched whenever the girl was within a three-metre radius. Truth be told, Chessie was terrified of her. The girl had done some truly nasty things at Bodlington and had proven to be an expert at covering her tracks.

Barclay Ferguson looked at the list of names. 'I'd like to give ye all ten points for inventiveness. Those team names are so ... Scottish. But I particularly like Clan Mac, so I am going to award them an extra ten points – in addition to Millie's problem-solvin' in gettin' Alice-Miranda here. So, by my calculations, that puts Clan Mac on thirty points and everyone else on ten. Ye will have plenty of opportunities to boost your scores, and I will be askin' the teachers and Miss Cranna and Miss Stuart for their observations too.'

'Is there a prize for winning?' Madagascar asked. She didn't really see the point if there were no riches to be claimed at the end.

Mr Ferguson ran his hand through his silver hair and smiled. 'Och aye, of course. I should have told ye that already, shouldn't I?'

The children leaned in, eager to hear what it was.

'There will be daily winners, but the ultimate team will receive a reward like no other.' The man paused for dramatic effect. 'Her Majesty has offered the winners an overnight stay at Evesbury Palace!'

Caprice folded her arms across her chest and smiled smugly. 'Been there, done that.'

'By accident,' Millie added. She just couldn't help herself sometimes.

Mr Ferguson gave Caprice the hairy eyeball. 'I hadn't quite finished. While yer there, ye will be given the opportunity to be real leaders – Her Majesty has said that she will agree to anythin' ye want for twenty-four hours. Nothin' is off the table, but ye must think about the consequences of yer decision-makin' as that's what bein' a real leader is all about,' the man said. 'In addition to which, the team will have the honour of helpin' to plan the next FLOP and attendin' as assistant leaders.'

'Yes!' Caprice hissed. 'We could make her fly in our favourite band and have a huge party in the ballroom, with chocolate fountains and giant lollipops and all the sweets we can eat! Or what if we make her give us the keys to the vault and we could take whatever we wanted? This is the best prize ever! Clan Mac had better win this thing.'

But Madagascar Slewt had other ideas. If her team won, she was going to get rid of that horrid old housemistress Mrs Fairbanks quick smart.

'Well, what are ye all waitin' for?' Barclay Ferguson leapt onto a chair at the front of the room as if propelled by excitement alone. 'Off ye go to the first challenge!'

He was met by a sea of confused faces.

Miss Cranna tapped him on the leg. 'Sir, I haven't yet given them their instructions or allocated teachers to their groups,' she said quietly. Davina Stuart chortled into her hand.

'Oh, forgive me. I'm a big-picture thinker, ye see – never been terribly good at the minutiae – which is why Miss Cranna and Miss Stuart are my right and left hands.' Barclay hopped down.

Davina grinned. It was nice to hear how much she was valued.

Morag waited a moment, then asked the captains to collect their folders. They each contained the itinerary for the program and some information about the activities. As well as the challenges and outings, there would be lectures in the evenings from prominent leaders in their fields and some leisure activities for the students to unwind. There would be extra material handed out each day so they couldn't be overly prepared for what lay ahead and to ensure there were still some surprises.

'The last thing I need to do is allocate a teacher who will be on hand to distribute clues for the treasure hunt at the castle this morning when certain checkpoints are reached,' Miss Cranna said. 'Please don't try to goad them or bribe them into helping you because I'm sure they won't. Your teacher supervisor will be making sure that the rules of the challenges are obeyed to the letter of the law, giving instructions and general support and supervision – and making sure that everyone is where they need to be when they need to be there. They also have a small budget for transport. So, without further ado, Clan Mac, you're with Mr Williams from St Odo's School in Christchurch; Nessie's Monsters, you have Mr Pienaar from Todder House in Capetown; Tartan Warriors, please introduce yourselves to Miss Patrick from Mrs Kimmel's School for Girls in New York; Highland Flingers, say *bonjour* to Mr Arnaud from Lycée International Paris; and the Pipers will be under the supervision of Miss Wall from Winchesterfield-Downsfordvale Academy for Proper Young Ladies.'

Caroline Clinch's ears pricked up from where she was standing at the back of the room. 'What am I supposed to be doing then?' she asked.

Morag gulped. She hadn't even thought about the woman who had escorted their missing student. 'Erm, I . . .' She cast a panicked glance Davina's way. 'Well . . . we thought you would do a wonderful job of supervising the supervisors and helping out wherever you're needed. It's an important role and we're fortunate that you came along,' Morag said, hoping that was enough for the woman.

'Is that really necessary?' Caroline snarked. 'Surely they're all trustworthy individuals. I should be back at school teaching my classes, keeping my program up to date, not gallivanting around Edinburgh in some fake role.'

'Come on, Caroline – it sounds like fun to me. Do you know how many teachers would love to be here?' Benitha Wall piped up.

'Well, I am not one of them. I'll be calling Miss Grimm and letting her know that this is a terrible waste of staff resources.' Even beneath her too-long fringe, the woman's contempt was plain to see.

'Seriously, Caroline. You're here now. I suggest you stop being an A-grade whiner and try to enjoy yourself. Given this is all about leadership, you're hardly setting a fine example,' Benitha chided.

Some of the children and staff chuckled.

'I'm sure that you'll feel differently in a day or so, Mrs Clinch, when you see how important your role is,' Morag said, wondering what else they could allocate to the woman so she had something useful to do.

The Maths teacher let out a sigh. 'I can't imagine so.'

The children were given a few minutes to acquaint themselves with the teacher in charge of their group. Alice-Miranda greeted Mr Pienaar in the usual way and was interested to learn that the man was a huge sports fan and on the weekends played drums in a rock band. Hansie Pienaar was a mountain of a man. He had a thick thatch of blond hair and matching eyebrows. He taught History and coached rugby and it was his first visit to Edinburgh, so he couldn't wait to get out there and see the sights.

Alice-Miranda had already thumbed through the information folder and noted the first activity was to take place at Edinburgh Castle.

'We're going on a treasure hunt this morning and there are all sorts of cryptic clues that we have to collect along the way. It says that the challenge involves working together and seeing how we overcome difficulties to solve problems. I suppose the first problem is getting to the castle,' the child said, pulling a map of the city out of the folder and holding it up.

'There it is,' Sep said, pointing to one of the squares. 'It's not too far. Perhaps we could walk down here.' He traced his finger along the proposed route.

'There's a tram stop right outside the hotel,' Madagascar said. 'I'm sure that would be faster.'

'What about a bus? Like those tourist ones that you hop on and off?' Sloane said.

Sep shook his head. 'Too expensive. We'd spend all our money and there'd be nothing left for emergencies.'

'I think we should take a taxi,' Alethea chimed in. She was wearing brand-new boots and could feel a slightly uncomfortable pinch on her left toes.

There was a chorus of noes and Madagascar, Sloane and Alethea all started talking over the top of one another.

Alice-Miranda clapped her hands. 'Quiet, please,' she called. 'We're never going to get anywhere if we can't speak sensibly and listen to each other's suggestions.'

Lucinda Finkelstein raised her hand. The girl had barely said a word the whole morning. Alice-Miranda hoped that she wasn't too overwhelmed by the bigger personalities in their group.

Alice-Miranda nodded in her direction.

'It's much quicker if we go this way,' the girl said, tracing her finger along an alternative route.

'How do you know that?' Madagascar said with a sneer. 'Have you been here before?'

Lucinda shook her head. 'I thought it would be a good idea to do a bit of homework prior to the trip, so I studied maps of the city. I knew which hotel we were staying in because it was in the letter. It should be a twenty-minute walk and, by the time the tram arrives, we could probably be there.'

Alice-Miranda smiled at the girl. 'And that, Lucinda Finkelstein, is why you are a leader of the future.'

Sep nodded and the dark-haired girl smiled. She had been wondering if she'd ever get a word in with Sloane, Alethea and Madagascar in her team.

'I still think the tram's a better idea,' Madagascar said with a pout. 'But I guess it's not up to me.'

Alice-Miranda glanced at the time and noted it was two minutes to ten. 'We'd better get a wriggle on, so let's go with Lucinda's suggestion. Okay, everyone, synchronise your watches,' the girl instructed. 'Edinburgh Castle, here we come!'

Chapter 12

Alice-Miranda led Nessie's Monsters through the foyer to the hotel's revolving front door. 'We have to stay together on our way there,' she reminded the group. 'Once we're inside the castle, we can have a different strategy, but I would hate for anyone to get lost before we've even started.'

They all nodded. A brisk wind had sprung up. Alice-Miranda looped her scarf around her neck and buttoned her coat.

There had been a great deal of discussion back inside about not following others, and about how the children were leaders, not sheep. It seemed that all of the groups were taking those words to heart. Every single one of them appeared to be heading to the destination by a different route.

Lucinda was in charge of the map and Sep had offered to assist. The pair of them plotted their path and were now looking up the street. Meanwhile, Millie and the rest of Clan Mac had decided to take the tram. It had been Neville's suggestion. He'd picked up a timetable from the hotel concierge the night before and worked out that the tram would get them to the castle quite quickly so long as they left the hotel right on ten o'clock.

Alice-Miranda and her group trotted off along Rutland Street, turning right into Lothian Road and then left into King's Stables Road, which was bordered on both sides by ancient stone walls topped intermittently with iron fencing. The children made a left turn into the Princes Street Gardens and, once off the public road, began to jog up the hill.

'It's just up there,' Lucinda called.

The children ascended the hill and spotted a

giant flight of stone steps that would lead them to their destination.

Madagascar noticed her cousin at the top of the stairs already. 'There's Millie! I told you the tram would be faster,' she grumbled.

Sloane couldn't help smiling as she saw Mr Williams, the teacher from New Zealand, having a stern word with Caprice. Who knew what havoc that girl had wreaked already.

'Doesn't mean they'll be any quicker on the treasure hunt,' Sep reminded Madagascar. 'It's about using your brain, not just being the speediest around the castle.'

'It helps if you're there first, though,' the girl retorted, and charged up the staircase, taking two steps at a time.

The six children reached the top with Mr Pienaar hot on their heels. There was still some distance to the castle gates across a large stretch of bitumen called the Esplanade.

'What a glorious view,' Alice-Miranda said. She stopped for a moment to take it all in. Back towards the east was a huge hill. 'I wish I could remember the name of that mountain there. Doesn't it look lovely in this light?'

'That's Arthur's Seat,' a man answered.

Alice-Miranda turned in the direction of the voice. A fellow dressed in a long grey overcoat, with a hat pulled around his ears and a black-and-tan glove on his left hand, was clutching a long stick with pincers on the bottom, trying to extricate something from a crevice in the stones near the top of the stairs. She noticed a large plastic bag full of bottles nearby.

'Oh, thank you for telling me that. I couldn't remember the name. I've only been to Edinburgh once before,' Alice-Miranda replied, smiling at him.

The fellow nodded.

She noticed that the fingers on his right hand were a deathly shade of white from the middle knuckle and almost blue at the tips. 'What happened to your other glove?' she asked.

'Lost,' he replied.

'Well, that won't do. They'll end up frostbitten – if they're not already. When my friends and I were in Switzerland, our ski instructor, Michaela, told us how quickly frostbite can set in – it's quite frightening really,' the child said. She glanced over at the row of shops on the other side of the road and saw that there was one selling woollen goods. 'Shall we buy you a new pair?'

'Oh, no need, miss. It's not that cold,' the man said. 'My hands are just old and I have something called Raynaud syndrome – don't worry, you canna catch it and it won't kill me either.'

Alethea scowled. 'Hurry up, Alice-Miranda,' she hissed. 'You know we shouldn't talk to strangers.'

'We won't be strangers if I tell the man my name and he tells me his,' the child replied, then proceeded to introduce herself in the usual way.

A smile tickled the old man's lips. It had been a while since someone had shown him such kindness. People didn't usually talk to him. They wrinkled their noses and called out horrible names. On the worst occasions, they threw rubbish or even rocks. 'I'm Gordy Onslow,' he said quietly.

'It's lovely to meet you, Mr Onslow. I'm afraid I'd better get going or I'll be in trouble with my team,' the girl said, and turned back to see that Madagascar, Sloane and Alethea had already scarpered. She spied them racing towards the castle entrance, but they were soon lost in a sea of tourists. She gave the man a wave and hurried away to find her team mates.

'I don't know why they ran off,' Lucinda said. 'Teams aren't allowed in until all of their members are present. It's one of the rules.'

Sep nodded. 'But we'd best hurry. We don't want the others getting too far ahead.'

Inside the castle walls, Alice-Miranda decided on a spot outside the New Barracks as the team's central meeting point. The castle didn't consist of a single building, but comprised a whole village at the top of the rocky mount protected by fortified walls. The barracks were about halfway up.

Mr Pienaar retrieved an envelope from the satchel he was carrying and passed it to Alice-Miranda. She opened it and read out the first clue.

I was the biggest and the best until I burst
and took a rest.
I've been restored to former glory, but my
work's no longer gory.
I am wide of girth and prominent –
gladly not so dominant.
I live my life outside and stand in iron pride.

Alethea groaned. 'What on earth is *that* supposed to mean?'

Sep thought for a moment. 'A weapon?' he said, looking to see where the battlements were located. 'It's outside and they used to do gory work.'

'That could be right,' Sloane agreed. It annoyed her no end to be outsmarted by her brother, but at least they were on the same team. Between him and Alice-Miranda, there were some pretty powerful brain cells.

'Okay, let's split up,' Alice-Miranda said. 'Sep and Lucinda, you go together with Madagascar and we can team up, Sloane and Alethea.'

'Should we meet back here in fifteen minutes?' Madagascar said.

Sep shook his head. 'Someone might find the answer faster than that. We need a signal so we don't waste too much time.'

'What about a whistle?' Alethea said, sticking her fingers in her mouth and creating an almighty screech.

Sep nodded. 'I can do that.'

'Me too,' Alice-Miranda said, and they both demonstrated their skills.

So it was agreed. The children headed off around the castle walls, and it wasn't more than five minutes before Sep found what they were looking for – a giant cannon called Mons Meg. He stuck his fingers in his mouth and, much to the horror of the woman standing beside him, whistled loudly, drawing his team mates back to their meeting point in no time flat. Sep whispered the answer to the others and scribbled it on the piece of paper Alice-Miranda had been holding. She popped it back into the envelope, resealed it and handed it to Mr Pienaar, who exchanged it for their second clue.

Alice-Miranda tore open the next envelope and read the clue aloud.

In the middle of the night a soldier
called out in fright.
It seemed that his bite helped his kinsmen
win a fight.
With his purple head, you wouldn't
want him in your bed,
but there's not so much to dread and
at least the rabbits will be fed.

Sloane's shoulders slumped. 'What's that supposed to mean?' she complained.

Alethea came up with the idea that it might

be a thistle – they have purple heads and rabbits like to eat them.

Lucinda nodded. She'd been reading something about thistles helping the Scots win a battle once. It had to be that. But where to start looking?

'Maybe there's a symbol or insignia in the Great Hall,' Alice-Miranda suggested. 'Let's have a look, but I think we should stick together this time.'

They all agreed and charged away.

The groups were crisscrossing the castle grounds like an army of ants. Given that there was no strict order to the way the envelopes were passed out, they were generally not looking for the same things at the same time, which made it harder for anyone to cheat.

Morag Cranna disappeared to get some warm drinks for herself, Davina and Barclay. She also had another phone call to deal with and didn't want to risk anyone listening in.

Chapter 13

Caprice was bored and cold. This treasure hunt was taking far too long and it wasn't nearly as exciting as she had hoped it would be. She detested taking orders from that ginger-haired bossy boots and Mr Williams wasn't very nice either. It wasn't her fault the old man fell over as she'd charged off the tram – he should have moved faster. There had to be an easier way to get the answers.

Clan Mac rounded the corner to the left while, up ahead, Alice-Miranda and her team were scurrying towards the Great Hall. Caprice suddenly had a brilliant idea. She cast a wary glance to either side and, without a moment's hesitation, hotfooted it after them.

Millie only realised that the girl was missing when the rest of them reached Mr Williams and she counted heads. 'Where's Caprice?' she asked with a note of impatience.

'She's probably batting her eyelashes at those French boys again,' Chessie said with a cheeky grin.

Despite Jacinta's best efforts, Mr Williams refused to hand out the next clue until all members of the group had returned. It was in the rules. Millie told her off for even trying as she didn't want Clan Mac getting a bad reputation.

'We've been doing really well until now,' Jacinta whined. 'Trust Caprice to go AWOL.'

Mr Williams was beginning to realise that he had his hands full with Caprice on the team – the girl hadn't seemed remotely contrite about what had happened on the tram.

'Perhaps you should check the ladies' toilets,' Neville suggested, blushing ever so slightly. 'She might have, you know, had an urgent call of nature.'

Lucas shrugged. 'Maybe she stopped at the gift shop to buy some souvenirs.'

'There's no point in all of us looking for her, in case she turns up here,' Millie said.

'I'll go,' Chessie offered.

After a brief discussion, Millie agreed that the rest of them would stay put while Chessie did a quick search of the nearby facilities. She recalled seeing a sign for some toilets close by and scurried off towards the Royal Palace. Chessie entered the stone building and wound her way down the steps, making sure to hold on to the iron rail. She could hear footsteps thumping towards her and hoped they belonged to Caprice. As Chessie rounded the corner, her breath caught in her throat.

Madagascar Slewt looked up and smiled. 'Oh, it's you,' she said sweetly. 'Were you looking for the loo?'

Chessie shook her head. 'Caprice,' was all she could utter.

'Haven't seen her.' Madagascar shrugged.

'Thanks,' Chessie whispered, backing away. 'I'd better go.'

'Why?' Madagascar lunged forward and grabbed the girl's arm. 'I was hoping we could catch up. I've missed you so much since you went off to that horrible new school of yours.'

'It's not horrible,' Chessie said softly. 'It's lovely.'

Madagascar's eyebrows jumped up on her forehead. 'Really?' she said, squeezing Chessie's arm. 'Perhaps I should see if I can move there too.'

Chessie's heart was thumping so hard she wondered if Madagascar could see it beating in her chest. 'B-but you love Bodlington, and your father is Chairman of the School Council.'

'That's true,' Madagascar said with a sigh. She released her hold of Chessie as though she were throwing a piece of rubbish on the street. 'Mrs Fairbanks is still so mean to me, though. And at least when you were there we had lots of fun – when you weren't crying, that is.'

Chessie thought of all the times Madagascar called her a crybaby. The girl even stole Rodney, Chessie's toy dog, and hid him for a week in Mrs Fairbanks's wellington boots. There was nothing fun at all about being with Madagascar. In many ways, Winchesterfield-Downsfordvale was a dream come true for Chessie. There was no way Madagascar Slewt was going to ruin everything.

Chessie drew herself up as tall as she could, even though she was trembling so hard she had to hold on to the railing. 'You never worried about me, Madagascar. You loved that I was sad. And then you did everything possible to make me even sadder.'

At that point Madagascar began to sob. Loudly. At full volume. No doubt she was expecting some poor unsuspecting tourist to come to her aid and then Chessie would be in trouble for upsetting her.

Chessie shook her head. 'Stop that nonsense, Madagascar. I know they're only crocodile tears.'

There was a sound of scuffling feet on the stairs. Chessie turned and was surprised to see Millie's head poke around the bend.

'What's happened?' the girl asked, looking from Madagascar to Chessie.

Chessie opened her mouth to say something, but the words wouldn't come.

Millie passed Madagascar a tissue and the girl wiped her face. Something about her tears gave Millie a funny feeling. She couldn't figure out why. It had been years since they'd spent any time together, but there was a memory scratching at the back of her brain.

Madagascar hiccupped and blew her nose. 'I ran into Chessie and then I was overcome because I'm so sad that she left Bodlington. We were best friends and now I don't have anyone,' the girl sniffled.

Chessie looked on in shock. If she'd been able to move, she would have pinched herself.

'Oh, Maddie, I'm sure Chessie misses you too.' Millie stepped down so she was level with Madagascar and wrapped her arms around the girl. It occurred to Millie that it was strange Chessie had never talked about any of the students from Bodlington. In fact, the girl had always said she'd been completely miserable in the short time she'd been there.

Madagascar peered over her cousin's shoulder at Chessie, her sad face immediately replaced by a smirk. She arched her left eyebrow.

Chessie shuddered. This did not bode well for the rest of the week. Who knew what that awful Madagascar Slewt was capable of?

Caprice ducked behind a tapestry wall hanging as Alice-Miranda and Sep surveyed the Great Hall, looking for their next answer. Sloane and Alethea were standing at the hearth of the gigantic fireplace gazing upwards, while Lucinda was investigating an odd-looking seat that was built in behind a partition wall.

'Up there!' Sep pointed to a spot where one of the beams was resting on the carved stones. 'It's a thistle.'

Caprice smiled to herself and, armed with the answer, stepped out from her hiding place as a tour group passed by. She attached herself to an elderly woman, who nodded and smiled at her. Caprice shuffled along with the senior citizens for a few metres before speeding away, almost knocking over a man with a walking stick.

She hadn't realised that Sloane and Alethea had spotted her.

'Stop cheating, Caprice!' Sloane called out, earning her a stern shushing from a guard.

Caprice turned around and poked out her tongue. 'As if!' she scoffed. 'My team just split up to find the next clue.'

But as Nessie's Monsters headed back to Mr Pienaar to hand in their answer, the fact that they saw Millie telling off Caprice for having disappeared was something of a dead giveaway.

'You know we're way behind now, thanks to you,' Millie grouched.

'No, we're not!' Caprice sniped, brushing past the girl and heading straight for Mr Williams. 'And you can thank me later.'

Chapter 14

It was just after half past twelve when Nessie's Monsters located the last piece of the puzzle.

'We'd better get moving or we'll be late back to the hotel,' Alice-Miranda said. 'But we should be thinking about what all of those answers mean if we put them together. Maybe it's a saying or a place?'

Sep nodded. 'Perhaps it has something to do with being a leader. Or someone important in Scottish history like Robbie Burns.'

Sloane wrinkled her nose. 'Who's he?'

The clues had led the children to various landmarks in the castle: the Stone of Destiny, a message in one of the replica embroideries that were originally created by Mary Queen of Scots and her gaoler's wife, Bess of Hardwick; the giant cannon, Mons Meg; a French prisoner's engraving in the cells; and a thistle carved into a stone in the Great Hall. It had been quite an adventure, though whether or not the answers they had were all correct wouldn't be known until later that evening.

Alice-Miranda spotted Millie on one of the parapets and called out to her. The girl turned and waved manically but didn't stop to talk. It was a competition after all and it seemed as though Clan Mac were a little bit behind.

'Are we catching the tram back?' Madagascar asked. She hadn't prepared herself for quite so much running around.

Sep had already consulted the timetable and said that he thought it would be faster again on foot. His statement was met with several groans.

'But my feet are hurting,' Alethea whined. 'Okay, I know I should have broken in my new boots before today. I'm just saying.'

Alice-Miranda smiled. The Alethea of old would

have whinged until she had her way. It was impressive to see the changes in the girl. Alice-Miranda looked over and noticed Miss Cranna was standing near the top of the stairs, holding a black-and-tan glove. She trotted over to say hello.

Morag greeted her with a tired smile. 'I was just wondering if any of you might have lost this,' she said, brandishing the glove, 'although it is a bit big.'

The children shook their heads and Alice-Miranda asked if she could take a closer look. She was almost certain she knew who it belonged to.

'I think it's Mr Onslow's,' the child said.

'Do you mean the man who was collecting the bottles?' Lucinda asked.

Alice-Miranda cast around to see if he was close by, but there was no sign of him.

'Come on, we don't have time to worry about lost gloves,' Madagascar said. She was itching to leave, having seen The Tartan Warriors boarding a bus five minutes ago.

'Who's Mr Onslow?' Morag asked.

'Some vagrant who Alice-Miranda was talking to earlier,' Alethea said. 'She's like that – talks to anyone.'

'Obviously. She talks to you, doesn't she?' Sloane said with a smile.

Fortunately, Alethea took the comment for the joke it was intended to be and smiled back.

'Just leave the glove here on the fence and perhaps the owner will find it,' Morag said. She didn't like the idea of Alice-Miranda befriending the city's homeless.

But Alice-Miranda wasn't so sure. 'Are we coming back this way again?'

Morag nodded.

'I think it might be best if I hold on to it and try to find Mr Onslow then,' Alice-Miranda said. She put the glove into her daypack and zipped it up. 'He did say he was going to buy another pair, so if I see him then he'll have an extra.'

Further down the hill, Davina Stuart and Barclay Ferguson were heading for a taxi. Davina turned and called for Morag to get a wriggle on.

Madagascar was tapping her foot, eager to get moving. 'You do know that we have exactly twenty-one minutes to get back to the hotel before we start losing points,' she glowered.

'Come on then, what are we waiting for?' Alice-Miranda grinned as the group charged off, retracing their steps from that morning.

For a moment, Morag Cranna was left alone with her thoughts at the top of the stairs. Onslow. That was a name she hadn't heard in a long time.

★

With seconds to spare, Nessie's Monsters sped through the hotel doors and into the conference room where they had to check in before one o'clock.

'We're here!' Alice-Miranda said as Miss Stuart counted heads and ticked them off her list.

They weren't the last to arrive, though. Clan Mac still weren't back and were losing one point for every minute past the hour. It was twenty past one when they finally skidded into the room and, from the dark looks on several of their faces, they had encountered a bump or two along the way.

Sloane looked at Jacinta. 'Caprice?' she said, and the girl rolled her eyes.

'Sounds like that one is trouble with a capital "T",' Lucinda commented to Neville, who could only nod his head in agreement.

Alice-Miranda frowned. 'For such a smart girl

she does some really silly things. Perhaps I should have a talk with her.'

'I don't know why you'd bother,' Sloane said. 'You know she never listens.'

Britt Fox waved from across the room and darted over to see Alice-Miranda. She hopped from one foot to the other and told the girl how she'd thought her team, The Tartan Warriors, were going to come last because their bus had broken down a couple of stops from the hotel. They'd had to run all the way back and were stunned to have beaten everyone else to the hotel. That said, she wasn't entirely confident they'd found all the correct answers up at the castle.

Barclay Ferguson entered the room with a spring in his step. He stood at the front with a broad smile on his face. 'Well done, everyone. It looks as if yer've made a sterlin' job of yer first activity, although I am disappointed Clan Mac were so late in gettin' back. We were beginnin' to think ye'd skedaddled aff somewhere. Unfortunately, I've had to dock twenty points from yer score, which brings ye back in line with everyone else.'

Caprice's team shot a collective round of daggers at the girl, who was sitting on her own apart from the group.

'What?' she hissed. 'It wasn't my fault. If it hadn't been for me, you would never have found that thistle on the stone.'

Sloane looked at Alethea. 'I knew she was cheating. Should we tell Mr Ferguson?'

Alethea thought for a moment. 'They've already lost twenty points. I'm sure she wouldn't be stupid enough to do it again.'

'Ye have until tonight to submit yer final answer,' Mr Ferguson continued. 'Captains, make sure to collect yer envelopes from yer teachers now and keep them safe until ye have to hand them in after dinner.'

Mr Pienaar took the envelopes from his bag and handed them to Alice-Miranda, who put them safely into the folder in her daypack.

Lucinda Finkelstein's stomach gurgled and grumbled so loudly it was heard by just about everyone in the room.

'Someone is starving,' Vincent quipped in his lyrical French accent. This not only garnered giggles from the children, but also set a few hearts aflutter.

'How embarrassing,' Lucinda whispered to Ava and Quincy, her cheeks burning.

'Yes, well, it seems that you've earned your lunch, which is being served now in the hotel dining room,' Miss Cranna instructed.

The children fell out of their groups and mingled together. Alice-Miranda suspected they were probably being watched to see how well they got along with all of their peers and she'd been thinking that, as the captain of Nessie's Monsters, she was going to share that role around. The idea of the forum was for everyone to develop their skills, so it seemed a little silly for one person to have that job the entire time.

They left their belongings in the conference room and headed for the dining room down the hall. Alice-Miranda was pleasantly surprised to find herself walking beside Neville.

'Oh, hello,' she said. 'Did you have a good morning?'

He pushed open the dining-room door and waited for her to walk through. 'I think we did okay, except for when Caprice wandered off. Between you and me, I have my doubts about what she was up to. She seemed to know exactly where to find the last answer even before Millie had read out the clue. I really hope Caprice didn't cheat. It goes against the spirit of the whole program.'

Alice-Miranda nodded. That settled it. She would have a quiet chat with the girl as soon as she could.

A long bain-marie like the ones they had at school was set up for a buffet lunch. The food smelt delicious, and Alice-Miranda could hardly wait to tuck in. She and Neville lined up with the others for a feast of beef stew and mashed potatoes, roast chicken with gravy and sausages and vegetables too. When their plates were filled, Neville led the way to an empty table with eight seats. Millie and Madagascar quickly joined them, followed closely by Sloane, Britt and Lucinda.

Millie spotted Chessie looking for somewhere to sit and waved her over. 'We've got a spare spot,' the girl called.

Chessie's stomach flipped. The vacant chair was right next to Madagascar. She looked around to see if there was anywhere else to go, but thought it would look too obvious and only give Madagascar more fuel for the fire.

'I thought you and Maddie might like to sit together,' Millie said when Chessie walked over. 'It sounds like you have a lot of catching up to do.'

'Thanks,' Chessie mumbled.

Madagascar patted the empty seat beside her. 'Hey bestie,' she said, grinning.

'So you two were friends at Bodlington?' Sloane asked with her mouth full.

'Chessie and I spent *loads* of time together. It mostly involved me trying to cheer her up,' Madagascar said, putting on an exaggerated frowny face. 'She was so sad – weren't you, Chessie? It almost broke my heart, and then she left and I thought I'd never see her again.'

Alice-Miranda looked over at Madagascar. It sounded like the girl had been very kind to Chessie, but for no good reason Alice-Miranda had a strange feeling there was more to the story. Chessie had not mentioned Madagascar once since she'd started at Winchesterfield-Downsfordvale.

Chessie had to turn away. It was a pity she'd never told Alice-Miranda and Millie who had made her life a living nightmare at school, and here was Madagascar putting on an award-winning performance. If Chessie told anyone the truth now, they'd likely never believe her.

'You can sit together on the bus this afternoon, if you'd like,' Millie said. 'But she's just on loan, Chessie. Maddie and I haven't seen each other in such a long time and I was hoping we'd become reacquainted, so don't keep her all to yourself.'

'Oh, I won't,' Chessie said tersely, causing Sloane to look up quickly from her stroganoff.

For the rest of the meal, Chessie pushed her food around her plate, having well and truly lost her appetite. Everyone else finished and returned to the servery for dessert. She was surprised when Sloane hung back and tapped her on the shoulder.

'Are you okay?' Sloane asked, sitting in the empty chair beside the girl.

Chessie's heart was stuck in her throat, but she managed a nod. 'I'm fine.'

'No, you're not. I can tell,' Sloane said, giving her a knowing look. 'You can't stand Madagascar, can you?'

Chessie didn't know what to say. If she agreed, Sloane might tell the others.

'It's okay. Your secret is safe with me,' Sloane added, patting the girl's arm. 'Perhaps we can talk later.'

Chessie managed to move her head up and down. She had no interest in getting Madagascar into trouble or making her fall out with Millie. She just wanted the girl to leave her alone. Perhaps she could speak to Sloane later when she'd found the words.

While Mr Ferguson was holding court at a large table with all the teachers, animatedly telling stories of his travel adventures to raucous peals of laughter, Caprice took the opportunity to sneak back into the deserted conference room. She picked her way among the clusters of daypacks until she found the one she was looking for. She unzipped the bag, pulled out the folder and flipped it open. She'd just borrow them for a little while, that's all. Clan Mac would be back in front again in no time, and her team mates would realise what an asset she was.

Chapter 15

That afternoon, the children were bundled onto a tour bus that wound its way along a well-worn route through the city. Morag had thought it would be a good way for the children to become better acquainted with the layout of Edinburgh, as well as an opportunity to have a rest before their first guest lecture that evening. The driver delighted them with all sorts of facts about the various buildings, parks and attractions. They'd seen the Queen Street Gardens, the monument to Sir Walter Scott, the

Princes Street Gardens and the Scottish National Gallery.

Before embarking on their excursion, Morag had given the driver explicit instructions to abstain from mentioning the landmarks on the worksheet the children had to complete during the journey. She was pleased to see the man was sticking to the script, until they pulled up at a set of traffic lights and a fellow crossed the road leading a little Skye terrier.

'Ah,' the driver sighed with affection. 'That wee pup reminds me of Greyfriars Bobby.'

The children peered around the seats in front of them to see what the man was looking at. Davina's eyes widened in alarm. She was certain the man wasn't meant to divulge that tidbit of information.

'Stop!' Morag shouted, but the man either didn't hear or was determined to tell the story.

'See that statue over to our left just outside the pub named in his honour? Well, that wee doggie sat on his master's grave no matter the weather for fourteen long years,' the driver continued. 'When the gun was fired at the castle at one o'clock each day, he'd run to the eatin' house for his food and then return to his master. People would come from all over to see him. Now, that's a faithful hound if ever I heard of one.'

Morag exhaled loudly. 'Thank you for not telling the children about Greyfriars Bobby.'

The man grimaced. 'Och, sorry about that. Just got carried away with meself. I promise not to point out the Parliament or the National Monument that was never finished.'

A ripple of laughter ran up and down the aisles of the bus as the kids realised the man had given away some other important clues.

'Thank you, sir! I think we have a good idea of what we will be looking for to complete our worksheets!' Junior called out in a thick South African accent.

Morag put her head in her hands. 'So much for getting any sleep tonight,' she muttered to Davina. 'I'll have to come up with another activity to replace this one. Perhaps you could give me a hand?'

Davina bit her lip and worried the hem of her cardigan. 'I'd love to, but I'm afraid I have a wee bit of organising of my own to do. If I manage to finish it early enough, I'll gladly give you a hand.'

Morag smiled tightly and nodded. She could feel her blood pressure rising. For the rest of the journey, she closed her eyes and tuned out. There was no point getting upset.

The children nattered away, getting to know each other and talking about which aspects of the program they were looking forward to most. After lunch, Mr Ferguson had asked them all to think about leaders they admired, and what it was about them they found particularly impressive.

Britt Fox was sitting with Lucinda halfway down the bus and across the aisle from Alice-Miranda and Millie. They'd just started discussing what Mr Ferguson had said.

'Katherine G. Johnson is my hero,' Lucinda said.

Britt had no idea who she was, but Lucinda soon filled her in on the incredible work the woman had done for NASA during the space race. The fact that Katherine Johnson, on grounds of being African-American, had only recently been properly acknowledged for her mathematical genius seemed so unfair. Britt had been a long-time fan of Nelson Mandela and could recite several of his speeches off by heart.

'I wonder who we're going to meet tonight,' Lucinda said. 'I never thought of myself as a leader at all until I met Alice-Miranda and she showed me what it meant to have strength and the courage of my convictions.'

Britt nodded. 'Well, you know what John F. Kennedy once said – leadership and learning are indispensable to each other.'

Alice-Miranda looked across the aisle at Britt and grinned. 'I used that exact quote in my application.'

'So did I,' Britt said with a laugh.

'Maybe you're secret twins,' Lucinda said. 'You look super alike – apart from the colour of your eyes and hair.'

'Perhaps we're kindred spirits like the sisters in *Little Women*, one of my all-time favourite novels,' Alice-Miranda said.

Britt gasped and clasped her hands. 'That's one of *my* favourite books!'

Caprice leaned forward and whispered to Millie through the gap in the seats. 'Looks like you've got some competition there.'

Millie plugged the gap with her scarf and ignored the nefarious girl, though it was hard to do the same with the uncomfortable twist in her tummy. Maybe it was something she ate at lunch.

A few rows along, Neville and Sep were catching up on news from Spain. Neville had the boy laughing out loud as he regaled him with stories of his mother's latest craze of making giant pans of paella and inviting half the neighbourhood round for tea. Last weekend the party had been going swimmingly until Sep's mother, September Sykes, had spotted a lizard and she was off home like a shot. The woman still hadn't got over her morbid fear of skinks – a phobia created by Sloane, who had told her they were poisonous so the girl could have some time in the garden on her own.

Amid the chattery buzz, Alice-Miranda turned her attention outside the bus window. She adored the architecture of the city, with its grand stone buildings and charming cobbled streets. Best of all, she loved watching the people going about their daily business: men and women in suits and over-coats on their way to meetings, mothers pushing prams with their babies rugged up against the cold, and tourists – lots of them, from all over the world – taking photographs and enjoying the sights.

Alice-Miranda was watching a young couple walking arm in arm when she spotted someone she recognised ambling along behind them. 'Look, there's Mr Onslow!' she exclaimed, grabbing Millie's sleeve. She pointed to a fellow who had just turned into the Royal Mile, which led up to Edinburgh Castle. 'Perhaps he lives there somewhere.'

Alice-Miranda had told Millie over lunch about meeting him at the top of the steps on the way to the castle that morning.

Millie noticed that the man still only had on one glove, and the weather was looking particularly grim. The blue skies of the morning had given way to a blanket of grey, with fat raindrops starting to splatter against the windows. She was glad they were touring inside the comfort of the bus and not on foot.

'The poor fellow looks as if he's freezing,' Alice-Miranda said. She thought for a moment, then jumped up and grabbed her daypack, as the bus had slowed to a crawl in the traffic.

'Do you want me to come with you?' Millie asked, knowing full well what her friend was intending.

'It's okay. I won't be long,' Alice-Miranda called back as she hurried to the front of the bus. She gently tapped Barclay Ferguson on the shoulder, jolting the Scotsman from his sneaky doze.

'Wha . . .? What's the matter?' he asked groggily.

'Is it possible for us to pull over, just for a

minute?' Alice-Miranda asked. 'I have something I urgently need to return to someone.'

Barclay Ferguson wondered what the girl was talking about, but the driver was way ahead of him. He spotted a bus stop outside a pub called Deacon Brodie's Tavern. The vehicle came to a halt and he opened the door with a *whoosh*.

The girl beamed. 'Thank you very much. I won't be a minute.'

Alice-Miranda ran down the steps and around the corner onto the Royal Mile. She sprinted up the footpath, her eyes darting about as she tried to find the man again.

'What in heaven's name is the girl doing?' Davina called loudly. She'd been busily going through the itinerary and checking arrangements when she realised the child had hopped off the bus.

'She's returning a glove to a friend,' Millie answered.

Morag was roused from her zen-like state as a gust of chilly air rushed in through the open door. Her eyes fluttered open and she gazed out the window. 'Oh, heavens be!' she gasped, leaping to her feet.

Seeing Mr Onslow up ahead, Alice-Miranda

wove her way through the crowd that was walking down from the castle. Although it was only four o'clock in the afternoon, it was getting dark and many of the city's attractions were already closing. She saw that he had finally stopped in a doorway. 'Mr Onslow!' she cried out.

This time the fellow turned around. He wore a look of surprise on his weathered face.

Alice-Miranda reached him, puffing hard. 'Thank goodness,' she said, unzipping her daypack and grasping for the glove inside. She handed it over with a smile. 'I think this belongs to you.'

The man's forehead puckered and he studied the item closely. When he looked up, his grey eyes took on a glassy sheen. In the distance, Miss Cranna's shouts were getting louder. Seconds later, the woman appeared right next to them.

'What were you thinking, young lady?' Morag panted. She glanced at Gordy Onslow and could barely mask her distaste. 'We need to get back to the bus. You're holding everyone up. Hardly the mark of a good leader.'

'Sorry, Miss Cranna, but I thought I mightn't have another chance to return Mr Onslow's glove and it's frightfully cold. I'd hate for him to get frostbite,' the child explained. She turned to the old man. 'Perhaps we should help you home. It's chilly now and you don't want to catch a cold.'

'Here,' he said, pointing at the door. 'I live here.'

Alice-Miranda peered around him. 'Oh, how lovely. What a beautiful street to live on – with all this history around you. You must see so many interesting things each and every day.'

Gordy Onslow managed a nod of his head. 'Thank you, lass. I willna forget yer kindness.'

Alice-Miranda smiled and hugged the man around his middle. 'You're very welcome.'

For a frozen moment, Gordy Onslow had no idea what to do with himself. It was the first time he had been hugged by a child in more years than he cared to remember. He dropped his bag of bottles and embraced the girl for just a few seconds before pulling away to dab at his eyes.

'I hope you'll take care and look after those hands,' Alice-Miranda said.

Morag Cranna hesitated. There was something disconcerting about the fellow, but she couldn't put her finger on exactly what it was.

'Goodbye, Mr Onslow,' Alice-Miranda said. 'Are you coming, Miss Cranna?'

The woman was still deep in thought. 'Aye, what?' She turned and looked at the child, who was waiting to go.

'We should get back to the bus,' Alice-Miranda said. 'I'm afraid I've probably thrown out our schedule a little. I'm terribly sorry about that.'

Morag nodded. As they walked down the road jostling with the crowds, she couldn't help turning back to look at the man, but of course he'd gone into his house. Morag felt an increasing uneasiness. She'd have to tell Mr Pienaar to keep a closer eye on the girl in future and make sure she didn't wander off talking to strangers. The last thing Morag needed was for one of them to disappear.

Chapter 16

The children arrived back at the hotel in time for afternoon tea followed by an hour of leisure. Dinner was at six and afterwards there was a lecture with a surprise guest. The teachers were off being hosted by Mr Ferguson and Miss Stuart in the posh parlour room at the front of the hotel, and Mr Ferguson had assumed Miss Cranna was supervising the youngsters.

'I can't believe you made friends with another homeless person, Alice-Miranda.' Ava Lee grinned as the children sat on the floor in the conference room they'd been in earlier. While they were out, most of the chairs had been removed and replaced with cushions and beanbags so the students could mingle more informally. There was a small station with hot chocolate, shortbread biscuits and fruit off to the side. The children had all got themselves something to eat and drink and had formed a giant circle.

'Now, why don't you believe that, Ava?' Quincy said. 'Remember when Alice-Miranda was talking to that homeless guy on the subway and he turned out to be a genius artist who knew her long-lost uncle? I think she's got a weird sixth sense about people, much like the way animals do. My mum used to love this really old show called *Lassie* that was about a dog with the best judgement of people ever. I think Alice-Miranda has that intuition too.'

Lucinda Finkelstein laughed. It was true. And that was just one of the things she admired about her friend.

'Aren't you ever a little bit scared of strangers?' Jacinta asked. 'The girls are absolutely right that you talk to everyone.'

Alice-Miranda shrugged. 'I suppose I like to

think the best of people. Being homeless doesn't make you a criminal and, actually, Mr Onslow has a home. He lives in a grand old building on the Royal Mile, not far from where I met him this morning.'

'Speaking of strangers, we should all get to know each other better,' Sep suggested. 'Seeing that we haven't had much of a chance to do that yet outside our own teams.'

'What do you recommend?' Vincent asked.

There was some murmuring among the group before Lucas spoke up. 'What about we say our name and where we're from, and talk about something that we love or that we're passionate about?' He looked adoringly at Jacinta, whose face turned a deep shade of crimson.

'Seriously, Jacinta, it's not always about you,' Caprice quipped, earning herself a volley of chuckles.

'It's hot in here, that's all,' Jacinta mumbled.

Blushing, Lucas reached for the girl's hand and gave it a squeeze. Jacinta was his girlfriend and he didn't care who knew it. He hoped she felt the same. She squeezed his hand back, which was something of a relief.

'So, who'd like to start?' Sep asked.

There was a very enthusiastic shout from Declan,

the Irish lad, who confessed his passion for potatoes, which of course earned him a huge laugh.

'No, no, I *really* love them,' the boy insisted. 'My da owns a potato farm and I'm keen on the biology. We're actually creatin' a strain of potato that can grow in the desert without any water. It's organic and we're usin' revolutionary techniques.'

Alice-Miranda's eyes widened in amazement. 'That sounds fascinating! I'd love to tell my father. A whole division of his company is dedicated to growing organic vegetables. I'm sure he'd be very interested to hear about your family's work.'

'That would be fantastic,' Declan replied eagerly. 'We'll talk later.'

Neville shot the boy a curious look. He hoped Declan wouldn't monopolise Alice-Miranda for too long. He'd barely had enough time with her as it was.

Following Declan was a girl and boy from New Zealand who'd definitely travelled the furthest to be part of the program. Hunter shared his love for the piano and violin, and said he was interested in becoming an orchestral conductor. Aimee was into snow skiing and adventure sports, and had already conquered the world's biggest bungee jump.

Apparently, she enjoyed hunting wild pigs too, but stopped short of describing the details.

It was Madagascar's turn next. She introduced herself and said that her passion was meeting people and being a good friend. Chessie almost vomited in her own mouth. More like beating people and driving them round the bend, she thought.

As expected, Neville talked about his love of lepidoptery, which conjured a few blank looks until he explained that he studied butterflies. It turned out that Christophe, from Switzerland, was equally entranced by the polymorphic creatures. The two boys arranged to meet up later to have a chat.

Britt Fox spoke about her interest in fashion, particularly sustainable products, and her vision to create her own ethical department store in Norway and hopefully expand the chain around the world.

Everything was going beautifully until they reached Caprice, who was determined to out-passion them all. The girl burst into song, with a rendition of 'My Favourite Things' from *The Sound of Music*. There was no denying her pure voice, but Millie couldn't help thinking she'd taken showing off to a whole new level. The song ended and Caprice took a bow, while the children gave her a rousing round of applause.

'Who's next?' Millie said curtly.

Caprice glared at her. 'Excuse me, I haven't finished. I have so many things I'm obsessed with. Singing, of course. I won the National Eisteddfod two years in a row.' She looked at Millie and added, 'I was runner-up in the most recent competition only because the judges were horrible and tone-deaf. Then there's acting. My first movie is coming out next month. It's called *Frontier Woman: The Life and Times of Nellie Williams* and I play the lead female part.'

'The lead female *child* part,' Millie corrected. 'She's only in the opening scenes, and we're in it too.' She pointed at Alice-Miranda, Sloane, Sep, Lucas and Jacinta.

'At least I had a *speaking* part, unlike some people,' Caprice retorted.

'We sing, Caprice,' Millie shot back. 'So we technically all had lines, not just you.'

Alice-Miranda wished she was sitting beside her friend as things were beginning to get heated.

'Anyway, shut up, I've got more to add.' Caprice flicked her hand in Millie's direction. 'I'm an outstanding equestrian and have never come less than top three in all of my classes. Oh, and my mother is a famous chef – she has her own television show called *Sweet Things*.' Caprice smiled smugly. However, if she'd been in tune with her peers, she would have realised that almost everyone in the circle was looking uncomfortable.

'And it's great that you're so modest too, Caprice. Very refreshing.' Millie rolled her eyes and several of the children giggled.

Unfortunately, Caprice had a tendency to bring out the worst in people and there was something she'd said that riled Alethea no end. The girl licked her lips and sat up taller. 'Your mother is famous, is she?' the girl asked.

'Yes, very,' Caprice boasted.

Given that half the time Caprice treated her mother horribly and seemed quite put out by the woman's notoriety, this sudden bragging about Venetia Baldini came as a bit of a surprise to her schoolmates.

'Pathetic,' Alethea scoffed.

Caprice was on her feet in a second and stalked to the other side of the circle where Alethea was sitting. 'What did you just say?' she demanded.

'You heard me,' Alethea replied, standing up.

Sensing trouble, Alice-Miranda hopped to her feet and positioned herself between the two girls. They towered over her, but she was undeterred. 'Alethea, Caprice, please calm down. Neither of you is acting like a leader at the moment – quite the contrary.'

Caprice looked at Alethea, a lightbulb going on in her head. 'You're Alethea Goldsworthy, aren't you? You ran away from school because of all the horrible things you did to Alice-Miranda, and then your father turned out to be –' Caprice gasped for effect – 'a criminal. Alethea's father is Addison Goldsworthy. He's in prison. What was it for again – embezzlement? And wasn't he involved in a big art heist when we were on camp?'

'How dare you!' Alethea spat. Her whole body tensed. 'I'm not my father and I didn't have anything to do with his misdeeds.'

'Really? What's that famous saying?' Caprice narrowed her eyes and jabbed the girl in the shoulder. 'The apple doesn't fall far from the tree.'

The rest of the children gasped in horror.

'Why, you brat!' Alethea shouted. Before she knew what she was doing, she clenched her fist, lined it up and threw a punch. Unfortunately, the girl was never good at contact sports.

Alice-Miranda gave a tiny yelp and clutched her nose. Tears streamed down her face and, no matter how hard she tried to quell them, the girl was racked with sobs.

Britt flew from the other side of the room and extracted a handful of tissues from her daypack while Neville rushed out to fetch a glass of water. Millie was already hovering over her friend, worry etched into her features.

Caprice turned to Alethea. 'Happy now?'

'I-I'm sorry, Alice-Miranda. I didn't mean to hit you,' Alethea said, her voice trembling. 'I'm so sorry.'

Gretchen jumped up to comfort her friend, although she planned to give her a stern talking-to later. No matter how much someone got up your nose, physical violence should never be an option.

Millie turned and glared at the querulous pair. Her hair looked as if it was full of static electricity and her freckles appeared to have caught fire. 'Shame on the both of you! I don't know how you ever got to come on this trip, but I'm sure you'll be sent home as soon as the teachers find out about this!'

'It was her fault!' Alethea said, pointing at Caprice. 'She was being awful about my father.'

'*You* hit her, not me!' Caprice screeched back.

The rest of the children were dumbfounded. Who knew that the Future Leaders Opportunity Program could be so dangerous?

Neville returned and helped Millie and Britt guide the tiny girl over to one of the chairs at the back of the room. Alice-Miranda placed her head between her knees and was pinching the bridge of her nose just as Barclay Ferguson strode into the room. In his arms was a towering pile of tartan scarves he had bought as a first-day present for the children's excellent teamwork.

'I trust ye've enjoyed a bite to eat,' he chirped before taking in the commotion. He dropped the woollen bundle on the floor, stunned by the scene in front of him. There was a seeping red stain on the carpet, children crying (several had been so distressed by what had happened they too had burst into tears), two girls screaming at the tops of their lungs, Alice-Miranda Highton-Smith-Kennington-Jones clutching a wad of tissues to her nose, while Millie, Britt and young Neville were hunched over trying to console her. 'Oh my!' the man exclaimed.

Caprice rushed towards him, explaining loudly that it was all Alethea's fault and that the girl should be sent home immediately. Alethea stomped over to defend herself, arguing that Caprice had started the whole thing by being such an intolerable show-off.

Barclay Ferguson looked at the pair in horrified bewilderment. At that moment he felt entirely vindicated for never having had the urge to procreate. 'Stop! Just stop!' he cried, pressing his hands against the sides of his head.

The room fell silent apart from the occasional whimper from Alice-Miranda.

Barclay sidestepped Caprice and Alethea, and made his way to the injured child. The bleeding had almost stopped, although the poor girl looked terrible. Her nose was beginning to swell, and he hoped it wasn't broken. Heaven help him if the Queen's favourite child had a wonky beak as a result of something that happened on his watch. He might as well kiss his knighthood goodbye.

He cast about for Morag Cranna, but the woman was nowhere to be seen. 'Neville, would you please ask the front-desk staff the location of the nearest emergency room?' he said, then turned to

152

face Caprice and Alethea. 'This is very disappointin'. Rest assured I do *not* condone violence of *any* form. I will be speakin' to yer teachers and we will decide on what punishment ye will receive. If I were ye two, I'd think about packin' my bags.'

'That's so unfair!' Caprice spat, stamping her foot. 'I haven't done anything wrong.'

Barclay held up his forefinger to shush the girl.

Caprice's face crumpled. 'But —'

'Zip it, young lady,' the man advised. 'What a pair of bampots ye are!'

Barclay didn't dare leave the room in case another brawl broke out. Fortunately, the doors opened and Benitha Wall breezed in, followed by the rest of the teachers.

'Hello, hello,' Miss Wall said cheerily. She had been enjoying the most invigorating conversation with Mrs Clinch and was feeling quite chipper. The old crone certainly had some life in her yet. Miss Wall halted, taking in the chaotic scene. Clearly, something terrible had happened. And while some of the children were visibly shaken, the rest of them looked as if they'd just been told they were eating sheep's brains for dinner.

Chapter 17

Alice-Miranda was about to place the icepack back on her nose when there was a quiet knock on the door. The child pushed back the covers and went to answer it, stretching up on her tiptoes to see through the peephole. She grinned when she realised who it was and then winced from the pain. Alice-Miranda swung open the door and pressed her finger to her lips. At least ten girls spilled into the room, led by Britt Fox, who was carrying a gigantic box of chocolates.

Britt was about to say something when she was interrupted by the sound of the toilet flushing and Millie's voice floating from the bathroom.

'Pooh! I wouldn't come in here for a while if I was you,' the girl declared. 'Must have been the cabbage.'

Millie opened the bathroom door and was confronted by a gaggle of giggling girls.

'What are you all doing here?' she blurted, her face turning the same shade as her hair. 'And you can forget I just said that. What happens on tour stays on tour!'

'Your secret is safe with us,' Lucinda promised, clutching her sides. 'We only dropped by to check on the patient.'

'You were so quiet tonight, Alice-Miranda,' Chessie added. 'We hope you haven't been suffering too badly.'

'I remembered that I had this in my bag in case of an emergency,' Britt said, passing Alice-Miranda the gold box wrapped in a royal purple ribbon. 'And I think what happened tonight constituted an emergency.'

'You really didn't have to,' the girl said with a shake of her head. 'But these are my favourites and

I think we could have at least one each before bed. As much as I love your company, you'd better not stay too long, though. I suspect Mrs Clinch will be around soon to make sure everyone's asleep.'

'She's on the warpath,' Millie added with a decisive nod.

Alice-Miranda lifted the lid and passed the box around. She noticed that the girls were wearing the cutest collection of pyjamas, from Sloane's gorgeous two-piece ensemble with a print of the night sky, to Britt's cute dalmation onesie complete with hood and long floppy ears. Susannah had on a nightie with a doll pattern, while Lucinda's harem pants and long-sleeved top looked good enough to wear in public.

Another knock on the door caused all the girls to freeze. If it was Mrs Clinch, they'd be in a world of strife. Ava took two more chocolates and stuffed them into her mouth just in case.

Millie tiptoed through the maze of girls to see who it was. She peered through the peephole and turned around, giving everyone a thumbs up, then pulled open the door.

'Quick, get inside,' she ordered.

Alethea darted into the room and frowned

when she realised it was full of girls. 'I thought you were in the bathroom,' she said to Gretchen.

Gretchen shrugged and grinned, her teeth covered in chocolate.

Alice-Miranda leapt to her feet. 'Alethea, are you okay? I've been worried about how you might be feeling. And before you even ask, I'm fine. It doesn't hurt that much and I know –'

'I'm so, so sorry,' Alethea blurted. She was painfully aware of the dozen pairs of eyes trained on her, but she'd come here for a reason and an unexpected audience wasn't about to stop her. 'I didn't mean to hit you and I feel horrible.'

Alice-Miranda looked at the girl. 'I know it was an accident,' she said and strode over, wrapping her arms around Alethea. 'There are no ill feelings on my part.'

Fat tears fell onto the top of Alice-Miranda's head.

'I used to think that no one could possibly be as nice and kind and smart as you, and that it must have all been an act,' Alethea blubbed through a watery haze. 'But, Alice-Miranda, you truly are the most wonderful girl in the world. I hope that we can be proper friends from now on. Forever, really.'

Millie sighed and jumped up to fetch the box of tissues from the bathroom. After offering them to Alethea, she quickly passed the box around as there wasn't a dry eye in the room.

Chapter 18

The girls' impromptu pyjama party had lasted far longer than anyone had intended. Millie had produced a pack of cards and they'd played two rounds of rummy and ate all the chocolates. Suffice to say, there was a contagion of yawns among the group the next morning.

'Pity Caprice didn't have the good grace to apologise to Alice-Miranda as well,' Sloane said to Chessie, as they boarded the bus.

Chessie nodded and rubbed her sleepy eyes.

'I think Alethea was really brave to apologise with an audience, and Alice-Miranda is so kind. She never ceases to amaze me. I'm not sure I'd have forgiven Alethea so easily. I imagine the only reason she and Caprice are still here is that Alice-Miranda asked Mr Ferguson and the teachers to give them both another chance.'

The girls sat down in the third row as the last of the children hopped on. Caprice trudged past in a filthy mood, glowering at anyone who cast a look in her direction.

Davina Stuart, who was sitting across the aisle from Chessie and Sloane, smiled to herself. There was no way Alethea was going home, and if that meant Caprice had to stay too, then so be it. She'd argued hard in favour of the girls last night. It had only been one misdemeanour, after all, and they'd travelled such a long way. There were so many more things in store for them.

'I'm just glad we didn't lose any team points,' Sloane said. 'I suppose, with twenty-eight witnesses all singing from the same song sheet, it was pretty clear that Alethea and Caprice were both to blame.'

The two miscreants were going to be on extra duties for the remainder of the program. One more hiccup and they were both on the first planes home at considerable expense to their parents. They would also be kicked out of the Queen's Colours program and have any past awards rescinded.

In light of what had happened, and the obvious distress it caused many of the children, Mr Ferguson had declared that teams had until the following evening to submit their answers from the treasure hunt at the castle. There would be no updating of the leaderboard until then either, so they were all even on ten points. There had been some disappointment among the more competitive members of the party, but Mr Ferguson assured the children it was the right thing to do.

He'd also organised for the group to attend a sound bath after breakfast to bring down everyone's stress levels. Barclay had discovered the ancient practice years ago during a sabbatical in the Himalayas, where he'd lived for a time in a Buddhist monastery. Proving he had a knack for improvisation – as there were no Tibetan bowls or gongs available at such short notice – Mr Ferguson had raided the hotel kitchen for an array of glassware and crockery. The children had to select an instrument and run their fingers around the rim, eliciting all manner of pitched hums and reverberations while others were given a saucepan and silver spoon that they banged and clanged. Millie hadn't found the exercise relaxing at all, especially after Aidan had marched up and down the hallway playing his bagpipes at the crack of dawn.

Sloane placed her daypack on the floor and fastened her seatbelt. 'Alethea shouldn't have hit anyone, but I can understand how mad Caprice makes people. She's always pushing Millie's buttons. I'd have been far less surprised if Millie had walloped her.'

'A little bit like someone else I know,' Chessie remarked. She and Sloane hadn't yet talked about the elephant on the bus, otherwise known as Madagascar Slewt.

'So, what's the *real* story with you and Madagascar?' Sloane said conspiratorially. 'Were you *really* best friends at Bodlington?'

Given the girl was sitting up the back with Millie, Chessie felt it was as safe a time as any to reveal the truth about the situation. While it wouldn't change Madagascar's horrid behaviour, having someone who understood what she was dealing with would probably help quite a lot. Chessie took a deep breath and explained in some detail the sort of relationship she'd had with Madagascar.

Sloane slammed her fist in her hand in outrage. 'What an impostor! We should tell Millie, you know.'

'Absolutely not,' Chessie said, shaking her head violently. 'Please, Sloane, I don't want to come between them. Maybe Madagascar is nice to everyone else, but for some reason has it in for *me*. Besides, blood is thicker than water and I don't want Millie to hate me.'

'Don't be ridiculous. Millie wouldn't hate you.' Sloane sighed. 'I'd have had no hesitation dobbing on Madagascar, but don't worry, I won't. I am going to keep a very close eye on her, though. If she puts one foot wrong, she'd better watch out. I might not have as good a right hook as Alethea, but my Chinese burns are brutal.'

Chessie giggled into her hand. Sloane was funny, and it made for a nice change to feel protected rather than harassed by a peer. Although Chessie was a little worried that Sloane was serious about the Chinese burns.

The atmosphere on the bus was surprisingly upbeat considering the events of the previous evening.

Alethea and Caprice had both been sent to their rooms without dinner and had missed an exhilarating lecture from a young man called Dion McDonagh, who had recently received the award for Scotland's Young Entrepreneur of the Year. He had spoken about his business, Senior Gadgets, which he had started after his grandad had suffered a fall in the middle of the night on his way to the loo. The lad had the idea of putting LED lights in the toes of slippers, which would automatically turn on in the dark. So, together with his grandfather, who was a retired engineer, Dion set about inventing glow slippers, which they marketed with the name 'Slip and Glow'. They were an instant hit, and not just among the elderly. Three years on, two factories and several hundred employees later, the business was a resounding success. Dion was keen to continue making life easier for the older generations and had just launched a new invention – glow-in-the-dark false teeth, to make dentures easier to find at night. Needless to say, the young man was beloved by senior citizens the world over.

Each of the children had come away inspired, none more so than Alice-Miranda and Neville, who were now enjoying a discussion of the previous night's lecture.

'I liked that Dion's central message was to not be afraid of running with an idea,' Neville enthused.

Alice-Miranda nodded. 'And the value of mentors and acknowledging that you don't know everything when you're young, even though sometimes it's tempting to think you might. I'm sure I was more certain about things a year ago than I am now. The older I get the less black and white things become.'

'I agree,' Neville said shyly. 'Growing up is a bit confusing at times.'

'It would have been lovely to meet Dion's grandfather, but I'd much rather he and his wife were off walking the Camino de Santiago trail in Spain,' Alice-Miranda said. 'I hope I'm doing things like that when I'm older too.'

'Maybe we'll have some adventures together,' Neville said, his face taking on a scarlet hue.

'I'd love that.' Alice-Miranda smiled. 'And you're awfully kind to be looking out for me, but I don't need a bodyguard. I'm sure I'm in no danger from Alethea or Caprice. It was my own silly fault for getting in between them,' Alice-Miranda said to the lad. It hadn't escaped her notice that he had opened every door for her and had hardly left her side since breakfast. 'If you want to spend some time with Lucas and Sep and the other boys, I quite understand.'

Neville blushed and stared holes into the seat in front of him. 'I just thought I'd make sure you're okay,' he mumbled. 'You probably should have gone to the hospital to check you didn't have a concussion.'

'I'm fine, really. My head isn't sore at all,' Alice-Miranda assured him. 'It's got nothing on the horrible concussion I had last year when I fell off my horse, Bony, and almost scared Millie to death.'

Neville looked at the girl admiringly. 'If someone punched me on the nose, I'd still be crying.'

'Oh, I don't think I put much stock in crying being a measure of bravery, anyway,' said Alice-Miranda. 'Besides, you're more fearless than I could ever be. You booked yourself a passage to America to meet the President of the United States. Not many kids would have done that.'

'They wouldn't be that deluded, you mean.' Neville grinned. 'It was kind of you to leave out the part about my getting on the wrong ship. I still can't believe I was naive enough to think that one of the suites on the *Octavia* was a second-class berth. Queen Georgiana must have thought I was a complete idiot. I suppose it all worked out in the end, though, and I'm much closer to my parents now than I was before. My dad drives me all over the countryside looking for butterflies. We've taken up cycling together as well. He doesn't even care that I don't like playing football, which is a relief because I was absolutely horrible at it.'

Neville was about to say something else when the bus pulled up at the Peffermill Playing Fields at the University of Edinburgh. It had been a very short ride from their hotel. Too short. Neville longed for more time to talk to Alice-Miranda. She was by far the most interesting girl he knew – not that he really knew that many girls.

Barclay Ferguson stood up and took the microphone from their driver. 'Well, I think ye only have to look outside to know what we're doin' this morning.'

The children glanced out of the bus windows to see several men and women clad in traditional Highland dress, armed with various weapon-like objects. The children looked back at Barclay blankly. It clearly wasn't that obvious.

Brendan Fourie decided to hazard a guess. 'Self-defence lessons, sir?' he called out.

Barclay frowned. 'Uh, no. Not exactly.'

Davina and Morag shared a look and stifled their laughter.

'As a leader of the future, ye must look after yer body as well as yer mind,' Mr Ferguson said. 'I take health and fitness very seriously and love nothin' more than some good competition. So today ye will be learnin' some new skills that will be put to the test later in the week when FLOP will culminate in our very own Highland games. And yes, Aidan, ye will be allowed to get out yer bagpipes then – but, please, not before. I don't want any more calls from hotel reception about ye practisin' at half-six in the mornin' and wakin' up an entire floor of guests,' the man said, raising his left eyebrow.

'I had to prise my fingernails out of the ceiling when that racket started up,' Millie declared loudly. 'I thought we were under attack.'

The children laughed. Alice-Miranda grinned, then grimaced. Moving her face was painful, despite having iced her nose for hours the night before. The swelling had mostly gone, but the shadows under her eyes were still a reminder. She had begged Miss Wall and Mrs Clinch not to call her parents, reasoning that her nose wasn't broken and, by the time she returned to Winchesterfield, she'd be fine. There was no need to upset anyone else unnecessarily.

Ava's hand shot into the air. 'Is this activity part of the competition?' she asked.

Barclay shook his head. 'No, you'll be told which of the activities contributes to the teams' competition, although I am not averse to givin' out points to groups I see cooperatin' and doin' the right thing,' he replied with a perfectly rolled R. 'Yer teachers and Miss Cranna, Miss Stuart and meself will be watchin' ye closely – some of ye more closely than others.'

Caprice swallowed hard. She really must return the pilfered items before someone noticed they were missing.

Each of the teams was met by a trainer and taken off to their first activity. Nessie's Monsters headed to the caber toss, which involved balancing a large tapered pole called a caber against one's shoulder, holding it with upturned palms and then throwing it as far forward as possible. The cabers were much smaller than those used in an actual Highland games

169

or the children wouldn't have been able to pick them up let alone throw them.

Their trainer was a fellow called Bryan, who was clearly a man of few words.

'Don' hit yerself, don' hit anyone else and chuck it as far from ye as ye can,' was the extent of his instruction. He demonstrated by throwing the caber a considerable distance, almost hitting Declan, who was halfway down the field at the third station.

'Hey, watch it!' the lad cried as the pole bounced along the ground beside him.

Bryan chuckled. 'Best don' throw it that far.'

The children lined up and each had a turn. Lucinda was the surprise package, tossing the caber the furthest.

Benitha Wall was with her group at the next station over. They were doing the stone put, which was like shot-put but with a smooth stone. She was itching to get her hands on the caber, though, never having tried throwing one before. When she spotted Mr Pienaar about to have a turn, she asked Caroline Clinch to take over watching The Pipers and strode across to introduce herself.

Bryan eyed the woman cautiously. She had a build to match her name and looked as if she could toss the thing the length of the field if she put her shoulder into it. 'Be careful. Ye don' want te cause a hospital run,' the man said. 'On secon' thoughts, I have a proper caber for ye. It's over here.'

He directed Hansie Pienaar and Benitha Wall away from the children to a couple of cabers that resembled large tree trunks.

Sloane clapped. 'Go Miss Wall!'

'Go Mr Pienaar!' Isabeau Pillay shouted.

The children began to chant, which caused everyone else on the field to stop what they were doing and look their way.

Caroline Clinch had been busy making sure that Benitha's group were taking the utmost care with the stones when she was distracted by the commotion. 'Oh, good heavens, what is that woman up to?' she said. Her eyes widened when she saw how close the children at the next station were to the action. Caroline began running down the field. 'Move! Get out of the way!' she screeched, flapping her arms.

Bryan squinted at the frantic woman. 'Is yer teacher tryin' to take off?' he asked, to the amusement of the children.

'You go first,' Benitha said to Hansie.

The man picked up the caber and balanced it against his left shoulder before running forward and tossing it halfway down the field. The children clapped and cheered. The rugby players on the pitch next to them stopped training and ran to the sideline to see what the children were so excited about. They'd already caught sight of the fellow's throw and were most impressed.

Bryan positioned the caber for Benitha's embrace. The woman managed to pick it up and rest it against her shoulder and neck, wobbling momentarily before regaining control. Benitha stood still for a second then began to stride out. Unfortunately, she soon lost her balance and was veering left and right in an effort to keep the pole vertical. Then, with a heft and a grunt, and having spun around completely, Miss Wall launched the caber into the air straight towards the rugby field.

The children cheered, the rugby players ducked for cover and the teachers were paralysed in terror as the stick bounced and catapulted not once but twice. A huge groan sounded as the caber flipped through the middle of the rugby posts, taking out the crossbar as it went. The crowd fell silent, transfixed as the two side supports swayed like drunken sailors before they both came crashing to the ground.

'Wow!' Sloane gasped.

Millie's mouth flapped open. 'You can say that again.'

Hansie Pienaar's eyes glazed over with admiration. The woman might have been a little off course, but she threw that thing much further than he ever could. 'You're amazing,' he breathed.

Benitha's face lit up and she felt herself tingling all over, although she wasn't sure if it was the embarrassment or something else. She hurried off to talk to the rugby coach about the damages.

Sep nudged his sister. 'Did you see the look on Mr Pienaar's face?'

'I think someone's in lurve,' Sloane said, chuckling.

The children undertook five different activities including the caber toss, stone put, hammer throw, weight over the bar and sheaf toss, which literally involved using a pitchfork to toss a sheaf of wheat over a bar – sort of like high jump, but more high toss instead. After a couple of hours, everyone was exhausted and ready for lunch.

'You're a natural at all of this, Lucinda,'

Alice-Miranda said to her friend as they walked back to the bus.

Lucinda grinned. 'Who knew?'

'I wish you could come to Winchesterfield-Downsfordvale for a while,' Alice-Miranda said. 'We would have so much fun.'

'My dad hasn't ruled it out completely,' Lucinda said. 'Maybe I can talk to Miss Hobbs and see if she's ready for an exchange program. If we don't do something soon, high school will be over and we'll all be off to college. Every year gets faster and faster, and my parents say that it's even worse when you're an adult.'

Millie looked over and saw Alice-Miranda loop her arm through Lucinda's. Her tummy twisted and she turned away.

'I love that we're friends,' Alice-Miranda said to Lucinda, 'and I'm glad that my mum and your dad patched things up after that silly misunderstanding that lasted far too many years. I'm so happy you and the other girls are here.'

'Maybe not all of the other girls,' Lucinda said pointedly. 'How's your nose today?'

'I think the cold weather must be helping. It's feeling much better already,' Alice-Miranda said as something tickled her eyelashes. She looked into the sky and realised it was snowing. 'And look how it's all turned out. Alethea and I are proper friends now and that's a very good thing.'

Lucinda and Alice-Miranda hadn't noticed that Caprice was right behind them. She thought she was going to be sick hearing Alice-Miranda's glowing appraisal of Alethea, but she didn't have time for that. She brushed up against the tiny girl's daypack and tried silently to undo the zip. Trouble was, they had already reached the bus.

Alice-Miranda turned and spotted the girl, who pulled her hand away just in time. 'Oh, hello Caprice. I haven't had a chance to speak to you all day. How did you enjoy the games?'

Caprice dropped her eyes to the ground. 'It was fine.'

As the children boarded the bus, Mr Ferguson gave another of his pep talks, saying how proud he was of them all and that he couldn't wait for the Highland games on Saturday, which would be a competition and a half if what he'd seen out there was anything to go by. He also mentioned that he hoped the groups had been thinking about the answers to yesterday's treasure hunt as he would be collecting them this evening. He was particularly looking forward to seeing which teams had worked out the bonus response.

Alice-Miranda swung into a seat halfway down the bus. 'We need to work out our answer to the bonus question when we get back to the hotel,' she said to Lucinda.

'Perhaps we can give it a go now,' Lucinda replied.

Caprice ducked into the row behind the pair and hoped no one would sit next to her. Luckily, everyone was avoiding her like the plague.

Alice-Miranda put her daypack onto her lap and unzipped it. She opened it up and looked inside. 'That's strange,' she said, her forehead crinkling.

'What is?' Lucinda asked.

'I could have sworn I put the envelopes in here yesterday. Maybe I took them out last night and left them in our room. My head was a bit of a muddle,' the girl said. 'I hope I haven't misplaced them. That wouldn't do at all.'

Caprice's heart sank as she listened between the seats. She had to get to Alice-Miranda's room first otherwise it would be a long, lonely journey home.

Chapter 19

The bus shuddered to a halt outside a mysterious gothic church on the other side of the city. Upon entering the building, the children were stunned to find that the pews had been removed, rendering the space empty but for a wall of mirrors down one side. Their lunch was sitting on a table near the front where the altar must have once been.

'What is this place?' Ava asked, as they were directed to sit and eat. The sound of bagpipes filled the air.

'My guess is it's a dance studio,' Alice-Miranda replied, 'if those mirrors are anything to go by.'

Just as the child spoke, a troupe of Highland dancers entered through a set of double doors at the back. There were five men and five women beautifully outfitted in traditional costumes. The ladies performed first while the men held their unsheathed swords upright with the tips pressed gently against the floor. When the women peeled off to the side, the men moved into the centre in formation and laid their swords on the ground, then jigged back and forth over them in various directions before performing a choreographed contest.

When the act concluded, the children leapt to their feet in applause. A man with a scraggly beard and wearing full Highland dress that was even fancier than the others burst into the room and took a slightly awkward bow. He walked with the aid of a timber cane, which had the most intricately carved head of a dragon on it.

Madagascar nudged Millie. 'There's something wrong with his leg.'

Millie stared. The man was wearing a kilt and long socks. There was only a small gap near the bottom of his knees, but Maddie was right. There was definitely something odd about his left leg.

'Good afternoon, laddies and lassies, and welcome to Duncraig's Academy of Highland Dance, where you will be learnin' exactly what yer've just seen in front of ye,' the man boomed. 'My name is Eachann Duncraig and I am the owner of this fine establishment. I am also a former world-champion dancer meself and will be teachin' ye the finer points of the sport.' He tapped the cane against his leg. The children were shocked to hear a knocking sound.

'How does he dance with a wooden leg?' Millie mused, much louder than she'd intended.

'Aye, ye noticed, did ye?' Eachann Duncraig looked at the girl with the flaming-red hair. She reminded him a lot of his granddaughter. 'I lost it in the loch.'

The children stared at him, wondering what he was talking about.

'Nessie,' the man whispered theatrically.

Madagascar rolled her eyes. '*As if.* There's no such thing, and even if she was real, I've never heard any stories about her chewing people's legs off.'

'Och aye, it wouldna be good for the tourist

trade, would it now? But I warn ye, if ye go up there, keep yer arms and leggies inside the boat,' the man said ominously. He gazed out at the crowd.

Lucas gulped and felt Jacinta's grip on his hand tighten. There was something not quite right about the man's left eye either. It looked to Lucas as if it were made of glass.

This time the children didn't know whether to laugh or squirm with fear.

'He's got to be kidding,' Madagascar said, although she didn't sound quite so sure of herself.

'Ye can make up yer own mind, lassie,' Mr Duncraig replied.

Caroline Clinch pursed her lips. She was seriously considering telling the man to pull his head in. The last thing she needed was for the children to be having nightmares, especially since they were heading north to Loch Ness the very next day. But there was a small part of her that wondered what if . . .

Barclay Ferguson slapped his knee and laughed. 'You almost got us, Eachann!'

He jumped up and walked towards the man with his hand outstretched, beckoning for Miss Cranna and Miss Stuart to join him. Morag quickly explained to the children that they would be learning to dance in their teams for the next half-hour and then Mr Duncraig would be judging them in a competition.

'But I've got two left feet,' Neville groaned.

Mr Duncraig winked with his good eye. 'At least ye've got two feet.'

Neville gulped and nodded his head.

'I'll have ye dancin' no matter if yer two feet are left or right or pigeon-toed, or one foot is real and the other a lump of wood,' the man said with a glint in his glass eye. Or was it the reflection of the crackling fire? 'My dancers are the best in the land.'

Eachann Duncraig organised the children into their groups to learn the first dance. The professional troupe spread themselves among the teams and assisted the youngsters to get the hang of it while the teachers formed their own group. Barclay Ferguson was tapping along to the pipes and drums and itching to take a twirl. He glanced over at Morag, who was swishing her skirt about and feeling secretly pleased with her choice of outfit, which had dancing kitties around the hemline. He was about to ask if she wanted to dance, but the woman was soon distracted by her phone and promptly disappeared. Davina was already spinning around with Dashiel Arnaud, the teacher from France, and giggling like a schoolgirl.

By the end of the first set, the children were completely done in and begging for mercy. Highland dancing took a lot of energy, that was for sure. But Mr Duncraig was a hard taskmaster and had them learning a modified version of the Reel of Tulloch before it was time for the competition, which involved the teams performing one dance that everyone would watch before they would all dance the Reel of Tulloch together. He would select places first to fifth for the team dance, and the most outstanding male and female dancer in the Reel.

The first team up were The Highland Flingers, who did an outstanding job. The Tartan Warriors were okay except for Philippe, who was devoid of coordination and kept treading on Britt's toes. You wouldn't have known it, though, as she gave the lad all the encouragement in the world, but the look of relief on both of their faces when it was over was palpable.

The Pipers were third and seemed to have everything under control. Miss Wall cheered them on and clapped her hands loudly.

Clan Mac were next, and Lucas and Jacinta were mesmerising. They both seemed to have the dance down pat and spent the entire time gazing into each other's eyes with smiles as wide as their faces. Caprice trod on Neville's toes about ten times then tried to blame him for it, which didn't go down too well with Mr Duncraig.

Finally, it was time for Nessie's Monsters. They were almost perfect except for Madagascar, who definitely had two left feet. When everyone else went right, she went left, and in the end she sent Sloane sprawling, tripping her over with the sword.

When they were all finished, Mr Duncraig asked the children to sit on the floor. 'Well, that was somethin' else,' the man declared. 'Some of it, I'm still not sure exactly what, but ye were entertainin' nonetheless. Now, I want ye in position for the Reel. Ye don' need to stay in yer groups, so find a partner and marry up.'

The children laughed at the man's turn of phrase and sought each other out all over the room. Neville took two quick puffs of his inhaler and made a beeline for Alice-Miranda, beating Sep by a whisker. The music started and half the children couldn't remember the first move, but the professional dancers helped them out and soon enough they were leaping and loping and flailing and flopping all over the place. Hansie Pienaar had asked Benitha to join him and the two were making quite the impression.

Mr Duncraig applauded loudly when the song finished. 'Well done, ye canny kids! In order from fifth to first, we have The Tartan Warriors, Nessie's Monsters, The Pipers, Clan Mac and – I don't know if they gave themselves this name because they had some experience – The Highland Flingers have come in at first place!'

There were claps and cheers all round.

Barclay beamed with pride. 'That was impactful work, kids!' he shouted above the din.

'What's he talking about now?' Sloane said, shaking her head.

Sep shrugged. 'Beats me.'

Barclay turned to Mr Duncraig. 'What about our individual dancers?'

'Well, I dunno the bairns' names, so I will have to point them out,' the man replied. He shuffled closer to Barclay and whispered in his ear.

'Aha, very good!' Barclay nodded. 'Ten points each to these dancers' teams. Congratulations,

Sep Sykes.' The children went wild clapping and cheering. 'And well done to Madagascar Slewt.'

The girl jumped to her feet and was leaping like a lunatic. Everyone else looked about in confusion. The girl had no talent for dancing at all.

Eachann Duncraig was horrified. 'No, no, no, not her!' he cried. He pointed to the child cowering behind the leaping girl. *'Her.'*

'Oh, I see,' Mr Ferguson said, the smile returning to his face. 'Please put your hands together for Miss Compton-Halls.'

'What?!' Madagascar screeched.

Chessie reeled in terror. She was going to cop it now – there was no doubting that.

'I'm going to tell my father about this, and he won't be happy!' Madagascar seethed. She turned on her heel and stormed off, pushing stunned bystanders out of her way.

Millie jumped up and ran after her cousin. With a bit of a nudge, the memory that had been niggling away at her began to come into focus.

Alice-Miranda cast around for somewhere to sit. Millie was looking after Madagascar, who was still teary, and everyone else seemed to have paired up. She spotted an empty seat beside Miss Stuart and hurried towards it.

'May I sit down?' she asked.

The woman glanced up and smiled. 'Of course you can, pet.'

Alice-Miranda settled onto the seat and sighed happily. 'The program has been absolutely marvellous so far. I have loved every single minute.' The girl felt a sneeze tickling her nostrils and tried to hold it in, but despite her best efforts it came anyway. She squeezed her eyes shut to stem the tears that had sprung.

'Perhaps not every minute,' Davina said with a wink.

Alice-Miranda giggled. 'Yes, I suppose everything but *that*,' she admitted. Her nose had started hurting a little with all of the vigorous activity, and she was quite glad that they would be sitting still for a while. She looked at the young woman beside her. 'May I ask how you became involved in the Queen's Colours, Miss Stuart?'

Davina thought for a moment. 'Oh, from the

second I learned about the organisation, I wanted to be part of it. It's been a dream come true, really.'

Morag Cranna leaned around from the seat in front of them. 'I thought it was a pure accident. I clearly remember Mr Ferguson saying something about walking smack-bang into you with his coffee one day and that's how you got talking and ended up with the job. It was just good luck, wasn't it? A bit like the way I got my position.'

Davina smiled tightly. 'Yes, Morag. Lots of good luck. No planning at all.'

'Oh, how serendipitous!' Alice-Miranda enthused, swinging her legs. 'I don't think you could go wrong working for Aunty Gee and Mr Ferguson. They're both incredibly inspiring. Are you two originally from Edinburgh?'

Morag nodded then slunk back around to face forward. She didn't like talking about her childhood.

Davina shook her head. 'I grew up further south,' she said, and dropped her eyes to the floor. She picked up her handbag and dug about inside it.

'How lovely. Uncle Morogh and Aunt Audrina live on the outskirts of the prettiest village south of Edinburgh. It's idyllic, with fields and animals gambolling about and rivers perfect for skimming stones. It must have been wonderful growing up there. Mummy says that I should make the most of every day of my childhood because one day you blink and it's all over.'

'It's not like that for everyone, I can assure you,' Davina snapped. Softening, she added, 'My childhood seemed to drag on forever.'

Alice-Miranda bit her lip. 'Oh dear, I didn't mean to upset you, Miss Stuart. Would you like to talk about it? I've always found that talking about things helps to make more sense of them. My daddy had a horrible time when he was a boy. His mother died when he was very young, and his brother too – except that he didn't really, but that's a whole other story. Grandpa didn't cope well, leaving Daddy to be raised by his nanny and housemistresses. I only found that out a little while ago. I felt so badly for him, but it's amazing what a happy and positive person he grew up to be in spite of it all.'

'But your father's family was rich beyond what most people can even imagine,' Davina said, to Alice-Miranda's surprise.

The girl frowned. 'It's true that Grandpa had a very successful business, but money can't make up for losing your family, no matter how much you have,' she reasoned with a wisdom beyond her years. 'It was still hard for Daddy – and for Grandpa too.'

'Try being raised by an aunt who treated you as her personal slave. Perhaps then you can lecture me on hardship.' Davina opened her folder. 'Excuse me, I need to check the schedule,' she said, and turned to face the window.

Even at her age, Alice-Miranda was well aware how unfair life could be. It really was a lottery which family you were born into. It sounded as though Miss Stuart had had a tough time indeed. No one can change their past, but hopefully the woman could see a brighter future ahead of her. As Alice-Miranda thought about what Miss Stuart had just said, her mind wandered to Mr Onslow. Clearly, he was having a tough time too. She hoped he was somewhere warm on this cold winter's day.

Chapter 20

As the bus pulled up outside the hotel, Mr Ferguson stood to announce that afternoon tea would be in the conference room for all staff and students, and then they would have an hour to work on their final answers from the Castle Challenge before dinner. Caprice was off the bus like a shot. She'd mumbled something to Miss Wall about needing to fetch an item from her room before racing off.

'Is everything all right with Madagascar?' Alice-Miranda asked Millie when they reached the conference room. The girl had managed to get away from her cousin for a minute while she went to the toilet.

Millie sighed. 'Hardly. She was awfully upset about missing out on being the most outstanding dancer and now she wants to go home. I'm trying to talk her around, but she seems pretty set on the idea. I think I'm beginning to remember what a stubborn streak she has. I have a vague recollection of a tantrum over a sippy cup when we were little, but I have a feeling there's more to that memory too. I wish I could ask Mummy.'

'Perhaps we can both talk to her later,' Alice-Miranda suggested. 'It seems a waste not to see the program through to its conclusion. Speaking of which, I've got to find my team's envelopes so we can work out the final answer. Be back soon.'

Alice-Miranda waved and hurried out of the conference room, passing Madagascar on her way back in. The girl's face was wet and puffy, as if she'd been crying. Alice-Miranda thought there must have been something else bothering the girl. She couldn't possibly be so upset about the dancing – that was just silly.

Alice-Miranda skipped upstairs to her room.

She was about to put the key card in the door when she heard a noise coming from inside. She paused for a second then pushed open the door.

The room appeared as she and Millie had left it. Nothing seemed disturbed or out of place until Alice-Miranda noticed the envelopes containing their answers sitting on the desk. She was sure they hadn't been there that morning. Alice-Miranda had a funny feeling there was more to it and the squeak coming from the bathroom only heightened her suspicions.

'There you are,' she said loudly. 'Silly me. How could I have forgotten?'

Alice-Miranda made quite a lot of noise before pretending to leave by slamming the door. She stood with her back against the door and waited. Not ten seconds later, Caprice Radford stepped out of the bathroom. She froze when she came face to face with Alice-Miranda.

'Oh, am I in the wrong room?' Caprice asked, quickly regaining her composure. She smoothed her copper tresses.

Alice-Miranda shook her head. 'Stop it, Caprice. You and I both know what you've been up to, and I think we need to have a long-overdue talk, unless you'd rather I have a chat with Miss Wall and Mrs Clinch. It would be a shame if Mrs Clinch got her wish to go home early and *you* had to accompany her.'

Caprice's eyes filled with tears. 'Please don't tell on me,' she pleaded. 'My parents will be furious and I can't afford to mess up again. I'll probably get expelled.'

'There's no need for drama,' Alice-Miranda said firmly. 'Surely you understand how many second chances you've had. Things *have* to change. Look at Alethea – she was a very difficult girl when I first met her, but she's made a huge effort to turn her life around.'

Caprice wiped her eyes and nodded.

'Why do you do it?' Alice-Miranda asked. She sat on the foot of her bed and patted the spot beside her. 'Why do you say mean things to Millie, and give Jacinta and Lucas a hard time, and show off constantly? You're a smart girl and extremely talented, but you make it awfully hard for people to like you at times. I really don't understand.'

Caprice's shoulders slumped as she sat down on the quilted bedspread. 'If I'm being truthful, which I guess I'll try to be from now on, I'm jealous,' she sniffed. 'And sometimes I have these nasty thoughts and, even if I know they're wrong or mean, I say them anyway. I can't stop myself. Or maybe it's because people have come to expect it of me. I don't know. Maybe I'm just a terrible person and there's no excuse for it. I embarrass Mummy and Daddy constantly. I want to be better – really, I do. I know you won't believe me, but it's true.'

Alice-Miranda placed an arm around the girl's shoulders and gave her a friendly squeeze. Perhaps there was hope for Caprice, after all.

The rest of the evening went well, considering Madagascar's histrionics and Caprice's confessional. Alice-Miranda promised not to report Caprice's thievery as long as the girl didn't participate in Clan Mac's final discussions about the answers to the castle treasure hunt. Alice-Miranda explained to Millie and Neville what had happened, and they agreed it was the best way forward. Millie didn't need any more theatrics given it had taken her hours to calm her cousin down.

In the end, Mr Ferguson announced that

Nessie's Monsters had won the Castle Challenge and the ultimate answer was revealed to be Mary Queen of Scots.

The leaderboard was updated with ten points for each correct answer in the Castle Challenge and an additional ten points for the overall solution. The scores from the dancing were also added. It was now neck and neck, with The Highland Flingers and Nessie's Monsters on a total of 120 points each, The Pipers on 100, and Clan Mac and The Tartan Warriors on 90.

The guest speaker that night was a young woman who had started a choir for homeless youth. She was a last-minute replacement for the actress Clotilde Heminger, who had taken ill, much to Caprice's bitter disappointment. It didn't matter, though, as this woman was equally impressive. She shared a clip of her choir's recent award-winning performance at the World Choral Festival. The children were mesmerised and even more so when the singers themselves entered the room and treated them to three bewitching tunes. Caprice was enthralled by the singers and hummed along with the group, resisting the urge to jump up and steal the show. She could hear Alice-Miranda's voice in her head and wanted to take heed – it just wasn't going to be easy.

A hot chocolate and a round of hugs later, everyone set off to their rooms. It was heartening to see that any resentment and hurt feelings had subsided – for the moment, at least. After a quick shower and brushing of teeth, Millie and Alice-Miranda compared notes as they lay in their beds.

'Do you really think Caprice was sorry?' Millie asked, turning over to face Alice-Miranda in the dark. 'Or was she just sorry she got caught?'

'I'm hoping the former. Anyway, she has a few days to prove herself,' the child replied with a yawn. 'What about Madagascar? Do you know why she was so upset about Chessie being named the best dancer?'

'She said that something similar had happened at school recently, when she'd had her heart set on a prize and lost out to someone else. She vows it wasn't because of Chessie, but I have to say, Maddie is very highly strung,' Millie said, her eyes beginning to close. 'I think I remember that memory from when we were . . .'

The girl fell into a deep slumber before she reached the end of her sentence. It was just as well, seeing as Alice-Miranda was also sound asleep.

✶

Alice-Miranda awoke with a start. She'd been dreaming about Mr Onlsow. They were sitting in a cafe sipping on the most delicious hot chocolate and he wanted to tell her something, but he couldn't find the words. Alice-Miranda hopped off the bed and padded over to the window. She ducked under the curtains and pressed her cheek against the cool glass pane. It was a clear night and she could see the moon and stars.

A movement in the street below caught her eye. There was a woman walking alone. She wore a long dark coat with the collar upturned and had on a familiar-looking beanie with cat ears stitched into it. Alice-Miranda was sure she'd seen that beanie before – on Miss Cranna, in fact. She wondered where the woman could be off to in the middle of the night. She hoped it wasn't on their account. The poor thing would be exhausted tomorrow.

Morag Cranna hurried along the street, pulling her coat tighter around her. She'd taken the call just after midnight and had pleaded her case not to go, but no amount of talking was going to change things. She was left with no choice. She prayed she would get back in time. She needed this job more than Mr Ferguson or Miss Stuart could ever know.

Meanwhile, in Room 303, Davina Stuart was also wide awake. Her mind was churning. When Mr Ferguson had told her that Madagascar Slewt was demanding he telephone her father and allow her to go home, she'd been horrified. It would undo all of her careful planning. The woman tossed and turned, unable to get comfortable. Thank heavens there were only a few days to go until the whole business would be over.

Chapter 21

Just after one o'clock in the afternoon, the bus pulled into Inverness, the largest city in the Scottish Highlands. It was another beautiful place full of ancient buildings, set against a backdrop of rolling green hills and the River Ness. A large body of water called Beauly Firth ran inland towards the mountains while, on the other side of the main bridge, the Moray Firth led out to the North Sea.

The children spilled into Whin Park on the River Ness, where they were to have lunch.

Glad to stretch their legs, they ran straight for the play equipment while the adults laid out the trays of sandwiches and fruit along a row of picnic tables. It was lovely that all of the teachers were getting along so well and were hatching plans for exchanges and professional development visits to each other's schools if they could wangle it with their bosses.

Morag stifled a yawn. She hoped there was some coffee in one of the thermos flasks Mr Pienaar was organising. Davina Stuart had been thinking the same thing.

'Right, everyone,' Barclay Ferguson called out, rubbing his hands. 'Lunch is up.'

The children and staff soon formed a single line. Lucinda Finkelstein was standing ahead of Mr Ferguson, deciding what she'd like. There was smoked salmon and crème fraîche, Coronation chicken, egg and lettuce, and ham and cheese. The girl ummed and ahhed before settling on the latter. She was about to head off when Mr Ferguson tapped her on the shoulder.

'There isn't any mustard on that ham, is there?' he asked. 'I can't abide the stuff. Gives me a terrible tummy.'

Davina Stuart was standing behind him, trying to ignore her own grumbling stomach.

Lucinda bit into her sandwich and shook her head. 'I can't taste any,' she said with her mouth full.

'Very good. Thank ye, dear.' The man nodded and helped himself.

The children spread themselves across the park for their impromptu picnic. Alice-Miranda scrambled to the top of an elaborate climbing frame that was comprised of three elevated cubby-houses with a tower at one end and two spiral slides. Millie scampered after her, and together they sat down with their legs dangling over the edge.

'I'm so glad I got to come after all,' Alice-Miranda said, smiling at her friend. 'I was perfectly okay about staying behind. Actually, I was a bit upset to begin with, but once I'd got used to the idea, I was all right.'

'I'm glad you're here too,' Millie said, wriggling forward on her bottom. 'It wouldn't have been the same without you. Luckily, it all worked out. Although I do have a confession to make.'

Alice-Miranda looked at her friend expectantly.

'I think I've caught Caprice's disease,' Millie said with a grimace. She put down her sandwich. 'I'm a green-eyed monster.'

Alice-Miranda's eyebrows jumped up. 'You're jealous? Of who?'

'You and Lucinda and Britt,' Millie replied sheepishly.

'Oh, Millie.' Alice-Miranda rested her head on the girl's shoulder.

'I know. Pathetic, right?' Millie leaned her head against Alice-Miranda's.

'Of course not. I'm sorry that we haven't been able to spend as much time together, but I thought you'd want to make up for lost time with Madagascar,' Alice-Miranda said. She leaned back to look her friend in the eye. 'You do realise that, no matter what happens, you're stuck with me – for life. You'll always be my best friend. I'm a bit like your bad smells – I stick around.'

'Thanks,' Millie said, a smile tickling her lips. She nudged Alice-Miranda. 'Ditto.'

'I suppose these funny feelings are all part of growing up,' Alice-Miranda mused. She picked up her sandwich and took a bite. 'Apart from the initial disappointment last week, I've hardly had any – except for the butterflies in my tummy since arriving here, but I think that's just because I'm having such a wonderful time.'

'Are you sure they don't have anything to do with Neville?' Millie wiggled her eyebrows.

Alice-Miranda giggled. 'We're just friends. He's such a kind boy – a lot like Sep, really.'

Millie gave her a look. 'You're the smartest person I know, Alice-Miranda, but maybe you're not that clever when it comes to boys.'

'Maybe.' Alice-Miranda hesitated. 'Perhaps I should ask Jacinta how she feels when Lucas holds her hand. I think I'd quite like Neville to hold my hand when we're a bit older.'

Millie smiled and shook her head. She hadn't told Alice-Miranda that she and Sasha Goldberg had been writing to each other ever since they'd finished filming the movie in Hollywood. She hoped they would be able to attend the premiere in Los Angeles so she could see him again. Millie now regretted having teased Jacinta about Lucas over the years, though it had been a good deal of fun.

Barclay finished his lunch and announced that they should take a group photo for Her Majesty. He asked Davina and the teachers to round everyone up and get them onto the play equipment as quickly as possible.

Chessie looked around in a panic. She didn't

want to end up with a foot in her face or, worse still, a hand on her back before she plummeted to the ground. Fortunately, she spotted Madagascar at the other end of the group. Chessie had successfully avoided the girl since the dance debacle the day before and wanted to keep things that way.

Davina snapped a few pictures before Mr Ferguson suggested the teachers join in. There were howls of protest from Mrs Clinch, who complained that it was completely undignified. Miss Wall, on the other hand, swung into action, clambering up one of the slides. Hansie Pienaar laughed raucously and followed suit, admiring the woman's flair.

'You should come up too,' Alice-Miranda called down to the FLOP organisers. 'Aunty Gee would be here in a flash.'

Millie nodded. 'She might be the Queen, but she's heaps of fun – remember when she played dress-ups with us at the palace?'

'What a sterlin' idea – glad I thought of it.' Barclay Ferguson grinned from ear to ear and passed the camera to the bus driver. 'Come on, ladies!'

Morag wished she'd worn her tartan kitty trousers instead of her ginger cat appliqué dress. Laughing, she grabbed Davina's hand and pulled her into the shot. The two of them ran into a spot of trouble climbing up the slide, though. Each time, they almost reached the top only to slip back down again. Despite this, Davina was having a ball and giggling like a schoolgirl.

Barclay Ferguson came to the rescue, giving them each the extra push they needed, before sprinting up onto the play equipment himself. Unfortunately, due to Morag's faffing about, the scene had descended into utter chaos, with several of the children now hanging precariously from the apparatus, pulling faces. The teachers proved just as unruly, chatting among themselves and giving each other bunny ears when the other wasn't looking. Miss Wall even took to pretending she was standing at the bow of the *Titanic*, perched as she was on the roof of the tallest cubby with her arms outstretched and Mr Pienaar behind her. Lucas and Jacinta, high above them all, decided it was as good a time as any to have their first proper kiss.

'Smile, everyone!' Barclay called.

But if the man thought he was sending that photograph to Her Majesty, he would have to think again.

Chapter 22

Davina Stuart hurried up the gangway into the cabin of the *Mairead*, a pretty wooden boat that would take them on their tour of the loch and on to their accommodation for the evening. Miss Cranna had ordered all the children to sit inside as the temperature had dropped significantly, and she didn't much like the idea of anyone being on the upper deck without close supervision. Actually, she didn't much like anyone being on the upper deck, full stop. She rushed around marking names off her list – twice – having no desire to leave anyone behind. That never ended well, in her experience. She'd checked her phone just before they'd boarded the *Mairead* and was relieved to see that the phone coverage was patchy at best.

There had been some protests from the children that they wouldn't be able to spot Nessie from inside, but Morag argued that the windows were so large that, if the monster did appear, they would absolutely be able to get a good look.

Once the children were seated, the captain, a sturdy fellow with a shock of ginger hair and a matching woolly beard, welcomed them all aboard. Millie remarked loudly that he looked a lot like their dancing teacher, Mr Duncraig. There were mutters of agreement from the rest of the children.

'Och aye,' the man said. 'I hear my brother was teachin' ye the finer points of Highland dance yesterday.'

'Are you Mr Duncraig's twin?' Lucas asked, surprised by the revelation.

'Aye, Jock Duncraig at yer service,' the man said with a twinkle in his eye. 'I bet that brother of mine told ye the story of how he lost his leg.'

'It was Nessie,' Jacinta said in her most authentic

Scottish accent yet. She'd been practising quite a bit and was enjoying the sound of it.

The man nodded solemnly. 'Och aye, 'twas Nessie.'

'But seeing as though the Loch Ness Monster is a myth, I'm sure there must be a perfectly rational explanation,' Quincy Armstrong said, arching an eyebrow. She wasn't about to be taken in. Monsters didn't exist – everyone knew that. Gretchen nodded in agreement, although there was a small part of her that was still apprehensive about the cruise.

The man let out a thunderclap of a laugh, causing everyone to jump in their seats. 'Yer a clever lass, but you dunno nothin' of these parts. 'Twas a dark and stormy night as Eachann rounded a bend on his way home from a ceilidh. He was ridin' his beloved motorbike, Nessie. They hit a patch of black ice and ended up in the loch. She took his leg, she did. He was lucky to survive, he was.'

'What about his glass eye?' Lucas asked. He wondered if Nessie had taken that too.

The captain's jaw dropped. 'He's never told me about that. Are you sayin' my twin brother, my own kin, has a glass eye and I dunno about it?'

Lucas shrank down in his seat, aware of at

least thirty pairs of real eyes drilling into his back. He felt like a complete fool.

Jock Duncraig winked at the boy. 'I'm just toyin' with ye, lad,' he said, grinning. 'My brother was playin' golf when we were bairns and the ball ricocheted off a timber-lined bunker and whacked him fair in the eye. You wouldna believed it, would ye? But it's the honest-to-God truth.'

'Well, that's disappointing,' Caprice remarked quietly, earning a snicker or two. 'It was a much better story before.'

Captain Duncraig went on to explain that they would travel as far as the ruins of Urquhart Castle before looping back to their hotel. He then indicated to a large screen on the wall. 'If ye're keen to know what's in the loch, just look up there,' he said. 'It's a sonar. We've seen all sorts of interestin' things over the years.'

He called out to one of his young crewmen to cast off, and the boat chugged away from the wharf. Captain Duncraig began his commentary, pointing out places of interest along their journey.

Davina Stuart found herself sitting between Morag and Alice-Miranda. She hoped neither of them were in a talkative mood as she'd counted on catching up on some much-needed sleep. Unfortunately, her wish was not to be granted.

Alice-Miranda looked up at the woman in concern. 'You look tired, Miss Stuart.'

Davina nodded. 'I didn't sleep well last night. I must have too many things flying around this head of mine,' she admitted with a light, tinkly laugh.

'It must be tricky orchestrating such an impressive program and looking after everyone at the same time. We are all incredibly grateful for the thought and planning that goes into an event such as this.' Alice-Miranda glanced down and noticed the colour of the woman's fingers. They were almost pure white, and the tips appeared to be turning blue. 'Oh goodness, would you like to borrow my gloves? They might be a little on the small side, but they should do for now.'

'Oh, aren't you a sweetheart.' Davina smiled. 'Not to worry. I should have some with me.'

Alice-Miranda gave a nod. 'Mr Onslow's fingers were a similar shade of blue. I was frightfully concerned he'd get frostbite.'

Davina rummaged through her bag and produced a baby pink pair of woollen mittens. 'Who's Mr Onslow?' she asked.

'Do you mean that vagrant from the other day?' Morag tutted.

Alice-Miranda's forehead puckered. 'Mr Onslow isn't a vagrant. He has a home and is actually very sweet.'

'Well, in future I'd prefer you don't talk to his type.' Morag pressed her lips together in distaste. 'It's not safe.'

Davina Stuart closed her eyes. The sound of Mr Duncraig's lilting voice through the microphone, combined with the gentle rocking motion of the boat and the warmth inside the cabin, was lulling her to sleep. Soon enough the woman was dead to the world. Alice-Miranda draped her coat over Miss Stuart and hoped that she would feel better when she woke up.

As the *Mairead* chugged on, the children snapped pictures of the surrounding mountains and some pretty cottages. They seemed to be the only ones on the water that day. Sitting at the rear of the vessel, Evelyn and Junior had both turned a nasty shade of green. It was Mr Ferguson who noticed them first and called out to Mrs Clinch that he thought the bairns were looking fair peely-wally. Caroline was on them like a shot. In her experience, there was nothing more contagious than a dose of the vomits. She recruited Andie Patrick to help her with Junior, and the pair of them had the sick bags out and the children onto the deck just in time.

'Now, this is one of the most famous spots for Nessie sightin',' Mr Duncraig said into the microphone. 'Here in the middle of the loch, it's two hundred and twenty-seven metres deep.'

'You wouldn't want to fall in,' Sloane remarked. 'Imagine how cold the water must be.'

'Och aye, it has an average annual temperature of six degrees Celsius. Interestin'ly, the water never freezes and people do swim in the loch in the summer, but ye'd need a full wetsuit and an empty head, if ye ask me.' Captain Duncraig eased off the power and the boat drifted along. He pointed at the ruins of Urquhart Castle, which stood proudly on the banks of Strone Point. 'That was an important castle in the Middle Ages, but ye can see it didna make it to present day.'

As the *Mairead* sat idle in the centre of the loch, several of the children ventured over to the windows to take photographs.

Sep, on the other hand, was rooted to the spot. He hadn't been able to take his eyes off the sonar screen. He'd spotted a blip that Captain Duncraig said was a sizeable fish – most likely a brown trout, an algal bloom and some eels, which were renowned to be whoppers. 'W-What's that?' Sep asked, just as a huge blip appeared. It seemed to be heading for the boat at an incredible pace.

The children gasped and Captain Duncraig's eyes almost crossed themselves. The creature was steaming towards them like a torpedo. They watched it close in until – BOOM! – there was a loud thud accompanied by the sound of splintering wood, as whatever it was hit the side of the boat with such force that Benitha Wall was thrown off her feet and straight into Mr Ferguson's lap, to Mr Pienaar's horror. There were a few squeals as the children scrambled to keep their footing while the boat rocked violently.

Davina's eyes flew open to find Alice-Miranda offering her a life jacket. The cabin was filled with the sound of shouting and children crying.

'Miss Stuart, it seems we have hit something or, more to the point, something has hit us and we have to get off the boat,' the child said. Her voice was calm and measured among the chaos.

Not two metres to their left, Madagascar Slewt was bellowing at the top of her lungs. Millie was doing her best to soothe her cousin, but the girl was inconsolable. 'I want to go home! *Now!*' she screamed.

'It's coming back!' Sep cried out, pointing at the screen.

'I'll teach ye to hit my boat!' Captain Duncraig roared. He charged out of the wheelhouse and stunned them all by diving into the murky waters.

'Man overboard!' Britt called, running to fetch a life buoy. She was immediately joined by Aimee and Declan, who all held their breaths, waiting to see if the man resurfaced.

'There he is!' Declan shouted, pointing over the side at a small circle of bubbles that had appeared.

Britt threw the buoy in that direction just as the man's head popped out of the water. The ring landed close by and he grabbed onto it. The children took turns heaving him back to the boat while the captain coughed and spluttered, cursing the mystery creature.

Meanwhile, Benitha Wall had righted herself and was standing on a seat, pulling life jackets from an overhead compartment and throwing them to the children, who were assisting each other in putting them on. Barclay Ferguson was on the case too, inflating the life rafts at the rear of the vessel and hoping they weren't all about to die a chilly death in the icy waters of Loch Ness. Mrs Clinch was making sure that everyone was properly kitted out. She'd left Miss Patrick in charge of the vomiting duo.

Paralysed in the corner of the cabin, Morag Cranna was as pale as a piece of paper. She didn't know what to do with herself. She pulled her phone from her pocket and looked at the screen, wishing now that there was a signal.

'No need to panic!' Captain Duncraig yelled, as the children hauled the dripping figure back over the side of the boat.

Lucinda ran to fetch a blanket for the man. Neville was helping one of the young crewmen direct everyone to the rear of the vessel, where they soon got into a rhythm while disembarking the boat from the transom. The Highland Flingers occupied the first of the rafts while Nessie's Monsters hopped into the second. Millie had practically pushed her cousin off the edge of the boat into Alice-Miranda's arms. Madagascar was still snivelling and carrying on. Just as The Tartan Warriors were about to depart, another crewman shouted from beneath the floorboards in the hull.

'I've plugged the leak and the bilges are pumpin'!' he called out. 'We can make it back to shore!'

Captain Duncraig hurried to the wheelhouse and checked the instruments. 'Get those children back on the boat and we'll head for the wharf,' he ordered.

Davina had finally collected her wits and was at the stern with Neville, assisting the crewman with the loading of the life rafts. Neville and Lucas were pulling The Highland Flingers back in and, moments later, the children were safely on board. Unfortunately, the rope had come loose on Alice-Miranda's boat. Nessie's Monsters were now drifting away and at quite a rate. The loch was well known for its strong currents and dangerous eddies.

'Why did we get off the boat if it's perfectly safe?' Madagascar shouted, leaning out over the edge above the dark water. 'Whose stupid idea was that?'

'Sit still or we're going to tip over!' Alethea grabbed the girl's arm and tried to drag her to the centre of the raft. But Madagascar fought back.

'Stop it!' Sloane yelled. She had had enough. 'You're not helping the situation by carrying on like a brat! Be quiet and sit still or I'll throw you into the loch myself.'

'And I'll help her,' Alethea added.

'How dare you both speak to me like that! I'm telling my daddy and I'm going home tonight. Mr Ferguson can't make me stay!' Madagascar shrieked.

Clutching to the railing of the *Mairead*, Davina watched on helplessly as the life raft floated away. The wind was beginning to blow, tossing the black inflatable about in the waves. She gasped as it almost overturned. But Alice-Miranda moved quickly enough to stop them from capsizing, throwing herself onto the other side to balance the load.

Neville Nordstrom appeared beside Miss Stuart. He was astonished the woman hadn't done anything to help, but then again some people froze in stressful situations. He grabbed a life buoy and lifted it from its hook, ensuring that the end of the rope was secured under his foot before he wound it up and threw it as far as he could. It fell short. With a grunt of frustration, Neville hauled it back in to try again.

Having calmed the children inside the cabin, Benitha raced out onto the deck to help. 'Here, give it to me!' she yelled.

Neville, recalling the woman's might in tossing the caber, gladly handed the buoy over. He hoped she wouldn't throw it past the children or, worse, clobber them with it.

'Incoming!' Benitha shouted. She lined up her shot and threw the buoy, landing it in the middle of the inflatable vessel. It almost took Madagascar's head off as it smacked against the vinyl.

Alice-Miranda lunged for it. 'Got it!' she called back.

With barely any effort at all, Benitha reeled in her catch. Neville leaned over the stern, watching on earnestly. Caprice was beside him, keeping an eye on the life raft to make sure it wasn't sinking.

Benitha grinned. 'We couldn't very well leave you out there to drift to shore – or spend the night in the middle of the loch with whatever it was that hit the boat.'

Alice-Miranda smiled as Neville took her hand and helped her aboard. 'That was a mighty fine effort, Neville. You almost got there.'

Madagascar fell onto the deck with a splat. Her hair was plastered all over her face and she looked the definition of miserable. 'Someone get me a phone!' she raged. 'I'm leaving!'

Millie shook her head in disbelief. She was beginning to recall that she and her cousin didn't always get along quite as well as she'd thought when they were little.

Davina Stuart marched up to the apoplectic girl and grabbed her roughly by the arm. 'Behave, *missy*,' she barked. All eyes turned to the woman, startled by her menacing tone. It was completely out of character for someone who, up until now, had been nothing but sweet. 'You are staying, whether you like it or not. You're not going to wreck everything.'

'Oh yeah?' Madagascar said, her eyes narrowing. 'Just watch me!'

The girl snatched back her arm and stormed off, almost trampling over Neville on her way.

The boy frowned. Who cared if Madagascar wanted to go home? The program would undoubtedly run a whole lot smoother without such an unbearable upstart in their midst. Neville glanced over at Alice-Miranda. He was just glad that she was back on board, safe and sound. He didn't know what he'd do if anything happened to her.

Chapter 23

The children's eyes were glued to the sonar screen as the *Mairead* chugged slowly along the shoreline. Whatever had hit them had disappeared into the murky waters and everyone was hoping it would stay there until they were back on dry land. The children alighted onto a slightly wonky timber dock and were all strangely quiet, no doubt still processing what had happened. Some had already concluded that they'd encountered the region's mythical creature.

'Do you really believe it could have been the Loch Ness Monster?' Chessie asked. She was beginning to think that was the only rational answer.

'Maybe it was a dolphin with a death wish?' Millie suggested, trying to lighten the mood.

'Or a seal?' Lucinda said. 'Or a small whale?'

The group congregated on the jetty.

No matter what it was, they were all relieved to be off the boat. Dashiel Arnaud was standing with Vincent and Philippe and they were all speaking in French at a rate of knots. The two kids from New Zealand, and Evelyn and Henry from Singapore, were speculating with Mr Williams about what the creature could have been. Henry said it might have been a dragon – they were popular in Asian folklore, so maybe one had emigrated to Scotland. Aimee thought it was more likely some sort of giant squid. She'd seen a television show recently about the creatures. Lucas was holding tightly to Jacinta's hand, just glad they were all okay.

'Children, good work out there,' Mr Ferguson declared. 'I will be awardin' some extra points to individuals who exhibited extraordinary leadership in the face of danger. But for now, let's get inside and warm those chilly bones.'

Alice-Miranda looked up past the soaring pine trees that partly obscured the view of the magnificent building where they were spending the night. There was a proper castle with turrets and towers hiding among the tall trees. 'This looks amazing,' she breathed.

Sloane gulped. She'd had more than enough excitement for one day and wished they were back at their cosy hotel in Edinburgh. 'It looks creepy, if you ask me.'

'There are probably ghosts,' Sep said with a glint in his eye, earning him a whack on the arm from his sister.

'Well, I'm not staying here,' Madagascar hissed.

'I bet there's a ghost or a headless highwayman or something equally hideous,' Alethea said loudly.

Gretchen clutched the girl's arm. 'Please don't say that.'

There was a ripple of conjecture among the children and staff as they followed Davina up a path from the castle's private mooring, through an overgrown garden to a cast-iron gate. An ominous 'Keep Out' sign was slung across it.

Caprice's lip curled. 'That's not very welcoming. Are you sure we should be staying here?'

Barclay Ferguson was inclined to agree, and wondered if Miss Stuart or Miss Cranna had actually visited this place before making the booking. Nevertheless, the children and adults continued in single file down a gravel path that was overhung with foliage.

Millie nudged Alice-Miranda. 'This reminds me of the time you took me to meet Miss Hephzibah at Caledonia Manor,' the girl whispered. She shivered and not just from the cold.

'There's nothing to be scared of, I'm sure,' Alice-Miranda said. She slipped her hand into Millie's and gave it a reassuring squeeze. Neville, who was walking right behind Millie, wished it was his hand the girl was holding. He didn't like the look of the place one little bit either.

The tunnel of trees and bushes finally opened up as the party reached a large lawn. The imposing castle was built of creamy sandstone with battlements on high, higgledy-piggledy turrets, windows ranging in size from tiny to huge, and gargoyles perched precariously along the roof. There was nothing even vaguely symmetrical about the place. It looked as if it had been built by a tag team of craftsmen over several centuries. Alice-Miranda thought it was positively charming, but it wasn't a sentiment shared by many of her travelling companions.

A rustling in the bushes caused everyone to jump. Two giant hounds emerged, followed by a man in full ceremonial dress. He had a thick tuft of pure white hair, which poked out from beneath a tam-o'-shanter perched at a jaunty angle. He introduced himself as Bronagh McDuff, and said his dogs were named Foxcliffe and Taffy.

'Welcome to Brokenwind Castle,' he said with a toothy smile. The man's voice had such a lilt to it that many of the children found it almost impossible to understand what he was saying.

Lucas glanced at Sep. 'Did he just call this place what I think he did?'

'Yep, must be the home of farts, flatulence, pop-offs, bottom burps and anything else that might gust from below,' the boy replied, twisting his lips to keep a straight face. But it didn't work.

The two lads were in tears, attempting to suppress their laughter, and had to inch their way to the back of the group so they wouldn't get into trouble. Benitha caught their eye and started giggling too until Caroline Clinch pinched her arm and told the woman to get a hold of herself, for heaven's sake.

The children followed Mr McDuff and Miss Stuart around to the front of the building, entering via a drawbridge over a moat. Inside a vast front vestibule, a huge coat of arms and crossed swords hung above an inglenook fireplace so large that at least twenty children could have stood in it side by side. Foxcliffe and Taffy ambled into the room and settled on a large patterned rug. A plume of dust rose in the air.

'Now ye might see our ghost, if ye're lucky this evenin',' Mr McDuff said to the children.

'Please,' Susannah sighed. 'I don't think anyone wants to see a ghost after what happened out there on the loch. We could have been killed.'

Meanwhile, out on the loch, Jock Duncraig was doing some investigations of his own. He was a practical man and had never put much stock in talk of the Loch Ness Monster, although he didn't mind making a living from tourists who came in search of her. But after today's event, Jock Duncraig might just have become a believer.

Chapter 24

The children were ushered down a steep stone staircase that seemed to wind on forever into the bowels of the castle. It was all very medieval, with fiery torches in steel brackets lighting a long corridor. Alethea jumped as she felt something touch her foot. She hoped the place wasn't alive with rats and mice – she wouldn't be able to sleep a wink if that were so.

Finally, Mr McDuff stopped at a low door, which he unlocked with a giant key that hung from an iron ring on his belt. 'Girls in here,' he said gruffly. 'Boys, come with me.'

Without so much as a cheerio, Mr McDuff and the lads continued along the seemingly never-ending passageway. Jacinta gave Lucas a forlorn wave before he disappeared with the others.

Millie pushed open the creaky door and stepped inside. What she beheld was a surprise, to say the least.

'I thought there would be cells and a couple of racks and other instruments of torture,' the girl said, visibly relieved. She wasn't the only one who had been thinking they were going to be spending the night in the castle dungeon.

Alice-Miranda followed her in, trailed by the rest of the girls. 'Oh, this is charming,' she declared, perhaps a little too enthusiastically to be completely believed.

The accommodation was basic, with a flagstone floor and bunkbeds lined up against the internal wall. There was a small fireplace with an electric heater in the grate. The lighting was moody, but not in a good way, with a couple of globes out and another struggling to survive.

'It might not be the dungeon now, but I'm pretty

sure it once was,' Sloane said, spotting the remnants of an iron chain that was forged into the wall. She reached up and rattled it, wondering how many unfortunate souls had met their demise in this very room. It wasn't something she wanted to linger on.

Caprice eyed a cluster of lead balls in one corner that looked as if they would have been attached to prisoners' legs with iron chains. 'I don't want to sleep here,' the girl whimpered. 'And I bet there *are* ghosts.'

'Think of it as an adventure,' Alice-Miranda said, flashing the girl a smile. 'What about we treat tonight as a themed slumber party? Does anyone have any goodies hidden in their bags?'

There were a few yeses from around the room and Britt suggested they could do some redecorating by using their coats and clothes to make the place appear less bleak. For a moment the mood lifted considerably.

'I'm sure the teachers aren't down among the dead men,' Millie remarked. 'Can you imagine if Mrs Clinch had to sleep in a room like this? She'd be on the phone to Miss Grimm and Miss Reedy quick smart.'

Loud footsteps echoed in the hall and there was a horrible scraping noise outside. Several girls gasped and clung to each other. The lights flickered as the door was pushed open. Alethea felt her stomach ripple with fear. But it was only Miss Wall. The woman stooped down low to walk into the room. Given the doorway height was about five and a half feet, and she was well over six feet tall, it was a sure indication of how much bigger humans had grown over the centuries – either that, or lots of them had gone around with bumps on their heads.

'Hello Miss Wall,' Alice-Miranda said cheerfully.

The other girls let go of each other.

Benitha surveyed the room, trying not to smile. 'Oh, this is . . . authentic, isn't it?'

Millie sat down on one of the squeaky beds, realising that there was a rather large lump in the mattress. 'So, your room doesn't look like this?'

The woman shook her head. 'I hate to say it, girls, but my room is gorgeous. I'm in one of the turrets and I have a perfect view over the treetops all the way to the loch. There's an ancient tapestry wall hanging and it's toasty warm with an open fireplace.' She eyed the dinky heater in the hearth and was glad that she wasn't down here tonight. There was quite a chill in the air. 'Anyway, I came to tell you that dinner is being served in about twenty minutes, so get yourselves organised and head back up. Don't be late.'

The woman turned and left the girls to it.

'I bags the bottom bunk closest to the door,' Caprice said, dumping her suitcase on the bed.

It didn't take long until everyone was sorted. Millie returned from the loo to report that the bathroom wasn't as creepy as the rest of the place. Although the clanking pipes were a bit of a worry. She hoped the noise wouldn't continue into the night.

Despite her protests that she wasn't staying, Madagascar had raced ahead of Alice-Miranda to claim the bunk above Millie's. Sloane and Chessie were positioned somewhere in the middle, with Alethea and Gretchen right next to them. Alice-Miranda happily found herself sharing with Lucinda. Jacinta was bunking with Susannah Dare, and was in a total fog of love ever since that kiss in the park. She didn't think there was anything that could dampen her mood. Not even an encounter with the Loch Ness Monster or a jibe from Caprice.

Chapter 25

The children and teachers gathered upstairs in the vast medieval dining room. The space boasted soaring arched ceilings and long tables with bench seating. Several stag heads adorned the walls, and there was another inglenook fireplace with a coat of arms above it.

'It's a bit creepy, don't you think?' Ava whispered to Quincy, who had just been thinking the same thing. She wasn't a fan of dead animals on walls, and this place seemed to have its own herd. At least none of the animals were rare and endangered – that was one saving grace.

The space was noisy and it didn't take long before the sound reached an unbearable level. Davina was about to call the roll when, out of the corner of her eye, she noticed Madagascar Slewt approach Mr Ferguson the way a lion stalks its prey. The woman sighed. She adjusted her glasses and briskly made her way over to put a stop to any histrionics the girl might be considering.

Sloane nudged Millie. 'What's Madagascar's problem this time?'

'Don't care,' Millie replied, rolling her eyes. She had officially resigned as her cousin's minder. All she wanted to do was enjoy a hearty, drama-free meal surrounded by her best friends.

Madagascar, meanwhile, had cornered Mr Ferguson. 'You have to call my father,' the girl demanded, jabbing the man's arm. 'I refuse to stay one more second in this horrid place.'

Barclay Ferguson tugged on his grey beard. 'I had high hopes for everyone on this program, ye included. Now, I don't understand what has upset ye so terribly, but I think ye should give it at least another night,' the man said. 'Leaders are not quitters. Perhaps we could sit down and peel the onion to see exactly what the matter is.'

Madagascar snorted. 'I am *not* peeling any onions,' she said evenly. 'If you don't call my father right this minute, I am going to tell him that you kept me here against my will and then he'll do everything he can to have you ALL sacked!'

Barclay clasped his hands and nodded. 'Right, well, perhaps we can reach out to yer father after dinner and see what he has to say.' He was loath to give in to the girl, but he had just about had enough of her antics. 'I suggest ye go and find a seat with yer friends.'

Davina leaned in to speak to the man in hushed tones. 'Sir, you're not really going to phone him, are you?'

Barclay shrugged with his palms turned upwards. 'I don't see it doin' any harm. I mean, the children have been very good about the no-phones rule – in this day and age of constant communication, it's a wonder we didna have more of this sort of thing.'

'But, sir,' Davina argued, 'the lass is letting the whole program down. You can't let her do that.'

Barclay patted her hand. 'Don't worry,

Miss Stuart. I'm sure that her da willna want to come all this way to get her.'

'You don't know Mr Slewt,' Davina spat. Her sweet features had contorted into something altogether formidable.

Barclay looked at her quizzically. 'And ye do?'

'O-Only by reputation,' the woman stammered. She took a second to regain her composure. 'The man's a fierce prosecutor. I hear he takes no prisoners.'

Mr Ferguson frowned. 'Oh dear, that is a worry. All the more reason to make sure the child is happy,' he said, and returned to his seat.

Davina clenched her fists. She had to do something, and fast. Madagascar Slewt wasn't going to ruin everything. Davina couldn't allow it.

Morag Cranna picked up a fork and tapped it loudly against her water glass. 'Good evening, children,' she said, and waited for the din to die down. It took a little while. 'Mr McDuff and his lovely family have prepared our meals, but they need our assistance getting the food from the kitchens, which are a bit of a hike from here. Could I have four volunteers from each of the groups to follow me? Oh, and a couple of teachers too?'

Alice-Miranda leapt up, as did Alethea, Lucinda

and Sep. Millie volunteered alongside Chessie, Caprice and Neville, although there was a brief argument with Lucas and Jacinta, who had also been keen to help.

Millie put paid to the fracas quick smart. 'You two,' she said, pointing at Lucas and Jacinta. 'You can stay right here where everyone can see you.' She arched her left eyebrow at the pair. 'Don't think I don't know what you did. And it had better not happen again while we're away. If we lose team points because of your smooching, I will not be happy.'

Lucas's face turned the colour of a ripe tomato and Jacinta's did too, but they both couldn't help giggling all the same.

'But good for you,' Millie said, softening. 'I mean, really, after China and that ridiculous peck on the cheek, I was beginning to wonder if you were ever going to lock lips properly.'

Davina hurried over to Morag. 'I'll go and help the children, if you like.'

'No, no, I can ...' Morag felt a buzz in her pocket. She hadn't imagined there would be any service within the walls of the medieval castle. She pulled out her phone and stared at the screen, gulping as she read the message. 'Okay,' Morag said absently. 'If you wouldn't mind. The kitchen stairs are in the sword room – we went through there on our way to the staff bedroom wing.'

Davina nodded. 'Rightio, see you in a wee jiffy.'

The children, Miss Wall and Mr Pienaar followed Miss Stuart into the front entrance hall and through a large sitting room furnished with overstuffed sofas, immense Persian rugs and heraldic banners that reached from the ceiling to the floor. Foxcliffe and Taffy were both sprawled on a sofa each, and received pats as the children passed by. Next up was a room that seemed dedicated entirely to armour and weaponry. They eventually came to a stone staircase and headed down into a cavernous space.

A veritable labyrinth of rooms, the kitchen was comprised of several separate areas, but they found Mrs McDuff and her daughters, Torna and Trevonna, carving huge sides of beef, which they were loading onto platters that were already piled with roast potatoes and pumpkin as well as cauliflower, cabbage, beans and carrots. The smell was mouth-watering and entirely unexpected, given that camp food usually consisted of mystery meat with white accoutrements. Two children were needed to hold either end of a platter, while the other two were to take a jug each of thick brown gravy and another of cheese sauce for the cauliflower, and some serving spoons. They quickly divided the tasks and organised themselves, heading back upstairs in no time.

Mr Pienaar carried one of the teachers' platters while Miss Wall managed the other. Davina insisted she could take the white sauce and gravy. She looked around and found a teaspoon, swiping it from the bench and tucking it into her jeans pocket.

'Do you have any mustard?' the woman asked Mrs McDuff, who was trying to wrestle the last butt of beef out of the one of the ovens with the help of her daughters.

The mistress of the house wiped the sweat off her forehead with the back of her sleeve and motioned to a wide opening to the left of the main kitchen. 'It's in the pantry, dear. I'll run and get it,' she said. 'I should have thought about that earlier – the adults might like it with their beef, although I can't imagine the bairns will.'

Davina smiled warmly. 'Oh, it's no bother. I'm sure I'll find it.'

Lucinda Finkelstein was halfway up the stairs when she remembered the serving spoons she'd left on the bench. She turned back and hurried down to fetch them, passing Mr Pienaar and Miss Wall on the way. Just as she was about to pick up the spoons, she noticed Miss Stuart in an adjacent room madly stirring something into a jug. The woman then quickly screwed the lid back onto a jar and placed it on one of the shelves. It was mustard by the looks of it. Lucinda hoped the rest of the gravy or white sauce was free of the stuff. Being a New Yorker, everyone presumed she loved mustard – it was a family favourite on hot dogs – but she'd never developed a taste for the condiment. Lucinda turned back to the kitchen bench and picked up the serving spoons.

'Is everything all right, sweetheart?' Miss Stuart asked, walking out of the pantry.

Lucinda waved the silver spoons in the air. 'I forgot these.'

'Ah, I see,' Davina said with a smile. 'You best hurry then. You don't want the delicious dinner getting cold.'

Despite the tyranny of distance, the children did a magnificent job getting back to the dining hall with their meals still piping hot. Neville and Chessie had quite the task of outmanoeuvring Taffy, who'd woken up and made a lunge for their platter.

Lucinda deposited the cheese sauce on her table and laid out the serving spoons as Miss Stuart offered Mr Ferguson the gravy boat. Mr McDuff stood up and bellowed something that could have been grace before they tucked in. The problem was, no one could understand whether he was giving thanks or further instructions. Mrs McDuff and her daughters soon arrived with the last platter of meat and vegetables in case anyone wanted seconds. It was quite the medieval feast and much better fare than a regular school camp, without a loaf of white bread or a tin of spaghetti in sight.

Mr Ferguson was full of compliments for their chefs. 'My goodness, this beef melts in yer mouth,' he said, loading his fork with meat and potatoes and swishing it in some gravy.

'Did you get your mustard, Miss Stuart?' Mrs McDuff asked the woman.

Davina looked up and shook her head. 'I couldn't find it,' she replied.

'Oh.' Mrs McDuff frowned. She could have sworn she'd placed a new jar on the shelf only a few days ago. 'Let me run and get it for you, dear.'

Barclay Ferguson swallowed his food and dabbed at his mouth with his napkin. 'Oh, don't bring it anywhere near me. Dreadful stuff – gives me awful tummy troubles.'

Lucinda looked over at Miss Stuart, their eyes meeting momentarily before Davina focused on her plate.

'Don't worry, Mrs McDuff, we're almost finished dinner,' Davina mumbled.

Lucinda watched with growing alarm as Mr Ferguson began to squirm. There was a loud gurgle and a pop too.

'Are ye sure there isn't any mustard in here anywhere?' the man said, his brows knitted together. 'Oh dear me,' he said, shooting out of his seat and making a run for the nearest toilet.

Chapter 26

The children almost inhaled their dessert of sticky date pudding with lashings of caramel sauce and vanilla ice-cream. Mr Ferguson reappeared, but from the perspiration on his brow and the uneasy way he was standing while conversing with Miss Cranna and Miss Stuart, he didn't look as if he would last the distance. Lucinda hoped the man was all right. She also wanted to mention what she had witnessed in the kitchens to Alice-Miranda, but the girl was sitting at the other end of the table deep in conversation with Neville.

'We'll be perfectly all right to organise tonight's activities,' Morag assured the man quietly.

'And I can telephone Mr Slewt,' Davina jumped in, noticing Madagascar was giving them all the evil eye from the other side of the room.

Barclay despised nothing more than admitting defeat. He was about to object when he clutched his stomach. A deep, sonorous gurgle rumbled from inside. Lucinda thought it sounded very much like a draining tub of bathwater.

'I'm sure we can sort it out, and I'll speak with Madagascar as soon as I get on to him,' Davina said with a sympathetic smile. 'Poor lass. I think you're right. There's no point making her stay if she doesn't want to be here.'

Morag knew the feeling. She really needed to be somewhere else right now, but that wasn't about to happen. After another gurgle and pop, Barclay Ferguson made a hasty exit. Morag turned to the group and announced that they were to proceed to the Baronial Hall for a team challenge.

The first activity involved building a tower out of newspaper. Each team could use existing towers as inspiration, or attempt to come up with a completely original design. The groups were only given sticky tape and a bundle of newspaper. They had to work out the best way to roll or fold the paper to create a base that would keep the structure upright. The building that stood tallest would receive points, as would the one that stayed intact the longest. Miss Cranna even hinted that they might have a bonus round for the most creative tower, so copying from each other was a definite no-no.

Sofia Ridout's hand shot into the air. 'What if we think of the same things?' she asked.

'If you see that your tower is the same as another one, I'd probably change it if I were you,' Morag said.

The teams assembled at their stations and began planning as soon as Miss Cranna blew a whistle. It transpired that Henry Yan was something of an expert at origami and was keen to create a replica of Tokyo Tower using small segments pieced together. However, no one else in his team could understand the lad's instructions, and there wasn't time for him to make it all on his own. Ultimately, he lost out and The Pipers managed something that vaguely resembled the Burj Khalifa in Dubai.

The Tartan Warriors, on the other hand,

accomplished a rather impressive leaning tower, which Vincent said was inspired by the one in Pisa. It mightn't have suffered quite the same tilt if anyone had noticed Madagascar sidling over and spilling half a glass of water on its base. By the time they realised it was wet, the challenge was just about over.

Clan Mac seemed to have attempted replicating the Eiffel Tower. Caprice had insisted the design would win them lots of points because not only was it sturdy, it looked good too. All was going well until one of the stanchions began to wobble and the entire thing collapsed before their very eyes. With only a few minutes up their sleeves, Clan Mac managed to slap something together, though it was rather less attractive than they'd hoped. Caprice was pouting most unattractively, too, until she caught a raised eyebrow from Alice-Miranda.

Nessie's Monsters went for a less traditional design, which gradually grew to look a little like the Seattle Space Needle but with a clumpier base. Ava Lee had recently visited the Petronas Twin Towers in Malaysia and used them as inspiration. In the end, Nessie's Monsters and The Tartan Warriors were both awarded thirty points in a tie for the win, and the other three groups scored twenty points each.

The second challenge of the evening involved a member of each team navigating a minefield of obstacles. Five identical courses were set out side by side along the room. The nominated team member was to negotiate the course while blind-folded. Another chosen member of the same team would shout instructions using the words: left, right, forwards, backwards, over, under and stop. The person with the blindfold was not allowed to speak at all, which would likely prove to be a challenge to some more than others.

The minefield was fascinating and concerning in equal measure. A few of the obstacles the children could see included a net fence, strung ropes, a small wading pool that contained something akin to green jelly, a whoopee cushion and mystery brown lumps that appeared to have steam rising from them.

The teachers and Miss Cranna watched closely as the groups worked out who would be involved. There were a few tussles that wouldn't be earning the children any additional points. Miss Wall and Mrs Clinch were watching the Winchesterfield-Downsfordvale girls in particular and noting how they were getting on. Benitha commented that this would be quite helpful when it came to writing her reports later in the year and Caroline couldn't agree more. Perhaps the week wouldn't be such a waste of time after all.

Morag yawned widely. She really just wanted the evening to be over and done with so everyone could get off to bed.

'You must be exhausted, Miss Cranna,' Alice-Miranda said to the woman. 'Were you working terribly late last night? I saw you leaving the hotel when I woke up after midnight.'

Morag's eyes widened. 'I don't know what you're talking about. I was fast asleep in bed by then.' She fiddled with her clipboard and turned away. 'Right, let's get this show on the road.' Morag raised the whistle to her lips and blew sharply.

Alice-Miranda frowned. She could have sworn it was Miss Cranna she'd seen the night before. With a shrug, the girl scampered off to rejoin her team.

Despite her moaning and groaning about wanting to leave, Madagascar seized the chance to boss someone around and nominated herself to give the instructions for Nessie's Monsters. Alethea followed suit by volunteering to be blindfolded.

Alice-Miranda would have much preferred one of the others to be in charge, but she decided to give Madagascar a chance. Wasn't that what being a good leader was all about?

Over at Clan Mac, Caprice insisted that she give the orders, and Neville was blindfolded. Millie was about to argue that perhaps she and Chessie would make a better pairing, then, like Alice-Miranda, decided to hold her tongue. It wasn't worth going into battle over the issue. The other pairings were Gretchen and Junior, Aidan and Evelyn, and Vincent and Susannah.

Miss Wall handed out the blindfolds then tested each of the subjects, asking them how many fingers she was holding up. She then shone a torch in their eyes as well. Nobody flinched, so she was certain they were all in the dark. Miss Cranna told the students responsible for giving the instructions to direct their subjects to the start of each course. There were a few bumps and stumbles, but the blindfolded contestants eventually managed to find their positions. When Morag was satisfied that all teams were ready, she blew the whistle to begin.

It was a tentative start for most, but Vincent had a different approach. He was more a bull at a gate, catching Susannah off guard as she'd barely uttered a couple of directions before he was ensnared in the net. His attempts to climb his way out of it only resulted in his getting an arm stuck and a foot too. The fact that his team was cheering him loudly didn't help matters, as Susannah was finding it almost impossible to make herself heard.

'Oh, do be quiet, will you!' Susannah screeched, which surprised everyone and instantly calmed things down. 'Vincent, you need to listen to me and do exactly as I say, and stop running off and thinking that you've got some sort of X-ray vision,' the girl scolded.

'Okay,' the lad squeaked, then remembered he could be penalised for speaking too. He hoped no one had heard him.

By now, he and the rest of the teams were well behind Madagascar, who was doing a sterling job with Alethea. It was unexpected to say the least. Alethea was listening to Madagascar's every direction and had made it past the net, under the ropes, around the first of several mystery brown lumps and was just about to pass the wading pool when she wobbled.

'Right!' Madagascar yelled, and immediately

realised she had meant to say left. But it was too late. Alethea stepped to the right and landed – *splodge!* – in the green slime.

'Yuck, what have I stepped in?' Alethea shouted, completely forgetting that she wasn't supposed to say a word. She tried to lift her foot, but it felt heavy and wet. 'Why did you tell me to go right? Did you put me in here on purpose, Madagascar?'

'Stop speaking!' Sloane called out. 'We'll lose more points.'

'Of course I didn't,' Madagascar spat back, her eyes brimming with tears.

Alice-Miranda cupped her hands around her mouth, careful not to bang her nose. 'It's okay, Alethea,' she said. 'It's not that bad.'

Alethea lifted her foot and tried to step out, but could feel herself slipping. Her arms spun like windmills and her feet slid from underneath her. She fell onto her bottom in the middle of the pool.

'Oh, gross!' Alethea grimaced, but to the girl's credit, she didn't lose the plot. Instead she pushed herself up and rolled out onto the ground.

Madagascar, on the other hand, was sobbing inconsolably. 'Why do I always get the blame for everything?' she wailed. 'Where's Mr Ferguson? Why hasn't he phoned my father?'

Miss Stuart arrived back just in time to witness Madagascar's latest meltdown. She hurried over to the girl and proceeded to tell her that she'd just got off the phone with Mr Slewt, and the man had insisted that his daughter see out the week. He'd be terribly disappointed if she tossed in the towel.

Madagascar's jaw dropped and she sucked in a breath so deep it was a wonder she didn't inhale the woman. 'No, he didn't! My father does *everything* I tell him to!' she bellowed.

Over on the course next to Nessie's Monsters, Millie realised right then and there why she hadn't seen her first cousin twice removed since they were very little. The memory hurtled towards her so fast it almost bowled her over. It had something to do with Madagascar's father taking the girl's side when she'd tried to strangle Millie with a skipping rope. She had marks on her neck – the evidence was clear – but Hutton Slewt would have none of it. Millie seemed to recall her mother had endured a similar incident with the man when they were children, and at the time Pippa McLoughlin-McTavish had decided enough was enough.

Chessie stifled a smile. She couldn't help feeling somewhat vindicated that Madagascar's true colours were on display for all to see.

'Madagascar, you need to pull yourself together,' Alice-Miranda called out. 'We're still in it, as long as you can guide Alethea to the end.'

Britt Fox had been watching the shenanigans from further down the hall and yelled some words of encouragement too, despite being on an opposing team.

Madagascar wiped her nose on the back of her sleeve and dabbed at her eyes.

'You need to tell her what to do because we can't,' Lucinda said. She hoped Madagascar's competitive nature would resurface. The other teams were still pitched in a ferocious battle to see who would be first to the end of their course.

Upon hearing they might still be in with a chance, Madagascar sniffled and drew herself up taller. 'Alethea, turn left!' she ordered.

Alethea did as she was told, then jumped over something she presumed to be one of the brown lumps. She hurried ahead as quickly as she could and leapt into the air only to stomp on the whoopee cushion, which had everyone falling about in stitches.

251

In the end, it was Neville who made it through the course first and without any mistakes. The Highland Flingers were next and, incredibly, Nessie's Monsters came in at third place, although they probably would have won if it hadn't been for the slime incident. It was lucky no one stepped on any of the brown lumps, but once it was all over, Mr McDuff admitted that they weren't real. They'd been his contribution to the courses as he liked to play practical jokes on the children who came to stay at the castle. A steaming pile of poo in the hallway was always a little disconcerting. Except there was one time when poor Foxcliffe did have an accident outside the children's rooms and, thinking it was another of Mr McDuff's jokes, a poor lad picked it up and got a very smelly surprise.

Chapter 27

The children went off to bed in high spirits, having enjoyed their challenges no matter the winner. Except, of course, Madagascar was still in a foul mood. She was convinced she would be blamed for landing Alethea in the slime, the way she got blamed for everything else. Strangely, Alethea hadn't seemed that fussed herself. Given the girl's reputation, Madagascar wouldn't put it past her to be plotting her revenge – the others probably would too.

On their way downstairs, Lucinda asked if she could have a quick word with Alice-Miranda. The girls stopped and waited until everyone else had passed by.

'Is something the matter?' Alice-Miranda asked.

Lucinda hesitated, unsure how to begin. Then she decided to just come out and say it. 'You know how Mr Ferguson felt unwell after dinner and Mrs McDuff asked Miss Stuart whether she found the mustard and she said no? Miss Stuart was lying. I'm certain I saw her stir mustard into the gravy while we were down in the kitchen.'

Alice-Miranda's eyes widened. That was quite a hefty accusation and a perplexing one at that. 'Perhaps Miss Stuart didn't know that he had a problem with it,' she said.

Lucinda shook her head and relayed that Mr Ferguson had spoken openly about his reaction to mustard that afternoon at lunch in the park. She was pretty sure Miss Stuart had been standing right behind him when he'd said it.

A voice called from the bottom of the stairs. It was Millie telling them to hurry up as they were under strict instructions from Mrs Clinch to be in bed by nine and no doubt she'd be around to check.

'Coming,' Alice-Miranda called back.

'I wish we could go down to the kitchen and I could check that jar,' Lucinda said. 'I need to be sure before I say anything to Mr Ferguson, and I know I won't sleep a wink until then.'

Alice-Miranda's eyes lit up. 'What about if we sneak out after everyone's asleep? It wouldn't take long and then you can rest easy.'

'Is that really you, Alice-Miranda?' Lucinda said, a grin spreading across her face. It was nice to know that her friend wasn't always a goody-two-shoes.

Alice-Miranda smiled and gave her friend a wink. 'Well, we can't have you awake all night, can we? We have another challenge tomorrow and I'd rather like our team to stay on top.'

The girls hurried into their room, where everyone was milling about getting ready for bed.

Madagascar eyed the two girls warily. She was sure they were up to something. They were probably planning to put her hand in a jug of water overnight so she'd wet the bed, or sprinkle itching powder all through her sheets. She was going to have to watch those two very carefully. In fact, she wouldn't sleep a wink until she knew they were fast asleep.

Chapter 28

Caroline Clinch poked her head in through the door of the girls' dormitory just before eleven. She hadn't seen the point in coming down any earlier – quelling a ruckus wasn't her idea of fun. Still, she was surprised to discover them all sound asleep. Then again, it had been a busy day and a strange one at that. On her way downstairs she had begun reflecting on their incident on the loch, and wondering if they'd ever learn what it was that had hit the *Mairead*. Perhaps it was best if that remained a mystery.

She turned to head back upstairs, pulling the door closed as quietly as she could. Caroline felt a wave of exhaustion roll over her and for a moment she didn't think she'd make it all the way back to her turret. It had been good to see the children working in their teams tonight. Certainly, there were some future leaders among them, and she'd begun to think she had been too harsh on Alice-Miranda. The child had handled Madagascar and Alethea with a deft touch this evening. Caroline couldn't imagine she would have kept her composure in quite the same way with Madagascar carrying on as she was. The woman shuddered at the thought. She was glad that Bodlington had to deal with that one.

Meanwhile, back in the girls' room, Lucinda Finkelstein was wide awake and ready to begin their covert mission. She prodded the bunk above her own and, not a second later, Alice-Miranda peered over the edge and grinned at her in the darkness. The child climbed noiselessly to the floor below while Lucinda swung her legs to the ground. Together, they tiptoed across the flagstones towards the door. Neither of them noticed that Madagascar Slewt was still awake too.

The girl waited for Alice-Miranda and Lucinda

to exit the room, then slithered out from under the covers. She managed to descend from the top bunk without waking Millie, who was gently snoring away. A couple of bunks over, it was a different story. Sloane and Chessie both woke with a start. Chessie catching sight of Madagascar scurrying out the door. She poked her head down over the edge of her bed and could see Sloane's eyes blinking in the sliver of moonlight coming through the window high above them. Sloane indicated towards the door and, before you could say 'shazam', she and Chessie were up and out of the room too.

Lucinda's mission to check out the pantry had turned into a potential midnight feast, although she and Alice-Miranda didn't know it yet. The girls scampered upstairs towards the sitting room, but pulled up short when they heard voices. They crouched around the corner of the doorway and listened.

'Goodnight, Mr McDuff,' they heard Mrs Clinch say.

'Nighty night,' the man replied.

There were a couple of clicks and the glow of lamplight dimmed. Lucinda and Alice-Miranda waited until they heard footsteps heading in the opposite direction. The grandfather clock at the end of the room struck eleven.

'Come on,' Alice-Miranda whispered to Lucinda.

Madagascar lurked in the shadows on the other side of the hall while Chessie and Sloane positioned themselves behind a pillar, waiting to see where Madagascar was off to next.

Alice-Miranda and Lucinda crept through the sword room and down to the kitchen. Flames danced in the hearth, and it looked as if the fire had only been stoked a little while ago. They hoped Mrs McDuff or her daughters weren't still about and planning an early start on breakfast. A shuffling sound stopped the pair in their tracks, but then they realised that the lumpy-looking rug that had just rolled over in front of the fire was actually one of the dogs. Thankfully, Foxcliffe had stirred but not woken, and Taffy was dozing beside him.

Once they were inside the pantry, Alice-Miranda flicked on her torch and shone the light around the shelves. Lucinda pulled down a jar and unscrewed the lid. The girls leaned in and an overwhelming smell of hot English mustard assaulted their nostrils.

Alice-Miranda grimaced, a tingling sensation running through her sinuses. 'There's no mistaking what that is, is there?'

'But why would she do it?' Lucinda said.

Alice-Miranda's mind was ticking over. It seemed a particularly cruel thing to make someone sick on purpose. Surely Miss Stuart wasn't deliberately trying to harm Mr Ferguson. Maybe she hadn't heard what he'd said at lunch after all.

After tossing and turning for hours, Morag decided to make herself a cup of hot chocolate. She hadn't turned her phone back on, but the wretched thing was like an itch she needed to scratch. She stuffed her feet into her kitty cat slippers and looked at the phone on her bedside cabinet before dropping it into her pocket and making her way towards the kitchen.

Back in the weapons room, Madagascar had been on her way to the stairs when her progress was halted by a ghostly apparition. She hastily looked around for somewhere to hide and spotted a suit of armour nearby with an opening in the bottom of the torso. Counting on the fact that the metal legs would hide her own, the girl ducked down and popped up inside the mid-section. She peered through a gap in the armour plates and had to stuff her fist into her mouth to stifle the scream that was building in her lungs. Dressed in white, with gossamer hair floating about her shoulders, a ghostly woman glided through the room and disappeared in the direction of the kitchen. Madagascar hesitated, wondering if it was safe to leave her hiding spot. She was about to step out when she heard whispers coming from the door. Her eyes narrowed as Chessie and Sloane emerged from the shadows. Madagascar attempted to duck down, hoping to give the two girls a nasty scare, but was alarmed to discover that her shoulders were jammed tight. In her haste to hide, it seemed she had wedged herself inside the suit of armour. It was as if the silly thing had swallowed her up and now she was stuck fast.

Downstairs, Alice-Miranda and Lucinda were just about to head back to bed when they were startled by the sound of footsteps approaching. They scuttled over to a large cupboard at the end of the pantry and bundled themselves inside it, pulling the louvred door shut behind them.

Madagascar was still struggling to get out of the suit when she heard footsteps again. It was as if half the castle was awake and wandering about. She squinted through a gap in one of the arms and blanched. Was the woman really wearing a stripy cat onesie with ears and a tail and matching slippers?

She thought about calling out and asking Miss Cranna to help her get out of the armour, but the woman would likely deduct points from Nessie's Monsters on account of Madagascar being out of bed. Then the others would have it in for her even more.

Madagascar watched as Miss Cranna took a phone from her pocket and held it to her ear.

'No, I can't possibly come now. I told you I'm away.' There was a short pause and Morag drew in a deep breath. 'I'll get someone . . . You can't expect that . . .' She took another deep breath and began to pace back and forth, as if she were trying to calm herself. 'No!' she snapped. 'They'll all be gone soon and then everything will be perfect. You know it will . . .'

Madagascar wondered who would be calling at this time of night and what the woman was talking about. Whatever it was sounded ominous.

The woman sighed loudly and dropped the phone back into her pocket then continued down-stairs to the kitchen, where surely there were enough people for a party by now.

Sloane and Chessie were wondering where Madagascar had gone, when they saw a shadow skulking to the other end of the room. The girls scurried past the dogs and found themselves in a room containing racks and racks of crockery. They were about to turn around when they heard foot-steps outside and decided to stay put.

In the cupboard at the end of the pantry, Alice-Miranda and Lucinda held their breaths as someone walked into the room. The girls peered through the slats and saw a woman dressed all in white.

'Who is it?' Lucinda mouthed.

Alice-Miranda shrugged and shook her head. There was a loud noise out in the kitchen, which caused the girls to jump.

'Oh hello, Taffy,' Morag said, sounding relieved. 'Where do you think I might find some cocoa?' She turned on the pantry light and got the fright of her life when she realised she wasn't alone. 'Good heavens, Davina,' she exclaimed, clutching her chest, 'what are you doing in here?' She looked at the jar in the woman's hands. 'Did you have a hankering for . . . mustard?'

Davina hesitated. 'Oh, Morag, I'm such a twit. I thought I was putting a smidge of horseradish into our gravy this evening and I realised, after poor Mr Ferguson had his tummy troubles, that I must have picked up the mustard instead. I felt so awful I couldn't say anything at the time.' Davina's voice cracked. 'I had to check for myself and now I feel absolutely wretched. You won't say anything, will you? It could cost me my job.'

Morag shook her head and patted the distraught woman on the shoulder. 'We all make mistakes, Davina. I've had plenty of personal experience with that. Would you like a cup of cocoa? I couldn't get to sleep and thought it might help. We've got a huge day tomorrow and then the weekend. I'll be glad when the children are gone.'

'Me too,' Davina said with a weak nod. She sniffed and wiped at her eyes. 'And yes please to the cocoa.'

Morag spotted what she was after and the two women stepped out into the kitchen.

'That's a relief,' Alice-Miranda whispered to Lucinda. 'And we have our answer.'

Lucinda shivered and rubbed her arms. 'That's true. I hope they leave soon. I'm cold and I want to go back to bed.'

The girls didn't have to wait long before they heard the women heading upstairs. As they emerged from the pantry, they were surprised to see Chessie and Sloane coming towards them from the other side of the kitchen.

'What are you doing down here?' Lucinda asked.

'We were following Madagascar, but she disappeared and then we heard Miss Cranna and Miss Stuart, so we hid until they left,' Sloane explained in hushed tones.

Alice-Miranda looked around. 'Where is Madagascar now?'

An almighty crash shook the air and was followed by a piercing scream. The sound of clanking metal came from the top of the stairs. The girls raced up and peered around the corner. Madagascar was crawling out from under the suit of armour that had previously been standing guard in the weapons room.

'What on earth are you doing, young lady?' Morag demanded.

Madagascar rubbed the back of her head and stood up. Her fringe resembled the crest of a perplexed cockatoo. 'I was following Alice-Miranda and Lucinda. If I'm in trouble, they should be too. And I saw Sloane and Chessie creeping about not long ago. They're all in the kitchen!'

'Preposterous,' Davina said, folding her arms across her chest.

'There's no one down there. Miss Stuart and I have just come from the kitchen,' Morag said sternly. It was hard to take her seriously in that onesie. 'I will be speaking to Miss Wall and Mrs Clinch in the morning to decide your punishment. Perhaps you *should* be sent home.'

Madagascar rolled her eyes. 'Which is what I've been saying this whole time,' she muttered under her breath.

Mr McDuff entered the scene in his tartan dressing-gown. 'What's gone on here?' he asked gruffly.

'Come on, let's go,' Sloane whispered, beckoning to the girls while Miss Cranna and Miss Stuart were busy explaining the situation to Mr McDuff.

The girls tiptoed their way around the party, keeping to the shadows, and broke into a run as soon as they were out of earshot.

Madagascar was ordered back to bed with Miss Cranna as her escort. Mr McDuff set about righting the armour, grumbling that it was a treasured family heirloom. In all the years he'd been hosting children in his castle, this was the first time he'd seen anything like this. He had apparently forgotten about the time a pair of lads had climbed up and taken a couple of swords off the wall and almost killed each other trying to see whether they could swing them around their heads.

'I don't go to Winchesterfield-Downsfordvale,' Madagascar said brusquely as they walked down the series of tunnels. 'So, it's no use telling Miss Wall and Mrs Clinch about what happened tonight.'

Morag shrugged. 'In that case, I'll decide your punishment now. You'll be up and dressed at six in the morning to help Mrs McDuff with breakfast. I'm sure she will be most grateful for an extra pair of hands to set the tables and do the washing up afterwards.'

'I don't do that for anyone,' Madagascar spat as they reached the girls' room. 'Especially not for *you*!'

'We'll see about that, young lady.' Morag raised an eyebrow at Madagascar, then opened the door and gestured for the girl to go to bed. She shone her torch around the room and found that all of the girls were tucked under their covers sound asleep.

Something inside Madagascar hardened. Those girls would pay for what they'd done. No one embarrassed her like that and got away with it.

Chapter 29

Although the castle visit had been fun, most of the children were keen to get on the bus and head south again. They were travelling to St Andrews to visit the home of golf and undertake another team challenge. Mr Ferguson was feeling much better and had dressed for the occasion in a pair of red-and-green tartan plus-fours, forest-green socks, and an argyle jumper also in red and green, with a collared shirt underneath. He had a dark green tam-o'-shanter on his head and suggested that the children might like to don their tams too.

'I hope we don't have to get outfitted exactly like *that*,' Neville said to Alice-Miranda. 'I don't mind wearing my tam, but the rest of it looks like a walking crime against fashion.'

The girl giggled. 'I love the tradition of it all, but I'm sure there isn't time for us to go shopping to complete the look.'

On the way, Mr Ferguson explained that, while St Andrews was best known for having the oldest golf course in Scotland, it was actually a sizeable town with a famous university as well. There wasn't just one golf course either – there were at least seven around the town. Located on the North Sea coast, the area had a reputation for wild and windy weather. Fortunately for them, it wasn't blowing a gale today. In fact, it was sunny by the time they arrived at the Royal and Ancient Clubhouse on the edge of the Old Course, which was quite unusual for that time of year. The man had also mentioned for at least the fourth time that there was a huge surprise coming before the end of the program, which had the children speculating wildly. Most of them thought Mr Ferguson was going to take them on an adventure challenge such as canyoning or ziplining, but the man wouldn't tell no matter how many times they asked.

'Are we actually playing a round of golf?' Chessie asked as they pulled to a stop. 'Because I've never even held a club before and I'm not sure that I want to, given what happened to Mr Duncraig and his eye.'

There were mutterings of agreement through the bus with several other children commenting that they hadn't realised golf was such a hazardous sport until they'd heard about the man's accident.

The bus doors opened and a young man bounded aboard to give Barclay a hearty handshake. The fellow had a thatch of curly hair and a broad smile. He couldn't have been a day over fourteen.

'Children, I've lined up something very special for today,' Barclay began, 'but first I want to introduce Rory Auchterlonie – he's the youngest professional on the PGA tour and is descended from a long line of golf champions. He's goin' to be speakin' to ye about his career and givin' ye some tips before we go out for today's challenge.'

The lad gave them a jovial wave. 'Hiya!'

'Yer'll be the only ones on the course as it's usually closed between the end of September and April,' Mr Ferguson said.

'There's a group over there!' Aidan said, pointing at the fairway.

'And another out there,' Ava called.

'Aye, the actual golf courses are open, but ye're goin' to be havin' yer team challenge on The Himalayas,' the man said, puffing out his chest.

Vincent frowned. 'I'm pretty sure the Himalayas are in Nepal.'

'Aye, ye're right, and Fergusons have some fabulous expeditions there, but this is a little different. It's The Himalayas puttin' course, and I can assure ye it's quite the challenge. As a member of the R and A, I've been granted special permission to host today's event.' Barclay failed to mention that he had had to persuade Mrs Marmalade, Her Majesty's lady-in-waiting and chief advisor, to put in a call to the chairman to ask the silly man to agree to host a FLOP delegation.

'What's the R and A?' Lucas asked.

'Oh, I know,' Alethea said. 'My father used to be a member until they kicked him out. He used to tell Mummy that the club was good for networking, but mostly everyone was just rude and arrogant.'

Barclay Ferguson burst out laughing and slapped his knee. 'I haven't heard that one in a while. And

271

ye're right, Alethea, the club has earned its reputation for bein' a bit stuffy, but the tide is turnin', lass.'

'Do you know how they get rid of members?' Alethea said to a sea of blank faces. 'Well, if someone places a black ball in your locker, you're out. You can't even appeal. It's where the expression "black-balling" came from.'

Madagascar would have liked to blackball a few members of her team right at that moment. She still had a bump on the back of her head. Getting out of that stupid suit of armour was akin to shedding snakeskin.

Barclay grinned. 'Ye are indeed very well-informed, Alethea. Now, as I was about to say, the club is called the Royal and Ancient. The organisation administers the rules of golf and is the most revered in all the world. It's considered a great honour to be a member. So let's head inside to chat with Rory and then out we go on the course!'

Alice-Miranda wondered how what amounted to playing a round of putt-putt golf had anything to do with leadership. Perhaps Mr Ferguson had wanted to take a side trip to St Andrews. But it turned out that there was a surprising twist to the event. The children had to decide on a team handicap, which involved quite a bit of discussion to work out what they believed the least number of shots would be required to get the ball into the hole. Then they had to take turns. It was very challenging and lots of fun. They quickly learned why the course was called The Himalayas, as there were undulating hills and quite a few peaks and troughs. If you got it wrong, your ball ran a mile, and often it took more than half a dozen shots to reach the hole.

When The Tartan Warriors scored a twenty, Philippe was thrilled to bits, shouting that his team would win for sure – until Sofia whispered that it was actually the team with the lowest score that would come out on top. Everyone had to play their role and it soon became apparent that the teams that supported each other did a lot better than the ones that niggled and poked fun.

Madagascar proved to have a dead eye, and Lucinda and Alice-Miranda were on song too. In the end it was Nessie's Monsters in first place with The Pipers in second. Clan Mac came third. Millie was beginning to lose her patience with Lucas and Jacinta, who were usually very reliable when it came to sports. However, they currently seemed to only have eyes for each other, and she was planning to give them another stern talking-to. At least there hadn't been any more public displays of affection. The Highland Flingers were fourth and, predictably, The Tartan Warriors took out the wooden spoon.

As the clouds rolled in and the weather took a turn for the worse, the children were glad to be back on the bus and heading for their hotel in Edinburgh.

'What are we doing tonight, Miss Cranna?' Alice-Miranda asked the woman, who was sitting across the aisle from her and Millie. Morag stared straight ahead and looked to be deep in thought. 'Miss Cranna?' the child tried again. 'Are you all right?'

The woman blinked and shook her head. 'Oh sorry, sweetheart, what did you say? I was just remembering how my father loved golf. He began teaching me when I was a girl.'

'Does he still play?' Alice-Miranda asked.

Morag shook her head again and tears sprung to her eyes.

Alice-Miranda quickly pulled out a tissue from her daypack and handed it to her. 'I'm sorry, Miss Cranna. Did I say something wrong?'

'Not at all,' Morag said, dabbing at her eyes.

'I just haven't thought about that for ages. He died when I was fourteen. It was so long ago yet the pain still feels as though I lost him yesterday.'

'I'm sorry to hear that,' the child said. 'It must be awfully hard to lose a parent so young. Mummy says it's horrible at any age. Grandpa has been gone forever, and Mummy and Granny and Aunt Charlotte all still miss him terribly. I didn't really know him, so it's different for me,' the child prattled. 'Was your father ill?'

The woman gazed at the little girl with the halo of chocolate curls. She had a goodness in her eyes that Morag realised she didn't immediately recognise in people. She suddenly felt bad for having lied to the child last night about leaving the hotel. 'He was killed in a fire,' Morag murmured.

Alice-Miranda's eyes widened. 'How awful. That must have made it even harder for you and your family.'

Morag trembled. She clenched her jaw and managed to stem the tears that threatened to fall.

Alice-Miranda patted the woman's arm from across the aisle. 'What about your mother?'

'She's never recovered,' Morag whispered, and squeezed her eyes shut. She hadn't slept at all last night, what with the phone call and then the shenanigans with Madagascar. Talking her mother down in person was difficult at the best of times, but with hundreds of miles between them, it was nigh on impossible. At least it was only another couple of days until this would all be over.

Chapter 30

The bus pulled up outside the Royal Hotel and in no time flat the children were back inside and settled again. It helped that they were keeping the same room mates as earlier in the week, although the room allocations had altered slightly due to the arrival of other guests. Alice-Miranda excitedly regaled Mr Campbell, the nattily dressed doorman, about their escapades in the north. He was particularly intrigued by their possible encounter with the Loch Ness Monster, but he wasn't going to tell his wife. They were heading up to the region for the summer and she might not want to go if she knew about it.

Dinner was served upon their arrival and this evening's guest speaker was Moira McKechnie. She'd started her own tech company when she was in high school and, while studying at university, had built it up to rival some of the biggest in the whole of Scotland. Now, at the ripe old age of twenty-eight, she employed over one thousand people and was renowned for being at the cutting edge of new leadership techniques.

Morag was sitting beside Davina at the back of the room. She looked at her watch at least twenty times during the lecture. Barclay Ferguson was behind her and wondered what was so pressing.

He leaned forward and tapped the woman on the shoulder. 'Everythin' all right?' he whispered.

Morag almost went through the roof, and her reaction wasn't lost on Davina. Morag was always on edge. Even when they were having their hot chocolate last night she seemed distracted.

'Of course, sir,' Morag replied quietly. 'I just want to make sure that we run on time as the children are exhausted and we'll be off quite early in the morning. There's a lot to do between now and the presentation on the weekend.'

'Yes, and I have had confirmation that Her Majesty will be attendin' the final fling on Saturday,' the man added casually. He hadn't wanted to get Morag and Davina's hopes up, but thought it was about time he told them so they could be appropriately anxious for the rest of the event.

Morag's heart felt as if it were about to beat right through her chest.

Davina's mouth dried up in an instant. She turned and faced the man, an angry rash creeping up her neck. 'What did you just say, Mr Ferguson?'

'Her Majesty will be joinin' us on Saturday for the last of the activities. I want to surprise the children – they'll be so excited. Gosh, I've done well to keep it to meself for this long,' the man said, jiggling up and down in his seat.

'Why didn't you tell us?' Davina said crisply. She was doing her best to keep her cool, but inside she was seething. Talk about making things more complicated than they needed to be.

Barclay grinned, completely impervious to the woman's tone. 'I wasn't one hundred per cent sure.'

Davina wanted to punch him on the nose.

Perhaps she could see if her left hook rivalled Alethea's. 'But, sir,' she hissed, 'some advance warning would have been appreciated. There are protocols to follow.'

Barclay rolled his eyes and sighed. 'Never mind all that, Miss Stuart. The Queen is comin'! I thought ye'd be thrilled. And it would be nice to see a smile from ye too, Morag.' He frowned at the woman. 'Ye both look as if I've invited Attila the Hun.'

Morag's mind was racing a mile a minute. She had been planning on ducking out for a few hours tonight, but she couldn't possibly if there was Her Majesty's arrival to prepare for. What was she to do now?

Alice-Miranda was sitting in the front corner of the room listening to Miss McKechnie's incredible tale. Out of the corner of her eye, she couldn't help but notice the tense scene between the FLOP organisers. Running the forum must have been a lot more complicated than they made it seem most of the time. It reminded Alice-Miranda of her mother's saying about ducks. How they may appear calm on the surface, but if you delve deeper you'd find their little feet were working ten to the dozen.

Chapter 31

The children were on the bus early the next morning and heading to the final destination of their trip – a tiny World Heritage-listed village called New Lanark. It was an hour south of Edinburgh and forty-five minutes from Glasgow. They were soon on a motorway, and not long after that turned off onto a narrower back road. New Lanark sat in a valley, hidden from the rest of the world on the banks of the River Clyde.

'I think I've been here before,' Alice-Miranda remarked to Millie. There was something vaguely familiar about the road. 'Actually, I'm almost certain Uncle Morogh and Aunt Audrina brought me here with Mummy and Daddy. If I'm right, they live quite close by in a beautiful old manor. I wish I could get a message to them that we're just over the river. You'd love them, Millie. They're a bit mad but loads of fun.'

'You've been to so many different places. How do you remember them all?' Millie asked. To be fair, since meeting Alice-Miranda, she'd travelled a considerable amount too.

A sign appeared on the crest of the hill, bearing the words 'New Lanark' and a little information about the historic village.

'It *is* the same place!' Alice-Miranda cried. She clapped her tiny hands excitedly. 'It's all coming back to me now. New Lanark was a cotton milling town far ahead of its time because the workers and children were treated to leisure days and education. That was a rare commodity for the lower classes in the eighteenth century because most people didn't believe they should have days off, or learn to read and write and do arithmetic. It was a way for the rich people to keep the poor in their place, which is horrible but true. Thank goodness times have changed a lot since then, although I think it still happens more than we know. Unfortunately, those privileges, which are considered basic human rights today, meant that the costs of running the mill skyrocketed and it sent the place broke. For a long time it was derelict, but then some clever people realised what an important place it was and sought to preserve it as a reminder of the past. How exciting to be back here again and this time I'm much older, so I'll remember a lot more!'

Millie thought Alice-Miranda remembered quite a lot already.

The bus pulled up at the top of a steep section of road. The valley below was shrouded in mist. The converted mill building had been beautifully restored and transformed into a hotel. The children were all staying on the third floor, with the teachers on the level beneath them. The girls in Alice-Miranda's group had a family suite with one queen bed, two singles and a rollaway.

Madagascar pointed at the queen bed. 'I'm not sleeping in there.'

'Me either,' Alethea said, and both girls raced for the two singles.

Alice-Miranda shook her head and chuckled. 'I don't mind sharing.'

Lucinda and Sloane said they were happy to as well, but in the end Sloane took the rollaway.

The children hurried downstairs to one of the conference rooms they'd been allocated for the program. Mr Ferguson was writing the points scores on a large whiteboard and had added some columns for the final challenges. No one knew what they would be except for the Highland games on Saturday.

'Look – we're in the lead!' Madagascar yelped, and pumped her fist. For someone who only hours before had been screaming about going home, she had certainly changed her tune.

'Quickly, children, please find a seat,' Morag said. 'First up, you'll be taking a guided tour of the village and becoming acquainted with the layout and history, and this afternoon you'll be involved in your first challenge of the day.'

Barclay Ferguson turned and grinned widely. 'Aye, it's fantastic too. Ye're goin' to be searchin' for an elusive creature.'

Sloane shuddered. 'Don't tell me there's another monster in these parts.'

'No, this one's as cute as a button and very friendly,' the man said, his eyes sparkling.

There was a spitfire round of conjecture from the children about what Mr Ferguson's creature might be, which canvassed the rabbit, badger, pheasant, weasel and hedgehog.

'Cat?' Gretchen said, even though she really hadn't meant to. She'd been mesmerised by Miss Cranna's jumper, which was one to outdo them all, with a montage of cats and kittens chasing after balls of wool.

The children giggled, but fortunately Miss Cranna had been distracted. She cast a look at her boss that pleaded with the man not to divulge what was in store, but of course Barclay couldn't help himself.

'Haggis,' he whispered indiscreetly.

Sloane grimaced. 'Haggis is food. Heart and liver and lungs all minced up in a sheep's stomach. Urgh, disgusting.'

Barclay shook his head, chortling. 'Haggis is a wee creature that roams about Scotland with the roundest little body and the cutest face ye ever did see and I can tell ye it's also delicious.'

'No, it's not,' Millie said loudly. Her father was fond of haggis, though she'd never acquired a taste for it herself.

'Miss Cranna, can ye put the picture on the screen, please?' Barclay asked.

The woman nodded and opened the file on the computer.

Ava Lee gasped as the picture filled the screen. 'Oh, that's so sweet!'

The creature looked like a long-haired guinea pig, although it had a face more akin to a baby bat and three claws on a very skinny leg that resembled that of a chicken. With tufts of long hair on its head, it was sort of glamorous and weird and multi-coloured to boot.

'Ye canna see it in the picture, but the wee thing has a problem with its legs. The ones on the right are longer than the ones on the left, so it walks with a limp or sometimes around in circles,' Mr Ferguson explained. 'Must be very frustratin', to say the least, not te mention difficult te get where yer goin'.'

'That's not real,' Madagascar scoffed. 'You just made it up to send us on some wild goose chase.'

'Well, if that's what ye think, then perhaps ye don't want te earn any points from the sightin's and never mind if ye capture the thing, what a prize yer'll be having then.'

At the mention of points and a prize, Madagascar closed her mouth.

'I think it sounds like fun,' Alice-Miranda said to her team mates, as they all set off with their teachers to explore the town.

There was plenty to see, starting with the textile mill, where you could watch the weavers at work with their giant looms. Then came the historic classroom in which the mill founder, Robert Owen, created the first Infants Class in the world. Last of all, they were taken on the Annie McLeod experience, where the children sat in pairs in pod-like chairs which moved around the exhibit, transporting riders back in time with ghostly apparitions, including young Annie herself talking about life in the mill town in the 1800s.

Mrs Clinch found the whole place to be absolutely marvellous. She couldn't help but think the venue would make an incredible excursion experience. Besides the obvious history of the site, there was a lot of maths and science at play too. Perhaps she might suggest it as an option for the senior girls when she returned to Winchesterfield-

Downsfordvale – a week-long trip here wouldn't go astray. Benitha Wall smiled to herself when Caroline shared her idea. If she didn't know any better, she would have thought the woman was actually enjoying herself.

Chapter 32

After lunch, the children gathered in their groups while their leaders read out the instructions for the Haggis Hunt. They weren't allowed to collaborate with any other teams and, to guard against collusion, their maps would send them off in different directions. Their teachers would tail them, but they weren't allowed to help in any way. Caroline Clinch was going to float between them all, overseeing things. She really did think it was the cutest challenge ever and hoped that they would find something.

'This is such a stupid challenge. We all know that it's a big joke,' Madagascar grumbled.

Sep gave her the evil eye. 'I thought you wanted to win this thing.'

'I don't even want to *be* here,' Madagascar replied tartly, 'but if I have to stay, I don't plan on losing.'

'Then I suggest we work together and enjoy it,' Alethea said, arching an eyebrow.

Lucinda grinned to herself. She was liking Alethea more and more each day. Maybe they would hang out at school when they got back.

Alice-Miranda scanned the page. 'It says that we should use the bags provided to collect evidence of the haggis and, if we are able to capture one, we should tie this leash around its neck.' She held up something resembling a dog lead. 'Apparently, they're friendly creatures and don't bite – not very hard, at least – and they don't carry any diseases.'

Neville grinned. He'd been standing as close to Alice-Miranda as he dared, given he was meant to be listening to Millie's instructions further along the room. He turned to the girl and smiled. 'I've spent half my life chasing butterflies, which lots of people think is weird. Hunting a haggis in Scotland doesn't sound that much sillier.'

Alice-Miranda grinned back at the lad, who quickly hurried to rejoin his group. The children were soon given the nod to get going. Alice-Miranda waved to Millie. 'Good luck!' she called out as they all set off.

Mrs Clinch rugged up against the cold and wondered which direction to head in first. The village was terribly pretty. She reached into her coat pocket for her phone and was annoyed not to find it. She must have left it in her room. Never mind, she'd have to take some photographs later. She watched the children in their groups striding off in several directions.

Nessie's Monsters took the trail along the River Clyde at the back of the main buildings. The clouds had cleared to the south, revealing a bright blue afternoon with barely a breath of wind, although jackets and hats were definitely still required.

'So, this thing is fluffy and has a sort of glamorous long hairdo,' Sloane said, walking along beside Alice-Miranda, who was thumbing through sheafs of laminated pictures of the haggis, its lair and footprints.

'There!' Sep shouted, pointing across the river into the woodland. 'I could have sworn there was something with a tuft of long hair on its head, just like Mr Ferguson's picture.'

The others were sceptical, but Alethea seemed convinced. 'I saw it too,' she confirmed.

'Okay, let's follow it,' Alice-Miranda said. According to their map, they were most likely to find the creature across the river in the woods. The girl smiled to herself. She suspected every group would find evidence of the haggis, having been planted by Miss Cranna and Miss Stuart. But the idea of it was fun all the same.

The threat of a storm on the horizon began to cloud Madagascar's features. 'It looks creepy over there,' she said.

'I'm sure it's perfectly safe,' Alice-Miranda replied. She pointed to a section of their map. 'There's an area circled here which I think is where we're most likely to find something. I can't imagine we'd be sent anywhere dangerous.'

It was settled then. The children scampered towards an exposed rock shelf, where it looked like they could get across. Lucinda glanced back towards the mill buildings and spotted Vincent and his group climbing the hill on the other side of the village. She gave a wave, but they mustn't have seen her. The Highland Flingers were close by too, which was strange because Alice-Miranda said they were all going to different places.

'Hurry up, Lucinda!' Sloane called from the other side of the river.

The girl picked her way across the rock shelf, her footsteps creating tiny splashes in the shallow water. It wasn't more than a couple of centimetres deep in the last section and had been almost dry the rest of the way. On the other side, the children chatted away as they walked along a path, keeping an eye out for the elusive creature. The trail narrowed as it took them deeper into the woods.

'Look!' Madagascar gasped all of a sudden, and dashed through the undergrowth. The rest of the children hurried along behind her.

Hansie Pienaar was bringing up the rear when he felt his phone vibrate in his pocket. He pulled it out and read the message. 'Kids, stop, we have to go back!' he shouted, and ran to catch up.

'Why?' Madagascar huffed. 'We've only been out here for half an hour.'

'I forgot the first-aid kit,' the man replied, holding up his phone. 'There's a message from Mrs Clinch.'

'Then you go and get it,' Madagascar said, folding

her arms. 'It's not fair that we have to walk all the way back because of your mistake. We'll stay here.'

The others nodded.

The man looked at the children. They were all fairly reliable, even if Alethea and Madagascar were a little on the bolshy side.

'We'll just explore this clearing,' Alice-Miranda said with a smile.

Mr Pienaar sighed. 'I'll be back in a jiffy,' he said, and thundered back down the track.

But Madagascar had no intention of staying put. She thought she saw something move up ahead and raced away.

'Hey! Where do you think you're going?' Sep yelled.

'Maddie, please come back,' Alice-Miranda called. 'We told Mr Pienaar we'd wait here.'

But the child was undeterred. Besides, Little Miss Goody-Two-Shoes would be in heaps of trouble if they didn't stay where she said they would, Madagascar thought, and that would be music to her ears. 'Hey, you should see this!' she shouted. 'I'm sure it's a haggis.'

'We can't just let her go,' Sep said to the others. 'And it's safer if we all stay together.'

Alice-Miranda nodded. The rest of the team sprang into action, chasing the girl down the narrow path with its overhanging branches. The children spotted Madagascar up ahead in a small clearing. Surrounded by trees, and almost completely obscured from sight, was a tiny cottage. It was built of stone, and the woods had enclosed themselves around it in a stiff embrace. Long tendrils of creeper snaked their way across the window frames and up into the eaves. The wonky chimney didn't look like it had vented a fire in years.

'Do you think someone lives here?' Sloane whispered. A shiver ran down her spine.

Before they could turn back, Madagascar darted inside. 'It's in here. There's a haggis!' the girl cried out.

'What do you want to do?' Sep said. 'We could just sit here and wait for her to come out.'

'It's going to get away!' Madagascar shouted from somewhere inside the rickety old cottage.

'Come on,' Alice-Miranda said, and pushed the squeaky door to reveal a teeny front room. A strong smell of damp thwacked her in the nostrils and she glanced around at the ghostly furniture draped in sheets. A bird flew out from a nest it had made in an overhead light fitting, causing her to jump.

The children's eyes took a minute to adjust to the gloominess. There was another door at the back of the room, but there was no sign of Madagascar or the haggis.

'Perhaps it went through the window there and back outside,' Sloane said, noticing it was slightly ajar. But so was the door to the next room.

Sep pushed it open and the children found themselves in the kitchen. There was a cooker and a large enamel sink alongside several cupboards, the doors of which were hanging off their hinges. It looked as if they were now homes to squirrels.

'Hey, look at this,' Lucinda said from the far corner, where a wooden trapdoor lay wide open.

Sep stuck his head down below and tried to have a look around, but it was no use without a light. 'It must be the cellar,' he said, his voice bouncing around the underground walls.

'Madagascar, where are you?' Alice-Miranda called. She took out the small torch she was carrying in her jacket pocket and turned it on. 'We need to go back. Mr Pienaar will be looking for us.'

'I'm down here!' came the reply.

'I know we're hunting for a mythical creature, but this is kind of fun,' Lucinda said, a shiver embracing her body. 'I wonder if everyone's hunt is as exciting as ours.'

'Come on then, let's go,' Sep said. He was hankering to see for himself. 'Maybe she really has found something.'

The children reached the bottom of the creaky mildewed steps and found themselves in a brick-lined cellar. There were even a few dusty wine bottles. Alice-Miranda shone the torch around and was surprised to see a passageway to their left. It was narrow and sloped downwards, and she thought she could just make out Madagascar up ahead.

'It's some sort of underground tunnel,' Sloane said. 'I wonder where it goes.'

'Maddie, come back!' Alice-Miranda called, but the girl didn't stop. She must have had a torch as well, because they could see the light bouncing ahead of her.

The children raced after the girl and managed to catch up to her.

'What are you doing?' Alice-Miranda panted.

'Exploring. This is way more fun than that stupid Haggis Hunt,' Madagascar said. 'Although I really did see something run into the cottage.' She grinned nastily. 'And I don't care if I get told off because this time *you* will too. Serves you right for getting me in trouble the other night.'

A horrible grating sound behind them stopped the group in their tracks. Alice-Miranda spun around and shone the torch in the direction they had come from. She was shocked to see a door sliding across the passage, blocking their exit. Madagascar ran towards it, pounding on what looked and felt like steel. Alice-Miranda chased after the girl.

Sloane's heart thumped in her chest. 'What's happening?' she asked in a small voice.

The light from Alice-Miranda's torch revealed that the panel was completely sealed, almost as if it were airtight. Sep ran his fingers across the metal surface, looking for a way to pull it back, but it yielded no answers.

'Is this a trap?' Madagascar shouted.

'Well, it's your fault for leading us down here,' Sloane muttered. She was trying had to battle the panic that was building in her lungs.

Alethea Goldsworthy was having none of it. She surveyed the area for clues. 'There has to be a way out. It must be part of the challenge – to see how we cope in a situation like this.'

As she spoke, there was another loud grating sound and the brick wall at the other end of the passageway, located further down the ramp, peeled back. The children's mouths gaped open.

'What is this place?' Alice-Miranda whispered.

Chapter 33

The children found themselves standing at the edge of a large room. It had four sets of bunkbeds lined up against one wall and a couple of couches sitting on a Persian rug in the middle. There was a dining table for eight people and, at the other end of the room, there was a kitchen with a huge cooker and cupboards alongside a very dated refrigerator and something that might have been a microwave oven, but it was hard to tell as it didn't look like anything the children were used to. There was a doorway on the wall opposite the bunks and paintings and a clock. If it wasn't so strange, you might have even called it homely.

Madagascar ran towards the other door and pushed it open, hoping it was an exit. She was surprised to find a bathroom not unlike one you would see in a school dormitory, with shower cubicles and toilets tiled in a style from long ago.

'When we were in St Andrews, I picked up a brochure for this place called Scotland's Secret Bunker,' Sep said. 'This kind of reminds me of that, except the one in the brochure looked much bigger. Apparently, hundreds of people lived underground during the War in case there was a nuclear attack. Maybe there were other bunkers in different places.'

Alice-Miranda surmised that there must have been some sort of heating, as the air was warm but not in the least stale.

'Do you think this is part of the challenge?' Sloane gulped.

'There wasn't a mention of anything quite like this in the instructions, but I wouldn't put it past Mr Ferguson to include a bit of extra fun to the hunt,' Alice-Miranda said. She didn't add that a strange feeling was niggling away at her. She walked towards the dining table and spotted an envelope. It was addressed to Nessie's Monsters. 'Here's something,' Alice-Miranda said brightly, picking it up.

'Well, what does it say?' Madagascar demanded.

Alice-Miranda ran her fingernail beneath the flap and pulled out a typed page. She scanned the contents then started again at the beginning, trying to comprehend exactly what she was reading.

'Out with it!' Alethea pressed.

Alice-Miranda sat down on one of the dining chairs. She placed the page on the table and stared at it. 'I think you should all take a seat.'

Back on terra firma, Hansie Pienaar was desperate to find the children. He hadn't expected someone as reliable as Alice-Miranda to have gone back on her word. When they weren't in the clearing, he'd pushed on and found a little cottage, but there hadn't been any sign of them there either. His heart was pounding. He'd never lost any kids before and the thought made him sick to his stomach. Surely they couldn't be too far away. He had to keep looking.

Hansie tore through the woods, which seemed

to be getting thicker and darker with every step. He pulled out his phone and contemplated the call he was going to have to make. He had one bar of service and the battery was almost flat. The man swallowed hard. It was as if the children had disappeared into thin air.

Chapter 34

Meanwhile, the rest of the groups had arrived back at the hotel and were in a spin trying to one-up each other with tales of their sightings. No one, however, had actually managed to capture the elusive beast. To say they were excited was something of an understatement. Davina Stuart was checking off the teams as they poured into the conference room. Outside it was almost dark, and the earlier blue skies had clouded over with the growing threat of a storm.

Barclay Ferguson ducked his head into the room.

'They've all arrived,' he said, rubbing his hands together.

Davina turned to the man and grinned. 'When's the big reveal?'

'I think now is as good a time as any,' he said, and dashed away before she could say another word. A couple of minutes later, the man returned. 'Children, I have a big surprise and I canna wait a second longer.' He was practically frothing as he pushed back the double doors. 'Look who's here!'

Millie spotted her mother first. She let out a squeal and leapt up off the floor, running straight into the woman's arms. 'Mum! Dad! What are you doing here?'

Pippa's blonde curls swished as she scooped up her daughter and twirled her around. 'Mr Ferguson wanted to surprise you all,' she explained, gently returning Millie to the ground. 'Apparently, there are some Highland games tomorrow and you know your father wouldn't miss that for the world.'

Millie hugged both her parents tightly. She missed them terribly during the school term, but that made time with them all the sweeter.

There were reunions taking place all over the room, with lots of hugs and even some tears.

Chessie was thrilled to see her mother and step-father and couldn't wait to tell them every detail of her amazing week, although she would save any mention of Madagascar Slewt for when they were in private.

Barclay Ferguson was thrilled that so many of the parents had been able to come along, but now he needed to get back to Edinburgh to meet Her Majesty's plane and escort her to the village. 'Davina, take care of things until I get back,' he whispered, then tapped the side of his nose. 'And make sure that everyone's ready and in place.'

'Of course, sir, it will be my absolute pleasure,' Davina said, smiling from ear to ear.

Hugh Kennington-Jones stood in the middle of the milieu with his hands in his pockets. He had cast his eyes across the crowd several times, but there was no sign of his daughter. He frowned and made his way over to Benitha Wall, tapping the woman on the shoulder. 'Hello Miss Wall. I was wondering if you've seen Alice-Miranda?'

'Oh, hello Mr Kennington-Jones,' Benitha greeted the man. 'Let's see. She should be around here somewhere.' Benitha surveyed the group for the girl and the other members of Nessie's Monsters and realised that, curiously, none of the children were present.

She wasn't the only one who was perturbed. September Sykes and her husband were standing in the corner of the room looking visibly peeved.

'We've come all this way and neither of our children could be bothered to say hello,' September said tetchily. She bit her bee-stung bottom lip and tried with all her might to frown. 'It's very disappointing. I thought they were training to be leaders, not brats.'

Over by the scones, another parent was grumbling about his daughter's absence. He was standing beside an impeccably dressed woman who appeared equally uncomfortable.

'Well, where is she?' Hutton Slewt muttered through gritted teeth. He bit fiercely into a scone, spraying the carpet around them with crumbs.

'Who knows, darling? Madagascar is a law unto herself at the best of times.' Pamela Slewt patted her husband's back and willed her daughter to appear in the next minute, otherwise things would decidedly get worse.

Pippa McNoughton-McGill had been shocked to see her cousin and his wife when they'd first arrived, and had been doing her utmost to avoid them. The fellow made her skin crawl. To think that poor Millie had had to put up with their brat of a child for a whole week.

Benitha strode over to Miss Stuart. 'Excuse me, Davina, have Nessie's Monsters returned?'

Davina looked up from her clipboard and pushed her glasses onto the bridge of her nose. 'Oh, I thought they had,' she said, and glanced down again at her list of names, 'but I see now I haven't ticked them off.'

Caroline Clinch had spotted a few of the childless parents too and walked over to speak with Benitha just as Morag entered the room, having spent an hour on the phone. There was much chatter and excitement as the children and their parents swapped stories. The catering staff had brought in trays of tea and coffee and some delicious scones. Things seemed calm again for now, although she immediately noticed Miss Wall's furrowed brow and the dark look hovering beneath Caroline Clinch's too-long fringe.

Benitha hurried over to Morag. She could hear raindrops begin to splatter against the windows and was well aware that the children's coats were not entirely waterproof. 'Miss Cranna, have you seen Alice-Miranda or the rest of her team?'

Morag's stomach dropped. 'They should have been back half an hour ago. Has anyone checked their rooms?'

'I'll go now,' Benitha said, and bounded away.

Mrs Clinch made her way over to Hugh Kennington-Jones. She tamed her nerves and put on a brave face so as not to alarm the man. 'Miss Wall's just gone to see if the children went straight to their rooms after the last activity. Your arrival was a complete surprise, so they're probably upstairs playing games.'

'Thank you very much. If I know my daughter, she's likely got a tournament in full swing,' Hugh said with a nod. He walked across the room to greet Morrie and Gerda Finkelstein, who had flown in from New York and were also wondering where Lucinda was.

Mrs Clinch decided to check with Millie, who was standing with her team and their parents laughing about their escapades. She was also quite keen to say hello to that dreamy Lawrence Ridley. She hadn't imagined he would be able to attend, but there he was in all his movie-star glory.

'We were so close,' Lucas said as the woman joined their circle. 'If only you hadn't scared it off, Caprice.'

The girl folded her arms across her chest. 'Why do I always get the blame when something goes wrong?'

Caprice's mother, Venetia Baldini, arched an eyebrow. 'Sweetheart, do you really have to ask?' she said, to everyone's amusement. Venetia grinned and wrapped her arms around the girl. Caprice may be a nightmare more often than not, but she was still Venetia's baby.

'Excuse me, Millie, have you seen Alice-Miranda?' Caroline asked with a smile. Lucas thought that was the most teeth he'd seen from the woman all week.

Millie shook her head. 'No. But they should have been back by now.'

'Maybe they'll lose some points,' Caprice said brightly. 'It is neck and neck.'

'I'm afraid points are the last thing on my mind, Caprice,' Mrs Clinch replied. The rain was getting harder and the wind was whistling through the window frames.

The colour drained from Neville's cheeks as he

realised the woman's meaning. 'Can we help?' he asked. 'We need to do something. It's horrible out there and I heard the lady on reception say that it might even snow.'

On the other side of the room, Morag Cranna held her breath, waiting for the children to charge through the doors at any minute. She spotted Benitha Wall making her way towards her through the maze of parents and children. The woman reported that she had checked every student's room and there had been no sign of Nessie's Monsters.

'Have you tried calling Mr Pienaar?' Benitha asked.

'Of course! I should have done that first,' Morag said, plunging her hand into her pocket. She didn't dare let out a breath just yet, though. She waited while the line clicked through, but it went straight to voicemail. She tried a second time and then a third. Morag thought she was going to be sick. This wasn't happening. Not again. Not on her watch.

Hugh Kennington-Jones walked over to Benitha. 'Any luck?' he asked with a winning smile.

'Um, no,' the woman replied, wringing her hands and finding it hard to meet the man's eyes. 'I imagine they've been caught in the storm and sought shelter in the village. Not to worry – they're with a teacher and he's very reliable.'

There was a huge clap of thunder overhead. The lights flickered and went out altogether, sending a hush through the room. Jacinta whimpered and held tight to Lucas. The sound of the rain was deafening.

Britt Fox gasped as the lights came back on and she spied a figure in the doorway. 'Mr Pienaar!'

The man was dripping all over the carpet and was completely out of breath. She ran to him with Miss Wall and Mrs Clinch hot on her heels.

'Where are the children?' Morag yelled over the noise of the storm.

'I don't know,' the man cried out. He shook his head, sending droplets flying every which way. He looked at her with pleading eyes. 'I'm so sorry.'

Morag blinked as the room began to spin. The last thing she remembered before she hit the ground was the look of horror on Hansie Pienaar's face.

Hugh Kennington-Jones swiftly rounded up the parents of the missing students and took them to another room across the hall. He rightly assumed that September Sykes would be hysterical and he didn't want her creating any more angst than was present already. Gerda Finkelstein took it upon herself to console the woman and had sent Morrie to fetch her and Mrs Slewt a strong cup of tea.

Hutton Slewt's lip wrinkled. 'Never thought I'd be suing the Queen.'

'I think we've got more on our minds than that at the moment,' Smedley Sykes said. He could hardly believe that was the man's first thought given the current situation, but people did react to bad news in odd ways. 'We need to do something.'

Hugh nodded, his face etched with concern. 'I couldn't agree more. My mother-in-law's cousin and his wife live on the other side of the river. I'll call them and see if they can loan us some vehicles. I'm keen to get out and start looking.'

'Have you seen the weather? We'll all drown,' Hutton Slewt said, recoiling at such a suggestion. 'I refuse to step foot outside this hotel.'

Morrie Finkelstein, having returned with a tray of tea, shook his head. 'Suit yourself, but I for one am joining Hugh. I'll go out of my mind if I stay here.'

Over in the conference room, Mrs Clinch had

taken charge of the situation while Miss Cranna had been carted off to bed. Britt Fox and Millie had organised soup and a blanket for Mr Pienaar and anyone else who was feeling a bit wobbly. Within ten minutes, Caroline had the teachers and a number of parent volunteers ready to head out. Venetia Baldini had put up her hand to help, along with Lawrence Ridley, Hamish McLoughlin-McTavish and his wife, Pippa. Len and Sylvia Nordstrom had also volunteered as well as, surprisingly, Alethea's mother. Hugh, Morrie and Smedley had joined them too. There was no way they were going to be left out of any search party.

Millie felt sick thinking about her friends out in the storm and begged Mrs Clinch to let her help, but the teacher said it was far too dangerous for the children, particularly as conditions were worsening. Feeling equally frustrated, Neville, Chessie, Jacinta and Lucas watched on helplessly as Mrs Clinch rallied the adults.

'Right,' the woman said. 'The children are to stay here with Mr Pienaar. Teachers and parents, meet me in the foyer in five minutes. Bring raincoats and boots, if you have them, and torches. As many as we can find.'

'What would you like me to do?' Davina asked. The poor woman looked as though she was at her wit's end.

Mrs Clinch scratched her head. 'What about the maps? Can you supply us with copies of the map that was given to Nessie's Monsters?'

'Yes, of course, I'll be back in a moment,' Davina said, and hurried away.

Caroline Clinch nodded. At least the children would be in good hands while the rest of them were out searching. Davina Stuart really was the loveliest woman.

Chapter 35

With a wavering voice, Alice-Miranda read out the contents of the letter.

Dear children,

I'm sorry it has come to this, but believe me when I say it's not about you. Your parents robbed me of my father, my childhood and every ounce of happiness in my life. Now it's their turn to suffer. They'll spend the rest of their days wondering and waiting and hoping – just like I had to.

Yours sincerely,
A bereft daughter

Lucinda sat back in bewilderment. 'It doesn't make any sense. What do our parents all have in common?'

'And more to the point, what have they done?' Sloane said, drumming her fingers on the table. 'I mean, we know your dad's a crook, Alethea. And, Sep, our mother's a vain piece of work at the best of times. But Alice-Miranda's parents are perfect. None of them are capable of murder.'

Madagascar pouted. 'My parents are perfect too, you know.'

'I wouldn't call my dad an angel,' Lucinda conceded, 'but he's paid for his crimes and I don't know of any others he's committed. Although, if I have learned anything in my short life, never say never.'

'There has to be some connection between them all and whoever has done this,' Alice-Miranda said, thinking hard. 'But that's not important now. First, we need to find a way out of here.'

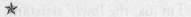

Caroline Clinch determined that the adults were to go out in pairs, searching strategically through the village and surrounding areas. Everyone was equipped with phones and she'd managed to procure a couple of sets of two-way radios from reception for good measure. The children were left at the hotel, pondering the fate of their friends with Miss Stuart and Mr Pienaar and a few of the parents who for one reason or another had decided to stay put. Morag had awoken from her faint, disoriented and panic-stricken. She made herself a cup of tea and nibbled on a biscuit to get her blood sugar back up, then ventured downstairs to see what was happening. An air of helplessness shrouded the room.

'We'll both be in terrible trouble if anything's happened to them,' Morag said to Davina, nervously picking at her fingernails. She couldn't fathom how calm her colleague was in the face of it all.

Davina's brow furrowed. 'I think you've got that wrong, dear. *You're* the one who devised the activities. I just do the paperwork. I think *you'll* find it's *your* duty of care – yours and Mr Ferguson's. I'm just the lowly assistant.'

Morag's head began to spin again and she thought she might throw up. 'B-But I'll go to prison,' she stammered, and reached out to steady herself.

'You know what happened before. I had no choice. My mother was having a breakdown. I *had* to go to her. I told the other staff, but they didn't listen and then the children disappeared – for three days. It almost ruined my life. You know all this, Davina. I confided in you. I trusted you.'

'Are you all right?' Davina asked, as if she were enquiring if the woman wanted a glass of water.

'Of course I'm not all right!' Morag screamed.

All eyes turned to the woman in alarm. It was clear everyone's nerves had begun to fray. Neville, however, noticed how incredibly calm Miss Stuart seemed among the chaos. It was especially apparent in comparison to Miss Cranna, who was behaving exactly how someone might if they'd just lost a group of children in the woods on a stormy night. There was something niggling him about the woman, and he wondered if this was what Alice-Miranda was talking about when she said she had one of her strange feelings.

Neville wandered over to Millie, who was standing in a huddle with their team, and took her aside to share his concerns.

'She seems so lovely, though,' Millie replied. 'I'm sure she wouldn't purposely put any of us in danger . . . Then again, it wouldn't be the first time I've overestimated an adult.'

Neville and Millie decided to gather all the children together. They couldn't just stand around doing nothing.

'Did anyone see Nessie's Monsters when we were out hunting?' Neville asked.

The kids all shook their heads except for Christophe, who recalled seeing them cross the river as his group climbed the hill on the other side of the village. He had been surprised at the time because his team's map had come with a note explicitly telling them to avoid the river. Several of the other children nodded in agreement, saying their maps had contained the same directive. Millie pulled out Clan Mac's map and noted that the instruction was also written in the top right-hand corner.

'That's not like Alice-Miranda to miss something so important,' Millie said. 'Nor to disregard it.'

'Well, that's it then,' Chessie said, her spirits rising for the first time in the past hour. 'The rain started and they're stuck on the other side of the river. They've probably taken shelter somewhere and they'll be back as soon as the storm clears and the water level drops.'

It sounded perfectly feasible.

Millie nodded, feeling slightly relieved. 'Alice-Miranda is way too sensible to try to cross the river if it's up at all.' She knew there had to be a rational explanation and she'd share it with Mrs Clinch as soon as the adults returned. Although perhaps they would find them in the village first and then there would be nothing to worry about.

But Neville wasn't convinced. He didn't like the sound of any of it.

Meanwhile, Barclay Ferguson was on his way back to New Lanark with Her Majesty and her entourage.

'I'm glad you turned on some good weather for us, Barclay,' Queen Georgiana remarked, the hint of a smile on her lips. She picked the tiniest piece of lint from her favourite woollen kilt, which she'd paired with a cashmere jumper for the journey. The outfit was suitably Scottish and toasty warm and far more appropriate than the gown Mrs Marmalade had laid out for her.

'I'm afraid that's Scotland for ye, Ma'am,' Barclay replied earnestly. He glanced out the window and sighed.

'Yes, it is,' Her Majesty said emphatically. 'For

heaven's sake, Barclay, lighten up. I've been looking forward to this for days and it wouldn't be Scotland if it didn't rain. You know I love the place regardless of the weather, unlike Marian here, who detests it.' She glanced over at her lady-in-waiting and chief advisor, Marian Marmalade, who was sitting between the pair in the back of the Bentley, her lips pursed. Her Majesty's personal bodyguard, Dalton, was up front beside the driver.

Mrs Marmalade rolled her eyes. The weather was truly atrocious. In her humble opinion, they really should have stayed in Edinburgh for the night. What was Her Majesty thinking?

Chapter 36

'Let's look at the map again,' Alice-Miranda said to Sloane and Lucinda. Sep and Alethea were busy hunting high and low for any evidence of a ventilation shaft while Madagascar was searching for signs of a doorway. She was looking in one of the kitchen cupboards when she suddenly remembered something, hitting her head as she backed out.

'Ow! Ow! Ow!' Madagascar hopped about as if she were on a pogo stick. 'I know who did this!'

The others turned and looked at her.

'It was Miss Cranna,' Madagascar said excitedly, rubbing her head. 'I heard her on the phone when we were at the castle. She was telling someone that we'd be gone by the end of the week and then there would be nothing to worry about.'

Sloane eyed the girl warily. 'How sure are you? Miss Cranna could have simply been talking about the program finishing at the end of the week and all of the students returning home. It doesn't mean she was going to literally get rid of us.'

Madagascar scowled from beneath her greasy fringe. 'It's definitely her! She's been on her phone the whole time and she's always skulking around corners and looking stressed. She probably had this planned for years. Plus, she was *really* mean to me.'

Alice-Miranda bit down on her thumbnail. She recalled the time she saw Morag leave the hotel at one o'clock in the morning and the way the woman had profusely denied it. 'From the few times I've talked to Miss Cranna, she seems to have had a tough upbringing. She said that her father was killed in a fire when she was young and that it wasn't an accident. Her mother hasn't been well ever since.'

'That's got to be it then,' Madagascar said smugly. She poked her tongue out at Sloane.

'Somehow our parents are linked to the fire. It says so in the letter – our parents need to suffer because of her father's death.'

Sloane frowned. She hated to admit it, but the brat might have stumbled her way on to something.

'Hey, come and look at this,' Sep said, his head inside the oven. He grabbed a knife and set about unscrewing the panel at the back. He pulled it off as the girls all peered inside with their torches. 'There's a hole where the wall should be.'

'I think I could get through,' Alice-Miranda said, although the opening was no bigger than the base of a bucket.

'What if you get stuck?' Sloane said.

Alice-Miranda shook her head. 'I have to try.'

Sloane trembled. 'What if it's a trap?'

'Well, we won't know unless someone gives it a go,' Alethea said. 'And let's face it, I don't want to be stuck down here for the next ten years. I've got flower girl duties to attend to.'

After three hours, Caroline Clinch and most of the search party returned to the hotel, half-drowned and empty-handed. There had been no sign of the children anywhere and, with the sheets of icy rain and gale-force winds, they had had no choice but to call off the search until first light.

Hugh, Smedley and Morrie had been picked up by Granny Valentina's cousin, Morogh Buchanan, and his wife, Audrina, who had driven them the long way around to the other side of the river as all of the low crossings were now well and truly under a torrent of water.

Hugh hadn't wanted to worry his wife, Cecelia, but when she had phoned from the United States, where she was still on business, he didn't have a choice. Cecelia had managed to remain remarkably calm on the phone to Hugh. Although ten minutes later, when Dolly Oliver called Cecelia to seek her advice about an upcoming dinner party, the woman was inconsolable.

September Sykes had been waiting in the hotel foyer with Gerda Finkelstein and Pamela Slewt. She had long abandoned her stilettos and sat with her stockinged feet curled up beneath her. Mr Slewt had gone up to his room hours ago, citing a headache. He had no real concerns, assured that the children were smart enough to find shelter. His daughter was such a princess there was no way she would tolerate being out there in this weather.

September looked up when the sodden troop trudged through the doors. 'Did you find them?' she asked, jumping to her feet.

Caroline shook her head. 'I'm afraid not.'

All three mothers had tears in their eyes. 'But it's dreadful out there,' September sobbed.

'We mustn't give up hope.' Gerda squeezed the woman's arm, but even she was secretly fearing the worst. What if the children had tried to cross the river?

Less than five metres away, Her Majesty's ruby Bentley pulled up under the portico outside the hotel. Barclay Ferguson was very disappointed that no one had remembered to roll out the red carpet he had specially ordered for the occasion. Miss Stuart and Miss Cranna were supposed to have the children form a guard of honour as the Queen made her way into the establishment. He hadn't been able to get hold of either of them and assumed the phones were out because of the storm, but surely they could have calculated the Queen's approximate arrival time. Instead they were greeted by the sight of a mob of staff and parents in raincoats, dripping all over the place.

'Excuse me, Ma'am, I'll just go and see what's, er, happenin',' the man said, making an awful job of bowing while alighting from the vehicle.

Mrs Marmalade bit back a smile while Dalton shook his head from the front seat.

Barclay Ferguson dashed inside, dodging puddles on the marble floor. He hurried over to Mrs Clinch, who seemed to brace herself for his arrival. 'What's all this?' Barclay asked, sweeping his hand around the room. He didn't recall any nocturnal events outside the hotel scheduled for this evening. Even if there had been, he would hope that common sense would prevail and alternate arrangements be made. Everyone looked miserable. Was that a child he saw crying? Besides, Miss Cranna and Miss Stuart were supposed to have everything ready for his second surprise.

Benitha Wall nodded at Caroline. They didn't want to alarm the man, but this was his show after all. 'One of the groups hasn't returned from their afternoon activity,' Mrs Clinch replied, trying for a gently-gently approach.

Barclay's eyes widened. 'But it's after dinner-time . . .' He took a deep breath. 'Are ye tellin' me there is a group of children missin' out *there*?'

Caroline and Benitha nodded gravely.

Mr Ferguson looked outside at the car containing Her Majesty. He needed to get her up to her room without anyone noticing. He squeezed his eyes shut for a moment, then opened them. 'Hang on a minute,' he said, holding his index finger aloft.

The man ran over to the reception desk, where he quickly exchanged words with a very confused-looking young staffer. He then raced out to the car.

'Yer Majesty,' he said tentatively, 'the hotel has suggested that, for yer security, we take ye around to the loadin' dock and use the service elevator to go straight up to yer room.'

Dalton pressed his lips together tightly. 'No.'

'Absolutely not,' Mrs Marmalade echoed. 'Whoever heard of the Queen riding in the *service* elevator?'

For once the two were in agreement.

'What's going on in there?' Queen Georgiana asked, indicating the hotel foyer.

'Umm . . .' Barclay's mind raced. 'Leaky ceilin'. Lots of puddles. Far too dangerous for ye, Ma'am, in the event that ye slipped.'

'Good heavens, Barclay. I've been on one of your blinking expeditions to the Amazon jungle – a few puddles inside the hotel aren't going to worry me.'

The Queen rolled her eyes. 'But I am feeling awfully tired, and there are quite a lot of people about, so perhaps it would be easier to use the tradesmen's entrance. We can hop up and order room service. I'm really not in the mood to make small talk.'

Marian frowned. 'But, Your Majesty, is that really . . . appropriate?'

'Oh, for goodness sake, Marian,' the Queen tutted, 'if it offends you to have to pass the garbage bins and linen bags, then I suggest you close your eyes. Which is exactly what I intend to do as soon as I've had a cup of tea and some googy eggs with soldiers. The children aren't expecting me, are they?'

'No, Ma'am,' Barclay replied humbly. He thanked his lucky stars that she was a pragmatic woman and that he hadn't told the children about the second surprise before he'd left. He assumed Miss Cranna and Miss Stuart hadn't said anything either.

'Then we're off,' the woman concluded.

'Wonderful decision, Ma'am. Splendid. Goodnight.' Barclay hopped out of the vehicle, bowing again, and gave a pinched smile as the car drove around to the back of the hotel. At least that was one less thing to deal with. He turned on his heel and sped back from the portico to the foyer.

Chapter 37

'It's as if we're in a real-life version of *Hansel and Gretel*,' Sloane remarked, watching Alice-Miranda wriggle inside the oven.

'Good luck,' Lucinda said. Her words were echoed by Sep and Alethea, but Madagascar just told her to hurry up.

Alice-Miranda flicked on her torch and clamped it in her mouth, then thrust her head through the opening in the wall, trusting that her shoulders would be narrow enough. As long as they were, she'd make it to the other side. Sep closed the oven door. Using all her might, Alice-Miranda pushed her feet against it, hoping that the latch would take her weight. She shoved and grunted and finally popped through, her legs snaking after her as she slithered out the other side into what appeared to be a cupboard. She stood up and peered through a gap in the door, but it was pitch black except for the torch beam. That had to be a good sign.

'I made it,' she whispered as loudly as she dared back to the others. Sep opened the oven door and she shone her torch back towards them.

'Good job!' Lucinda called.

Sep shushed her and quickly closed the door again. They couldn't be too careful – someone could be waiting on the other side.

Cautiously, Alice-Miranda pushed open the cupboard door and stepped into a small room. It was much like a command centre with desks and other office equipment. The walls were covered in pinboards, and they in turn were covered in news-paper clippings and photographs. Threads of cotton wound tightly around pins led from one pinboard to the next, creating a spider web of sorts.

Alice-Miranda shone her torch on one of the

pages and gasped when she read the headline: *Father and husband killed in shopping centre blaze*. Alice-Miranda scanned the article but became distracted by a photograph of her father and another of herself. She followed the trail around to the next board, the dots slowly joining in her mind. Everything she needed to know was in this room and the more she read, the more she was aware of the urgency of the situation. She had to get out of here. Their lives depended on it.

Neville Nordstrom couldn't sleep. The children had been sent to bed after playing some inane board games, which no one had been remotely interested in. He pushed back the covers and, as he slipped to the floor, a hand reached out of the darkness and grabbed hold of his arm.

'Where are you going?' Lucas whispered.

'I can't stay here and do nothing,' Neville whispered back.

Vincent sat up. 'Well, what are we doing just sitting here?'

Neville grinned. 'I was hoping you'd say that.'

The boys quickly got dressed and put on their warmest, most waterproof clothes. They snuck out into the hallway and were stunned to find Millie, Jacinta and Chessie leaving their room across the hall at the same time. A second later, Britt Fox poked her head out from behind a door two rooms along. It seemed their operation had just tripled in size.

'What are you doing?' Neville whispered to Millie.

'Going to look for them,' the girl replied. 'We know they went across the river, and we've found a trail map in our room and there's a suspension bridge further up. We should be able to get across even if the river is flooded.'

'Then what?' Lucas said.

Millie shrugged. 'Who knows, but it sure beats waiting around here.'

The others agreed. Just as they were about to leave, Caprice stepped out of her room fully dressed.

'Where are you all going?' she demanded.

'Go back to bed, Caprice,' Millie whispered.

The girl shook her head. 'They're my friends too.'

Millie's eyebrows jumped up and, despite herself, she smiled. 'Okay then, but make sure you keep quiet. I don't need Mrs Clinch cottoning on before we've even left.'

Neville had checked the fire stairs prior to lights out and had planned on leaving the hotel via the service entrance. That way, the adults would be none the wiser.

Someone else seemed to have had the same idea. The figure of a woman darted from a room ahead of them and through the emergency exit. She was wearing a dark raincoat that hid her features. Intuitively, the children hung back for a minute or so.

'Where do you think she's going?' Jacinta asked.

Neville shook his head, his eyes narrowing. 'I'm not sure, but something tells me we should follow her.'

Chapter 38

Alice-Miranda used her torch to highlight the walls and ran her fingers over them as well. There were a few wonky sections which she'd hoped were secret doors, but so far she'd found nothing. The children had all agreed that the bunker must have been built during the Second World War – they'd found lots of things from the 1940s when they were searching for a way out. Alice-Miranda racked her brain for a place the military would put a door no one would ever think to look. She got down on her hands and knees. Still nothing.

A tall filing cabinet caught her attention. Alice-Miranda systematically opened each drawer until a faint click sounded. The entire unit rotated away from the wall as if it were on a conveyor belt. Behind it was what looked to be a circular vent shaft with ladder rails concreted into the side. It seemed to go up and up forever. Alice-Miranda placed one foot on the bottom rung and scurried as quickly as she could to the top, where a round metal lid blocked her path. There was no way she could push it up – the lid looked as if it weighed a tonne. But then she spotted a green button.

'Here goes,' she whispered, and pressed it. With a *whoosh* of stale air, the metal lid slowly opened. The girl poked her head out the other side and shone her torch around. She was in a cellar by the looks of it. Alice-Miranda lifted herself up and scrambled through, the metal door slowly closing behind her. When it was back in place, she saw it was covered in bricks that matched the cellar floor. No one would ever know it was there, which was slightly troubling because she now had no clue how to make it open again either.

Alice-Miranda took a deep breath and climbed the stairs. She came to a door and, after pushing it open, found herself in a carpeted room. A bolt of lightning lit up the sky, briefly illuminating her surroundings. She was in a cottage, only this one wasn't derelict. Alice-Miranda shone her torch around. Someone must live here – there was furniture and the hum of a refrigerator. She picked her way across the floor to the kitchen. There were clean dishes stacked on the drainer beside the sink and biscuits in a jar on the bench. Her stomach grumbled, but she didn't dare take one.

Alice-Miranda made her way into a small sitting room with an unlit log fire. With the aid of the torchlight, she searched the walls for clues and stopped at a photograph of a man and a child. A gasp escaped her lips. Alice-Miranda finally understood. She hunted high and low for a telephone, but came up empty-handed. With a sinking feeling, the girl realised she'd have to brave the storm to get back to the hotel and sound the alarm.

Alice-Miranda scampered to the front door when she spied something on a side table. She picked it up and opened it, stunned to see the licence inside. Why was that here? She put it into her pocket and unlatched the front door. Outside, the storm raged on. The girl braced herself against the driving sheets of rain and pulled her scarf up around her neck. She shone her torch into the trees and took a small compass from her pocket, wondering which was the best way to go. She would head north and hopefully come across a track along the way. If there was a cottage out here, there had to be a way of getting to it.

Stumbling through the undergrowth, and blinking to keep the rain out of her eyes, Alice-Miranda pushed on until she heard someone calling her name. She turned in circles, trying to work out where the voice was coming from.

'I'm here!' she called back.

Alice-Miranda heard a rustling in a nearby bush and was blinded by a yellow light. She shielded her eyes with her arm and froze when she realised who was holding the torch.

'How on earth did you get out of there?' said a familiar voice. 'You're incorrigible! It's fortunate I had the cameras linked to my phone.'

Alice-Miranda's heart sank. 'You don't have to do this, you know,' she shouted over the noise of the storm.

The woman advanced upon the tiny girl. 'You have no idea what you're talking about. The lies spun by *your* father and those other *criminals* sent an innocent man to prison,' Davina spat. Her hair was soaked and plastered across her face.

'But it was Miss Cranna's father who was killed in that fire,' Alice-Miranda said, backing away. 'Your father set it on purpose to get the insurance money. Why do you think he's innocent?'

'Lies!' Davina screeched, her face contorted with hate. 'My father was an honourable man – a good man – and he went to prison, and I wasn't allowed to see him any more. Then he died.' A sob escaped the woman's lips. 'Do you know what it's like to live with an aunt who despises you and makes you wait on her hand and foot?'

'I'm sorry for what you had to suffer as a child,' Alice-Miranda said, and she meant it. 'But you can't imprison innocent children to pay for something you think their parents did.'

Davina lunged at Alice-Miranda, but the tiny girl managed to duck away. There was shouting in the distance, and torchlight danced among the trees.

'I'm here!' Alice-Miranda called, hoping against hope that she would be heard.

Neville came running out of the darkness with Lucas and the others charging along behind them. The rain thumped down and the sky erupted as lightning forked overhead.

'Get her!' Vincent yelled. He and Sep launched themselves at the woman, pinning her to the ground.

'Stop it!' Davina screamed, thrashing in the muddy leaves.

Caprice was having none of it. She hurried over and sat on the backs of the woman's knees while Britt held Davina's feet as tightly as she could.

Millie ran to her friend and wrapped her in a fierce hug. 'Are you all right?' she asked, her eyes combing the girl for signs of injury.

Alice-Miranda nodded and smiled. 'I'm fine, but I've got to get back. And we can't let her get away.'

'You're just a bunch of stupid children!' Davina bellowed. The venom in her voice was almost palpable. 'No one will believe a word you say. They never believed me when I was a child!'

'What shall we do with her?' Vincent asked. They couldn't very well sit on her in the rain until dawn.

'I know a place,' Alice-Miranda said. 'You'll have to tie her up to make sure she doesn't escape.'

The others followed the girl's lead, and within ten minutes the woman was tied to a chair in the kitchen of the cottage Alice-Miranda had just come from. The children would all stay put until Alice-Miranda and Neville could find help.

The pair ran through the woods and along a fence line until they spotted headlights. But there was no road as far as they could see. The vehicle was in a field along with a herd of shaggy Highland cattle huddled together against the rain. Alice-Miranda waved her arms in the air, hoping that whoever it was could see them. She was stunned when the clattering Land Rover pulled up and Uncle Morogh hopped out in his tartan dressing-gown and kilt. Alice-Miranda was even more surprised to see her father beside him.

'Daddy!' she cried, running into the man's arms.

'Oh, darling heart, thank heavens you're all right.' Tears mixed with rain streamed down Hugh's cheeks. 'Where have you been? And, Neville, what are you doing out here?'

'It's a long story, but we can tell you on the way,' Alice-Miranda said hurriedly.

Hugh's forehead creased with confusion. 'On the way where?'

'Edinburgh. The Royal Mile,' Alice-Miranda said. 'This is Neville, Uncle Morogh,' she added, introducing the lad. 'He just saved my life.'

Neville bit his lip and tried not to smile. After all, none of what had happened was a smiling matter.

Once they were on the road back to the city, Alice-Miranda regaled everyone with her very strange tale. Hugh telephoned Miss Cranna and Mr Ferguson to tell them what had happened. Morag almost fainted with relief to know that the children were safe, but she almost fainted again when she heard about Davina's evil plot. Uncle Morogh and his cargo only just made it out before the swollen river cut off the road, leaving no way to the bunker until the water subsided.

Hugh then phoned Aunt Audrina, who had been driving on the other side of the property with Smedley and Morrie. It was decided they would stay at the manor until the morning. The woman was mesmerised by the tale and made a note to write down all the details once she got home. It sounded like a winning plot for their next novel, although they would have to add some romantic leads. She was already pondering a title and thought *Bunker Down* had a nice ring to it. She and the men would meet the police at the bunker at first light. She knew exactly where it was. It had been sealed up and decommissioned by the government years ago.

By the time Alice-Miranda was on her way back to the hotel, the storm had passed and dawn was breaking clear. Thankfully, the rivers dropped as fast as they had risen, allowing the children to return to the village without any troubles. Alice-Miranda organised her guest a cup of tea and some toast while they waited for everyone to waken.

Chapter 39

With some additional instructions from Alice-Miranda, Aunt Audrina had guided the police to the cottage and then to the bunker, where the rest of Alice-Miranda's team was released and Davina was placed under arrest. However, they didn't immediately whisk her away to be charged. Alice-Miranda had kindly asked the inspector to instead bring the woman back to the hotel. It was just before nine when the missing children spilled through the hotel doors and were reunited with their distraught parents. Alethea's mother hugged the girl like there was no tomorrow.

'I don't know why Miss Stuart picked on me,' the girl said while being smothered by her mother's kisses. 'Daddy wouldn't care.'

Her mother reassured her that certainly was not the case. Although the man had done some terrible things, he was still her father and loved her very much.

Hutton Slewt was incandescent with rage and vowed that he was going to put that insane woman away for a very long time – even longer than her murderous father. That revelation came as something of a shock to the others, but certainly helped the adults whose children had disappeared to work out how they were all connected. It didn't take long for them to realise their links to the man.

'I was the face of the shopping centre,' September gasped. 'I testified against him in court – I'd seen some dodgy things and I knew he'd set the fire.'

And it turned out that Morrie Finkelstein had got cold feet about expanding his department stores into Scotland due to a downturn in the economy and had pulled out of a deal with the man. Addison Goldsworthy, who had been the financial backer, had also withdrawn his support at the last minute. Hugh Kennington-Jones had been the chairman of the board of the insurance company that had denied the man's claim before the police had enough evidence to put the fellow away. Hutton Slewt was the crown prosecutor who ensured that Davina's father went to prison for a considerable length of time.

The group gathered in the conference room, awaiting further instructions. Barclay flitted about nervously. He hoped Her Majesty had ordered breakfast in her suite and wasn't planning on appearing until the start of the morning's program. Little did he know that Dalton, upon realising that the hotel was swarming with police, had made his own enquiries and had tasked Mrs Marmalade with keeping Her Majesty occupied until he gave the nod.

'I'm so relieved everyone's okay,' Gretchen said to Alethea, who had just finished relaying the whole miserable ordeal.

Davina Stuart was waiting in another room, her mind roiling over how her plan had gone wrong. All those years following their movements and working out how she could exact her revenge, only to be outsmarted by a bunch of kids. She was cradling her face in her hands when the door opened and Alice-Miranda walked through.

'Excuse me, Miss Stuart,' the child said.

Davina looked up. 'What do you want now?' she asked wearily. 'Have you come to rub my nose in it and tell me how clever you are?'

'No,' Alice-Miranda replied gently. She stepped to the side. 'I've brought someone to see you.'

Davina struggled to raise her head. She felt as though she had a lead weight around her neck. A man shuffled into the room, his back bent and his skin pitted by the ravages of time. At first she didn't recognise him, but then she saw his eyes. They were now framed by wrinkles, but they were *his*.

'Davina, what mess have ye gone and got yerself into?' he said sadly.

She gasped, clutching her chest. 'No, it's not you. It can't be.' Davina could feel the tears pricking her eyes. 'They told me you had died.'

'My darlin' Davina. I ruined everything. I didna want to do ye more harm. I'm so ashamed,' he began.

'But you didn't do it. You never set the fire,' Davina said, her eyes pleading. 'It was Morag's father. He was there when he shouldn't have been.

His business was going badly and he set the fire, but then the stupid man got caught up in it.'

Gordy Onslow shook his head. 'I told ye that because I couldna burden ye with the truth. I didna want my own girl to think her father was capable of such a thing. I couldna face ye. That's why I sent ye away to live with yer aunt. She said she'd take good care of ye. Did she?'

Davina froze and clenched her hands into fists. 'She was the worst kind of woman. I waited until I was old enough and then I ran away,' she said bitterly. 'And I started planning – for years I planned. I was going to make them pay for what they did to you. I've become a monster like Aunt Hortense and like you.' Davina's hands flew to her mouth and tears streamed down her cheeks as the reality of the situation set in. She looked at the tiny girl with cascading chocolate curls. 'Oh, Alice-Miranda, what did I do? I could have let you all die down there, and what for? A lie? My whole life is a lie.'

'I should have told ye the truth,' Gordy Onslow said, his voice trembling. 'I set the fire because we were on the brink of financial ruin. Everythin' I had was invested in that centre. I needed the insurance money, but I didna know that Ray Cranna was there that night. I checked the buildin' and it was empty. Or so I thought. Money makes people do terrible things and that night I became the worst version of meself. I've loved ye every day, Davina, and I have prayed to be forgiven for what I have done.'

Davina Stuart began to sob. Her father hesitated before walking over to hug his daughter tight for the first time in more than twenty-five years.

'Do you have to take her away?' Alice-Miranda asked the detective inspector.

The man nodded. 'Aye, but how bad it gets depends on what the parents want to do.'

'Could you wait a moment?' the child asked.

The detective said he would, and Alice-Miranda ran across the hall to the other room. She rounded up Nessie's Monsters and asked them to follow her. Alice-Miranda's team mates blanched when they saw Davina was in the room.

Alice-Miranda turned to her group. 'I want you all to listen. I think Miss Stuart has lived her life based on a lie, and although revenge is never a good idea, she had her reasons.'

Madagascar looked at the girl as if she were mad. 'She didn't care if we died down there,' the girl spat. 'She's a vile excuse for a human being.'

Davina nodded. 'Aye, you're right about that.'

'See? She even agrees with me,' Madagascar said.

But Alice-Miranda wanted them to hear the whole story. And while she knew that Miss Stuart would be punished for putting them in danger, perhaps the children could try to put themselves in her shoes.

'What did our parents do to you, anyway?' Alethea asked, taking a step towards Davina.

'It's a long story,' the woman began. But for the first time since she was a girl, Davina Stuart shared the experiences that had driven her to form her diabolical plan.

Her revelations got Madagascar thinking that perhaps revenge wasn't the best course of action after all, especially if it could land you in prison. Although, as her father was a lawyer, she reasoned that she'd never end up in the clink anyway.

Alice-Miranda made her way to the man sitting on his own in the vast hotel dining room and handed him a cup of tea. Davina had gone with the police for questioning and he was waiting for a lift back to Edinburgh.

The man looked at her, his eyes red-rimmed and still wet with tears. 'Hello lassie. How did ye know she was mine?'

Alice-Miranda pointed to the man's hands. 'I read about Raynaud syndrome – they say it can be hereditary. And your eyes. I suppose the fact that Miss Cranna paused and looked at you so long when I gave you back your glove and then there was the portrait in Miss Stuart's cottage. You were a lot younger but the resemblance was unmistakable.'

'I never thought I'd see her ever again,' the man said with a faraway look in his eyes. 'I hurt her so badly. I didna deserve such a beautiful girl.'

'She needed you,' Alice-Miranda said.

'I know that now,' he sighed. 'I was a fool. I've been a fool all my life.'

The child smiled and put a hand on his shoulder. 'You've got another chance to spend some time together.'

'How did ye get to be so smart for someone so small?' Mr Onslow said.

Alice-Miranda was surprised to see Morag

standing in the doorway. She felt her heart thump in her chest.

Gordon Onslow turned and looked at the woman. 'I'm sorry, Morag,' he said quietly. 'I didna know your father was there that night. I wouldna have done it. And, worse, I lied because I couldna face my own family.'

Morag nodded. She'd been waiting to hear those words ever since she was a teenage girl. 'I'll never understand it, but I can see your remorse and I thank you for that,' she said, and walked away.

Alice-Miranda stood up to leave. She didn't say a word but leaned in and gave the man a hug.

'Thank you, lassie, I canna tell you what ye've done for me. It's a pity life doesn't give us the chance to start over and erase our mistakes,' Mr Onslow said. 'All I can do is my best each day and that I can promise ye.'

Chapter 40

By half-past ten, and with the help of Miss Wall and Mrs Clinch, who stepped into the breach left by the departure of Miss Stuart, Morag Cranna had everything back on track for the final event of the program. They were due to start the Highland games at eleven o'clock sharp. The children had been sent to their rooms, where they were to get changed into the surprise outfits that had just arrived from the tailors in Edinburgh. They were to meet back downstairs and, at the sound of the bagpipes, head into the ballroom for the official start to the games. It wasn't long before the children were milling about in the conference room, closely appraising one another's dress.

'I wonder if this is one of my family tartans,' Millie said.

'But which one?' Chessie raised her eyebrows. 'You've got a few to choose from.'

The girls thought the boys looked fabulous in their kilts and sporrans.

'What are you wearing under there?' Sloane asked her brother.

'Wouldn't you like to know?' the boy replied cheekily.

'Ew, gross,' Sloane said, wrinkling her lip, and the others all laughed.

'Where do we all stand on the competition ladder, Miss Wall?' Caprice asked.

Benitha grinned. 'Looks like it's neck and neck between Clan Mac, Nessie's Monsters and The Highland Flingers. But with the Highland games and the debate this evening, it could be anyone's race.'

'It's ours, for sure,' Caprice said with an air of confidence, then seemed to have second thoughts. 'If we work hard as a team, of course.'

Madagascar Slewt rolled her eyes.

Outside in the foyer, the sound of bagpipes sent the children scurrying to the grand ballroom, with its crystal chandeliers and tartan wallpaper. They filled the front rows of chairs, and their were parents seated behind them. Aunt Audrina and Uncle Morogh, in all his kilted glory, were there too. Caroline Clinch couldn't resist commenting to Benitha about the man's unusually coloured scalp. The two of them shared a giggle until Audrina turned and shot them a death stare.

Aidan marched into the room playing the bagpipes, followed closely by Barclay Ferguson banging a large drum. The man was resplendent in full Highland dress, although he was finding it difficult keeping time and poor Aidan was working hard to play to the beat. Barclay marched to the podium and nodded at Aidan to stop. Unfortunately, the boy missed his cue and continued until Benitha Wall hopped up and tapped him on the shoulder.

'Children and parents,' Mr Ferguson began, 'I would like to welcome ye all to this final event of what has been a magnificent and somewhat surprisin', perplexin' ... and distressin' week. Children, ye have come so far. Yer leadership skills have served ye well and many of ye have exhibited bravery and courage beyond expectation. Parents, thank ye for makin' the journey. I hope very much that ye will be as impressed with yer bairns as I have been. But I have one last surprise.' He looked towards the double doors. 'I give ye our patron, Her Majesty, Queen Georgiana.'

The ballroom doors swung open to reveal the royal entourage, with Queen Georgiana dressed in a rather fetching tartan kilt and jacket. She had a tam upon her head and a diamond brooch in the shape of a thistle at her throat. She was trailed by Mrs Marmalade, who was wearing a slightly simpler outfit and her trademark pearl choker. Finally, Dalton brought up the rear. The man seemed ill at ease in his Highland dress, tugging constantly at his kilt like a self-conscious teenage girl.

Alice-Miranda leapt up from her seat. She ran down the aisle, practically launching herself at the woman's middle. Dalton charged towards them, then retreated when he realised who it was. The child was lucky not to have been taken out.

'Darling girl!' Queen Georgiana hadn't been expecting such a warm greeting, but she lapped it up. Being royal, people were reluctant to touch her most of the time. It was supposedly in the rules, but it wasn't one she lived by.

Alice-Miranda gazed up at the old lady and smiled. 'Hello Aunty Gee.'

Queen Georgiana leaned down to whisper in the tiny girl's ear. 'I hear you've had quite an adventure. Don't worry, I suspect Miss Stuart will have some time to think about her misdeeds, but given her past and the age of her father, I think she's suffered quite enough. Wouldn't you agree?'

Alice-Miranda wrapped her arms around Her Majesty's neck and kissed the woman's powdered cheek.

'Now, you must tell me,' said the Queen, her eyes sparkling, 'what's on the agenda for this afternoon? Will I get to toss a caber and eat some haggis?'

Alice-Miranda grinned. 'It wouldn't be a Highland games if you didn't.'

And just in case you're wondering . . .

The Highland games were quite literally a smashing success. Benitha Wall had cajoled Mr Ferguson into adding some adult events given there were parents present too and many had expressed an interest in having a go. She hadn't counted on such stiff competition, not only from Hansie Pienaar but from Her Majesty too. The Queen clearly didn't know her own strength, as she tossed the caber right through a window.

The children were surprised and thrilled to see Eachann Duncraig and his brother, Jock, who arrived to judge the haggis cooking competition and to lead the dancing after dinner. Aidan played his bagpipes to his heart's content until Barclay Ferguson decided that six renditions of 'Scotland the Brave' was quite enough. However, Her Majesty didn't agree and asked the lad to give it another whirl.

At the end of the day, after the final debate, the topic of which was 'Leaders are Born, Not Made', the children and adults retired to the hotel conference room, thoroughly exhausted and eager to learn the final results. In a surprising twist, The Tartan Warriors had come from nowhere to scoop the pool, much to Madagascar's disgust. She planned to ask her father to lodge an official complaint.

Lucas and Jacinta snuck in one more kiss before they all headed home. Jacinta told him that she didn't want to get into trouble back at school, so maybe that one would have to last for quite a while to come. Meanwhile, Alethea and Gretchen couldn't wait to get back to New York for their parents' wedding. They jointly decided that, if there was an exchange program with Winchesterfield-

Downsfordvale in the offing, they would both like to apply. Lucinda vowed she would too.

Much to Millie's surprise, Caprice apologised to her for her bad behaviour and vowed that she would do her best to keep any nasty thoughts inside her head from now on. Millie was very pleased to hear it and said she'd try harder too. It was far less of a surprise to hear Chessie's confession about her true relationship with Madagascar. At Sloane's urging, the girl had come clean to Millie and Alice-Miranda. Millie told her that, sadly, you could choose your friends but not your family.

Despite the kidnapping business, Alice-Miranda had had a wonderful time. She had made lots of new friends and a particularly special one in Britt Fox, who everyone commented was the girl's Nordic twin. Perhaps a visit to Norway would be on the cards soon.

Davina Stuart had spent years plotting her revenge on the children's parents. She'd followed their every move and, when she realised quite a few of the children were linked via the Queen's Colours, she saw her opportunity. Her job was no coincidence and neither was Morag's. Davina had paid a young thug to take the woman's handbag in a robbery gone wrong. Morag had been stunned when Alice-Miranda returned her missing wallet, which she'd found in Davina's cottage. It was further proof of the lengths the woman had been prepared to go to. Davina had also got rid of Alith, Barclay's former assistant, by landing the woman her dream job working at the Scottish seabird centre in North Berwick. She had applied on the woman's behalf and, when the offer came in, Alith thought she'd been headhunted. How could she possibly resist, obsessed as she was with puffins?

Davina had even orchestrated who was invited to the program. She'd meant to shred Neville's invitation, along with a heap of others, but had missed it on her desk. The boy was very glad that she had. Alice-Miranda's letter, however, had merely been misplaced and Davina just hadn't realised. Her mistake could have ruined everything.

Jock Duncraig reported that they still hadn't found out what had hit the *Mairead*, but he was going to keep searching, if it was the last thing he ever did. In brighter news, several of the locals reported a haggis sighting in the woods.

The bunker actually belonged to Aunt Audrina and Uncle Morogh. Once it was cleared of evidence, they decided to convert it into a tourist attraction like the one further up north. Uncle Morogh was always looking for ways to make money so their manor house didn't fall down around their ears.

Her Majesty declared the inaugural FLOP a resounding success. She loved the acronym too and couldn't wait to see what Morag and Barclay came up with for next year's event. In the meantime, she was going to make sure that Morag's mother had a full-time carer and limited access to a phone – at least while her daughter was on duty.

Neville Nordstrom really didn't want the week to end. He was so proud of Alice-Miranda and what she'd done, leading her friends from danger and unravelling the riddle of Miss Stuart's life. He told her so and asked if she'd like to visit Barcelona during one of the holidays. She could stay with Sloane and Sep, and Neville could take her butterfly hunting. Alice-Miranda replied that she would like that very much.

Cast of characters

Future Leaders Opportunity Program teams

Nessie's Monsters

Alice-Miranda Highton-Smith-Kennington Jones	Winchesterfield-Downsfordvale student
Sloane Sykes	Winchesterfield-Downsfordvale student
Septimus Sykes	Fayle School for Boys student
Madagascar Slewt	Bodlington School for Girls student
Alethea Mackenzie	Mrs Kimmel's School for Girls student
Lucinda Finkelstein	Mrs Kimmel's School for Girls student

Clan Mac

Millicent Jane McLoughlin-McTavish-McNoughton-McGill	Winchesterfield-Downsfordvale student
Francesca Compton-Halls	Winchesterfield-Downsfordvale student
Neville Nordstrom	Barcelona International College student

364

Jacinta Headlington-Bear	Winchesterfield- Downsfordvale student
Caprice Radford	Winchesterfield- Downsfordvale student
Lucas Nixon	Fayle School for Boys student

The Tartan Warriors

Declan O'Connor	St Gerald's School student
Vincent Roche	Lycée International student
Philippe Le Gall	Lycée International student
Britt Fox	Hartvig Skole student
Susannah Dare	Winchesterfield- Downsfordvale student
Sofia Ridout	Winchesterfield- Downsfordvale student

The Highland Flingers

Ava Lee	Mrs Kimmel's School for Girls student
Quincy Armstrong	Mrs Kimmel's School for Girls student
Gretchen Bell	Mrs Kimmel's School for Girls student
Junior Brown	Todder House student
Brendan Fourie	Todder House student
Isabeau Pillay	Todder House student

The Pipers

Aidan Blair	Burns School student
Aimee Anderson	St Odo's student
Hunter Martin	St Odo's student
Christophe Meier	Geneva College student
Evelyn Seow	Mandeville College student
Henry Yan	Mandeville College student

Future Leaders Opportunity Program staff and guest speakers

Barclay Ferguson	CEO
Davina Stuart	Assistant to Barclay Ferguson
Morag Cranna	School liaison officer
Andrew Williams	St Odo's teacher
Hansie Pienaar	Todder House teacher
Andie Patrick	Mrs Kimmel's School for Girls teacher
Dashiel Arnaud	Lycée International teacher
Dion McDonagh	Young entrepreneur
Rory Auchterlonie	Pro-golfer
Moira McKechnie	Tech entrepreneur

Parents

Hugh Kennington-Jones	Alice-Miranda's doting father
Pippa McNoughton-McGill	Mother of Millie
Hamish McLoughlin-McTavish	Father of Millie
Lawrency Ridley	Father of Lucas
September Sykes	Mother of Sloane and Septimus
Smedley Sykes	Father of Sloane and Septimus
Pamela Slewt	Mother of Madagascar
Hutton Slewt	Father of Madagascar
Len Nordstom	Father of Neville
Sylvia Nordstrom	Mother of Neville
Jemima Tavistock	Mother of Chessie
Anthony Tavistock	Stepfather of Chessie
Venetia Baldini	Mother of Caprice

Winchesterfield-Downsfordvale staff

Miss Ophelia Grimm	Headmistress
Miss Livinia Reedy	Acting headmistress and English teacher

Miss Benitha Wall	PE teacher
Mrs Petunia Clarkson	Housemistress of Caledonia Manor
Mrs Caroline Clinch	Maths teacher
Mrs Philomena Reeves	English teacher
Mr Percy Pratt	Science teacher
Mrs Doreen Smith	Cook

Others

Dolly Oliver	Highton-Smith-Kennington-Jones' family cook
Aldous Grump	Miss Grimm's husband
Agnes Grump	Daughter of Miss Grimm and Aldous Grump
Gordy Onslow	Old man
Bryan	Caber toss instructor
Eachann Duncraig	Owner of Duncraig's Academy of Highland Dance
Jock Duncraig	Captain of the *Mairead*
Bronagh McDuff	Owner of Brokenwind Castle
Mrs McDuff	Wife of Bronagh McDuff
Torna and Trevonna McDuff	Daughters of Bronagh and his wife
Morogh Buchanan	Granny Valentina's cousin
Audrina Buchanan	Uncle Morogh's wife
Aunty Gee	Queen Georgiana
Mrs Marian Marmalade	Queen Georgiana's lady-in-waiting and chief advisor
Dalton	Queen Georgiana's bodyguard
Frazer Campbell	Doorman
Loch Ness Monster	A lake monster of Scottish folklore . . . or is it?

About the Author

Jacqueline Harvey taught for many years in girls' boarding schools. She is the author of the bestselling Alice-Miranda series and the Clementine Rose series, and was awarded Honour Book in the 2006 Australian CBC Awards for her picture book *The Sound of the Sea*. She now writes full-time and is working on more Alice-Miranda, Clementine Rose, and Kensy and Max adventures.

www.jacquelineharvey.com.au

Jacqueline Supports

Jacqueline Harvey is a passionate educator who enjoys sharing her love of reading and writing with children and adults alike. She is an ambassador for Dymocks Children's Charities and Room to Read. Find out more at www.dcc.gofundraise.com.au and www.roomtoread.org.

Enter a world of
mystery and adventure in

OUT NOW

CHAPTER 1

BKDIXKA

Max woke with a start as the car crunched to a halt. He yawned and looked around at his sister, who was still asleep in the back seat. Her blanket had slipped down and she was drooling on the pillow that was wedged in the corner. She wouldn't thank him for noticing.

The boy peered out at the jewel box of stars in the clearing night sky. It had only stopped raining a little while ago. On the other side of the car, Max could see what looked to be a hotel. A dull glow shone from one of the windows high in the roofline. For a second, he glimpsed a face, but it was gone as soon as it had appeared. 'Where are we, Fitz?' Max asked.

Fitz turned and gave him a weary smile. 'This is Alexandria,' he replied, as if that was supposed to mean something. 'Be a good lad and take the daypacks with you, and mind the puddles. No one will thank you for tramping mud inside.'

Fitz opened the driver's door and hopped out of the Range Rover.

Max stretched, yawning again, then reached over and gently shook his sister's leg. 'Kensy,' he whispered, 'we're here.'

The girl groaned and flopped her head against the pillow but didn't wake up. It was to be expected given they'd just spent the past sixteen hours driving from Zermatt, near the Swiss–Italian border, across France and then to England.

Fitz reappeared at the open driver's window. 'Don't wake your sister unless you want your head bitten off,' he warned with a wink.

Kensy let out a grunty snore, as if to agree.

Max heard footsteps on the gravel and looked up to see a tall man approaching. The fellow was wearing a red dressing-gown and matching slippers. His dark hair had retreated to the middle of his head and he sported large rimless glasses. Fitz walked towards him and the two shook hands.

As the men spoke in hushed tones, the boy slipped out of the car. The stars had disappeared again and fat drops of rain began splattering the driveway. Max quickly collected the packs from the back seat while the man in the dressing-gown retrieved their suitcases from the boot. Fitz swept Kensy into his arms and carried her through a stone portico to an open doorway.

'Are we home?' she murmured, burrowing into the man's broad chest.

'Yes, sweetheart,' he replied. 'We're home.'

Max felt a shiver run down his spine. He wondered why Fitz would lie. This wasn't their home at all.

The four of them entered the building into a dimly lit hallway. Without hesitation or instruction, Fitz turned and continued up a staircase to the right.

That's strange, Max thought. Fitz must have been here before.

'Please go ahead, Master Maxim,' the tall man said.

Too tired to ask how the fellow knew his name, Max did as he was bid. The hypnotic thudding of their luggage being carried up the stairs made the boy feel as if he was almost sleepwalking. They followed Fitz down a long corridor and eventually came to a bedroom furnished with two queen-sized beds and a fire-place. Max's skin tingled from the warmth of the crackling fire. He deposited the daypacks neatly by the door and shrugged off his jacket as the tall man set down their bags and drew the curtains.

'Sweet dreams, Kens,' Fitz whispered, tucking the girl under the covers.

Without any urging at all, Max climbed into the other bed. He had so many questions, but right now he couldn't muster a single word. The soft sheets and the thrum of driving rain against the window panes made it hard to resist the pull of sleep. He closed his eyes as Fitz and the tall man began talking. Max roused at the mention of his parents' names followed by something rather alarming – something that couldn't possibly be true. He tried hard to fight off the sandman to hear more, but seconds later Max too was fast asleep.